P9-CAN-142

I met the Love Talker one evening in the glen,
He was handsomer than any of our handsome
    young men,
His eyes were blacker than the sloe;
His voice sweeter far. . . .

> His other name was Ganconer. He appeared
> to maidens in lonely valleys and made
> love to them before fading away and leav-
> ing them to pine away and die. . . .

Also by Elizabeth Peters:

STREET OF THE FIVE MOONS

SUMMER OF THE DRAGON

The LOVE TALKER

Elizabeth Peters

FAWCETT CREST • NEW YORK

THE LOVE TALKER

This book contains the complete text of the original hard-
cover edition.

Published by Fawcett Crest Books, a unit of CBS Publications, the Consumer Publishing Division of CBS Inc., by
arrangement with Dodd, Mead & Company

Copyright © 1980 by Elizabeth Peters

All Rights Reserved

ISBN: 0-449-24468-7

Printed in the United States of America

First Fawcett Crest printing: December 1981

10 9 8 7 6 5 4 3 2 1

The
LOVE
TALKER

CHAPTER

1

Once upon a time there was a nice big girl named Laura. She had rosy cheeks and nut-brown hair and three dimples, one in one cheek and two in the other. This nice big girl (no, she was not a nice *little* girl; she was five feet nine inches tall and weighed one hundred and twenty-seven pounds). . . . As I was saying, this nice big girl lived in a nice little house. (It was little, even if it wasn't a house. It was actually an apartment, the kind they call an efficiency; so you see, it was very little indeed.) One winter day she was sitting by her window watching the snowflakes make pretty patterns on the pane when there was a knock at the door. A messenger dressed in blue, with gold braid, had brought her a letter. Little did she know it then, but the letter was from the elves, inviting her to visit them in their woodland haunts.

An hour after the mailman had handed her the special delivery letter Laurie was still sitting by the window staring at the big fat snowflakes. Instead of thinking pretty thoughts about their exquisite patterns she was wondering how many more inches the snow-beleaguered city of Chicago was due to get this time. She swore aloud, in language unbecoming a nice girl, big or little. What evil imp had possessed her to select Chicago as the place in which to write her dissertation? Why not Florida or California, for God's sake?

There had been sensible reasons for the decision. The chance to sublet a friend's apartment, at a reasonable rent; the proximity to the university, with its excellent library. And there was the real reason: Bob. Bob was majoring in philosophy at the university. Bob was big and blond and adorably homely . . . and selfish and lazy and arrogant. She had not discovered that he possessed these additional attributes until after they had tried a brief experiment in communal living, and she thanked heaven that some residue of common sense, and the terms of her lease, had persuaded her to keep her own tiny apartment. Well, she should have known better. No doubt Bob's field of study had given her a false impression. She wouldn't have been surprised to find that a budding lawyer or doctor or business executive was a ravening chauvinist in sheep's clothing, but philosophers were supposed to be gentle, rational, and fair-minded. She should have remembered Nietzche and the Superman, Plato's views on slaves, women, and other inferior creatures, and similar philosophical aberrations.

The storm-gray skies were so dark that she could see her face reflected in the window glass, and its malevolent expression and dim transparency suggested something out of a horror story—a wind-blown demon, pausing in its flight over the cities of men to perch for a moment and leer in at her window. A doppelgänger, the phantom double of the soul, whose appearance portended danger and death.

8

The externalization of her own evil thoughts, grimacing and glowering at her. . . .

Laurie's wide mouth curved in a smile of amusement, and the reflected features changed from diabolical to benign. Malevolence sat strangely on her face; it was round and pink and healthy-looking, with big brown eyes—the Morton brown eyes, so dark they looked black in most lights—and a generous, full-lipped mouth. Normally her mind was as healthy as her face; hostile thoughts were alien to it. She had spent too much time thinking up rude descriptions of Bob. At least the letter had given her something new to worry about.

Laurie should not have been staring out the window. She had a towering pile of notes on the table, on the left side of her typewriter, and a stack of virgin typing paper on the right side. She should have been working. Instead, she reached for the letter and read it again.

The beautiful, Spencerian handwriting was a little tremulous, but that was not surprising. Great-Aunt Ida was getting on. She and Laurie shared a birthday, so it wasn't hard for Laurie to figure out the old lady's age. Ida had been sixty-eight the year Laurie was sixteen. She had spent most of that summer at Idlewood, and they had had a joint birthday party. So Ida was now seventy-five.

Her mind was as sharp as ever, though. The meticulous grammar and formal phrasing learned in Ida's long-ago school days were still faultless.

"My dear Laura," the letter began. "Far be it from me to place an additional burden on your time; I know the demands of a scholar's life and realize you must be 'burning the midnight oil' with your books."

Laurie grinned again at that. She had been burning the midnight oil, all right, but not with her books. How typical of her great-aunt to enclose that phrase in quotation marks, as if it were a bit of daring slang.

"However," the letter continued, "it has been some

weeks since we last heard from you, and naturally we are concerned over your well-being. I trust you do not leave your apartment after dark. The news broadcasts these days horrify us with their accounts of violence in the cities. I wish you would seriously consider coming to us to finish your dissertation. Our library is excellent, as you know; your old room is waiting for you; you would have the advantages of healthy country air and good food, instead of the sandwiches on which you no doubt subsist. I cannot believe you would patronize establishments of the sort we see on television; surely the waiters and waitresses constantly singing and dancing in the aisles would be enough to disturb one's digestion, even if the food were edible, which I understand it is not."

Laurie's grin broadened. Did Ida really suppose that the overworked employees of MacDonald's and Roy Rogers' burst into song whenever someone ordered a hamburger? The old lady had never set her sensible oxfords inside such a place. Indeed, the very idea of Ida, or Uncle Ned, or dear fluttery Aunt Lizzie munching french fries at a fast-food restaurant set Laurie's imagination reeling.

So they wanted her to return to the old family homestead, safe from the dangers of the city. Naive as they were, they watched enough television to be aware of those dangers, including some Ida was too proper to mention. Wouldn't they just love to have her there at Idlewood, firmly under their collective thumb, supervising her diet and her "young men," as they had done when she was sixteen! Remembering some of the young men Ida had considered suitable, Laurie rolled her eyes heavenward. Hermann Schott, for instance. Ida had mentioned that Hermann was still at home, still unmarried. Heaven save her from Hermann, and from Great-Aunt Ida's matchmaking habits.

And yet ... Her cynical smile softened as the memories flooded back. There might be worse fates than spending a few months at Idlewood; many advantages to balance the horror of Hermann and his kind. Idlewood had been her summer home for over ten years, and she loved it as much as the old people did.

The stone house had stood on the hilltop for more than two hundred years. Walls three feet thick resisted the cold winds from the western mountains; cedars and pines formed a protective barrier around it. The first Morton to come to Maryland, fleeing the harsh retaliation of a Hanoverian king, had carried his Stuart loyalties and his threadbare kilt to the new world, his only wealth the cut-glass goblet with the Stuart rose, which had been used to drink the forbidden toast to Bonnie Prince Charlie. In the fertile farmlands of western Maryland he had won a grant of land and founded a family. Unlike many a feckless Highland cavalier, Angus Morton had been a hard worker and a shrewd businessman. He and his descendants had prospered. In the early part of the twentieth century Idlewood had been one of the great studs of Maryland, producing two Derby winners. The lovely blooded horses no longer graced the white-fenced pastures, but the original grant of over three hundred acres remained. Fields and pastures had been leased to neighboring farmers, but acres of tangled woods were untouched, giving sanctuary to Uncle Ned's beloved birds and animals. No hunter ever carried a gun onto the Morton property. The local people knew that Ned haunted the woods like a benevolent troll, and that he was perfectly capable of smashing an expensive rifle to tatters against a rock if he caught someone violating his No Trespassing signs. Despite his age—Laurie realized he must be nearing seventy-eight—he was in superb physical condition, probably because he spent most of his waking hours out of doors.

Ned had been the first one to welcome her to Idlewood. He had been a hale and hearty sixty-three then; she had been a bewildered, unhappy eight-year-old. Arriving at the bus station in Frederick, she found herself handed over by the driver to a terrifying apparition—a tall, burly, red-faced man in high laced boots and a heavy plaid shirt, who towered over her scrawny frame. But when he leaned down to take her hand she saw that the brown eyes behind his steel-rimmed glasses were soft with an emotion he was too reticent to express; and his big, hard fingers were very gentle as they clasped hers. They continued to reassure her as he led her toward the door, although he was muttering to himself in angry tones.

". . . little thing like that, come so far alone . . . always was irresponsible . . . *birds* make better mothers than Anna!"

Even at eight, Laurie had known why her mother had sent her away. Her parents were both actors; lots of her friends had several daddies and mommies. Dad and Mother were getting a divorce, and they didn't want her around while they went through the process, which Laurie knew must be unpleasant. "Breaking up," they called it, and they certainly had smashed a lot of dishes while they discussed it. No doubt, Laurie had thought, the divorce itself involved an awesome amount of broken crockery. But until Uncle Ned's muttered criticism of her mother Laurie had harbored a vague, nagging feeling that she might be at fault in some way. His blunt comments swept away guilt she hadn't even known she possessed.

So the ride to Idlewood, which she had dreaded, became a pleasant experience. A city child, Laurie had never seen such wide, rolling fields, or a sky so broad and blue. Black-and-white cows, all in a row along a fence, peering interestedly at her, made her giggle. Uncle Ned hardly spoke to her, which was good; most adults asked such silly questions, and she never knew what to answer. He whistled through his teeth, a most fascinating sound; Laurie determined to ask him how he did it. Long before they reached the tree-lined drive that led to the house she had decided she liked him. Then—the wonder of that moment would never be forgotten—she found out he was a magician.

He stopped the car under a canopy of green boughs and opened the door. With a gesture that cautioned her to be still, he walked away from the car and began making strange chirping noises. Something moved among the trees. Before Laurie had time to be frightened, a deer and two fawns stepped delicately onto the grassy bank.

From one of his pockets Uncle Ned took a handful of grain and held it out. The fawns danced skittishly; but the doe walked up to Ned and ate from his hand.

The moment had imprinted itself on Laurie's mind, not with the vagueness of most childhood memories, but as brilliant and perfect as a tiny scene from an illuminated manuscript—the vivid emerald green of the summer leaves washed with sunlight, the soft brown velvet of the doe's coat, the bright reds and blues of Uncle Ned's shirt. When the animals finally left, in a flash of lovely movement, Laurie's chest ached from holding her breath.

"Teach you how to do that," Ned had remarked, as he got into the car. "Takes patience. But you can learn."

Reluctantly Laurie returned from that glowing memory picture to snow and gray skies and the boring realities of adulthood. Had any child ever had a more magical introduction to a place? No wonder she had thought of Idlewood as her private fairyland—Oz, Middle Earth, Avalon, Narnia, a land where the animals could talk and no one ever grew old.

But the aunts and Uncle Ned *were* getting old. Ned was seventy-eight, Ida three years younger. It had taken Laurie some time to get over her awe of the stately, gray-haired lady who had addressed her, from the first, as an adult. Ida, who never admitted weakness or asked for help, had done so now, in the letter Laurie held. It was not a direct appeal; but

13

knowing her great-aunt as she did, Laurie was able to read between the lines.

"Please consider this suggestion seriously, Laura. I feel I must warn you that you will find *some of us* sadly changed. Your Uncle Ned continues in excellent health, and I have nothing of which to complain, considering my age. I only hope I will be taken *before my mind fails.* As you know, your Aunt Elizabeth has always been subject to fancies; but this latest affectation exceeds everything. Fairies in the woods, indeed!"

With this incredible statement the letter ended. Ida's signature was squeezed onto the bottom of the page.

Laurie knew quite well that her meticulous great-aunt would never have concluded a letter so awkwardly if she had been her usual calm, controlled self. There must have been another page, or part of one, in which Ida had enlarged on Lizzie's fancies, but for some reason the old lady had decided not to send it.

Aunt Lizzie, the baby—now seventy years old. . . . Aunt Lizzie had always been something of a problem to her strict, literal-minded elder sister. Ida was the only one who called her Elizabeth.

Again Laurie's memory returned to the past—to that first visit. Her eight-year-old mind had still been bemused by the magic of the deer when they reached the house to find both aunts waiting at the door. Ida, grave and tall in her sober dark dress, had shaken her hand and greeted her formally, but Lizzie had emoted enough for two people. She immediately dropped to her knees and enfolded Laurie in her arms, dripping tears all over her. Marshmallows, chiffon, goosedown pillows, whipped cream . . . Lizzie was all the soft, sweet, gooey things Laurie had ever known, coalesced into the shape of one plump old lady. Aunt Lizzie called her "darling" and "sweetheart," and hugged her a dozen times a day, and stuffed her with cookies when Ida wasn't looking.

Lizzie was "the domestic one." She cooked superbly, she embroidered and crocheted, and she made Laurie inappropriate, exquisitely stitched Kate Greenaway dresses, tucked and trimmed with lace and ruffles. Laurie would have preferred jeans, but she wore those dresses without a word of complaint.

And now, at the tender age of seventy, Lizzie had finally flipped. That was what Ida's terse hints meant.

Aunt Lizzie's fancies were a family tradition. Over the years she had enjoyed every psychic fad from spiritualism to a firm belief in flying saucers. Once, when investigating astral projection, she had hypnotized herself so thoroughly that it took a doctor to snap her out of it. Another time she had hired a strange young man from a local college to erect a tower from the top of which electrical impulses would be beamed toward distant galaxies, in the hope of getting return greetings from Arcturus. ("But, Aunt Lizzie, why Arcturus, of all places?" "Oh, I don't know, darling; it just seemed like the logical spot, don't you think?") The doctor had to come again, two years later, when Aunt Lizzie, attempting some form of yoga, had found herself unable to get her foot out from under the opposing elbow. Laurie's favorite fancy was the reincarnation bit; Aunt Lizzie, having concluded that she was the reborn soul of an ancient Egyptian princess, had gone jingling around the house in gold jewelry, draped in a sheet, emitting cryptic sentences in what she fondly believed to be the tongue of Ramses and Tutankhamon. She had bought a dictionary and a grammar and had taken up the study of hieroglyphs, which she scribbled on every flat surface in the house.

It had all been very entertaining and harmless. True, Aunt Lizzie had limped for a few days after the doctor finally got her foot out from under her elbow, but that had only been a slight sprain. Lizzie had a restless, imaginative mind; it was childish in the same sense that children's minds are unconfined by convention, open to wonder. That very quality had made Aunt Lizzie a wonderful companion for a small girl, and she had unquestionably shaped Laurie's mental development. She had supplied Laurie lavishly with fairy tales and books of fantasy; the two of them had told each other ghost stories by the light of the dying fire in the parlor, and had scared one another half to death.

So Laurie was not surprised that her aunt should be pursuing fairies. She had tried everything else, and "the little people" were in fashion. The bookstores had several new books on the subject—not, as one might expect, in the juvenile section. Gnomes and fairies and the fantastic worlds of Tolkien and Richard Adams were quite respectable hobbies for intelligent adults.

No, the alarming thing was not the subject itself, or Lizzie's interest in it. It was Ida's reaction. She had never been other than scornfully contemptuous of Lizzie's fantasies; neither had she ever been particularly worried by them. She was worried now. Her concern was implicit in every guarded word, in the very handwriting of her letter. The fact that it had been sent special delivery was a cry of alarm in itself. The Mortons didn't have to worry about money, but they did not waste pennies. They were still Scots at heart.

Laurie switched on a lamp. It was only four o'clock, but the sky outside was night-dark with winter. Two more hours until the telephone rates changed. She had her own share of Scottish blood, but in her case frugality was necessary; she was supporting herself, and a graduate student's stipend left no cash for extras. Anyway, Aunt Ida would have a fit if she wasted the money.

As she sat staring at the telephone, it began to ring. The strident shrilling sounded abnormally loud in the silent room. Laurie reached for the phone, and then hesitated. Once before, after a quarrel, Bob had called her and made extravagant promises, which she had been stupid enough to believe. She didn't want to go through that again. The phone insisted. Reluctantly, Laurie picked it up.

Her heart jumped at the sound of a masculine voice, but even before she had said, "Yes," in reply to the questioning, "Laurie?" she knew it wasn't Bob.

"You sound funny," the voice said. "Didn't you ever have those adenoids taken out? Or is it just your corn-fed Midwest accent?"

Laurie removed the telephone from her ear and stared at the mouthpiece. Then she replaced it.

"Who is this?" she demanded.

"Break, my heart," the unfamiliar voice moaned. "She has forgotten. And I had hoped I had left an indelible impression. Dear sibling, don't you know your one and only brother?"

"Doug?"

"Have you other brothers? I didn't think so, but with Mother you can never be entirely—"

"Really, Doug!"

"Prissy as ever. How long has it been, sister mine? Five years?"

"Longer than that," Laurie said.

She remembered only too well. The summer she was sixteen, when she and Ida had celebrated their July birthdays with high revelry.

Doug had been seventeen, going on ten; preparing for college in the fall, and insufferably superior as only a boy that age can be. He wasn't her brother, he was her half-brother, a souvenir of Anna's first marriage. After Laurie was born her mother had decided that the joys of motherhood were overrated; she had not had other children. Which was a good thing, Laurie thought, if Doug was a specimen of what Anna produced. His father had received custody of him after the divorce, and he was supposed to spend his summers with Anna; which meant, as in Laurie's case, that he spent them at Idlewood with the Mortons. For six or seven summers she had seen a good deal of him, and had hated every moment of the time they spent together. After he started college he managed to visit Idlewood for a week or so every year, but somehow these visits had never coincided with Laurie's increasingly infrequent trips east. Normal sibling rivalry had been intensified by other factors, quite obvious to her now. She had no memories of Doug except unpleasant ones.

Doug stuffing himself with cookies so there would be none left for her (and he never even got sick, which added insult to injury); Doug beating her at Scrabble, Parcheesi, and Monopoly every time they played, and jeering at her for being stupid; Doug teaching her to play football, and tackling her every time she got her hands on the ball. It was many years later before she discovered that kicker and passer were supposed to be exempt from late hits.

"How did you get my number?" she demanded.

"Ida."

"Why did you. . . . ? Oh." Her mind, usually so quick at putting the pieces together, was slow today. "You got a letter from her too?"

"Right. She sounded so worried I thought I'd better call her."

"I was about to telephone her myself," Laurie admitted. "Though I can't figure out why she's so upset."

"She's upset, all right." Doug's voice deepened portentously. "My letter was sent special delivery."

Laurie couldn't help laughing.

"Mine, too. So being richer or not as cheap as I am, you called her. What did she say?"

"Not much. You know how she is about long-distance calls. I had a hard time convincing her I wasn't on the verge of death, and when she found out I was okay I had an even harder time keeping her from hanging up on me. I couldn't get much out of her. But I've decided to take her up on her invitation. I don't like the sound of things, and I want to see for myself."

"You really think the situation is that serious?"

"Yes, I do. All the more so since you tell me she

sent you the same distress signals. I won't go into laborious detail about why I think so; you know the old girl as well as I do. You and I are the only ones who care about them. The only ones Ida would call on for help."

"I know."

"So," Doug went on rapidly, "I figured I had better call you. There's no point in both of us going if you're tied up with work. I mean, if it's hard for you to get away . . . No point in both—"

"Tom Sawyer," Laurie interrupted.

"Huh?"

"The old 'don't help me whitewash the fence' technique," Laurie muttered. "Never mind. I don't suppose you are aware of your own foul subconscious motives. How is it you can take time off to go chasing little green elves? I thought you were working for a firm of architects in Atlanta."

"No, no, nothing so plebeian. I'm my own boss. Left Banks, Biddle, and Burton to start my own show."

Laurie grinned fiendishly.

"Aha. You've got no clients."

The ensuing silence vibrated with unexpressed emotions. Then Laurie heard a muffled sound that might have been, and in fact was, a laugh.

"Got it in one," Doug said. "I'm starving. If I don't accomplish anything else, at least I can fatten up on Lizzie's cooking. You coming or not?"

Laurie glanced at the window. It was frosted over, but the hiss of sleety snow was clearly audible.

"I'm coming."

"I could pick you up at the Baltimore airport . . . when?"

"I'll call you back after I've made a reservation."

"Good. If I'm not in," Doug said grandly, "just leave a message with my secretary."

He hung up before she could ask the obvious question: if he was broke, how could he afford a secretary?

19

The following afternoon, when Laurie's plane took off from O'Hare, it was snowing again. She was glad she hadn't waited any longer; a little more of this, and by nighttime the airport might be closed. She settled back in her seat, beamed at the stewardess, and ordered a drink. The pilot announced that it was raining in Baltimore, and that the temperature was forty-three. Rain! Forty-three! Practically tropical, by Chicago standards. A further source of satisfaction was the fact that her phone had been ringing as she locked the door of her apartment, and some psychic sense told her that the caller was Bob. She hoped it had been, and that he would continue to call an empty apartment and wonder where she was.

However, as the plane descended for its landing at Baltimore, Laurie was conscious of a mounting discomfort. She knew its source. She hadn't seen Doug for years, and she had detested him. Modern psychology had relieved her of any old-fashioned need to love her brother; all the same, she was nervous about seeing him again. She wondered if she would recognize him.

Nor did she. Her eyes passed over the tall, sandy-haired man in the leather jacket, though her basic instincts registered his appearance with approval. He knew her, though. Before she had time to look further, she was enveloped in a leathery embrace, her nose mashed against a shirt front smelling of tobacco, aftershave, and . . . Chanel Number Five? As he held her at arms' length, caroling joyful greetings, she saw the smudge of lipstick on his collar and understood the perfume. She also understood how Doug could afford a secretary.

"Dearest sister," Doug murmured, and pulled her toward him again. This time, prepared, she fended him off with a hard hand against his chest.

"You'll never see any of these people again," she

said coldly, indicating the passing throngs. "Why put on a show for them?"

"Why not? Gives them a warm, happy feeling about the nuclear family which, as we all know, is in serious trouble. I'd know you anywhere, dear. Same plump face, same buckteeth. . . . Too bad nobody in our family believed in orthodontists."

"I have been told," said Laurie, "that the teeth give me a piquant air. I'm so glad your acne didn't leave bad scars. I mean, in a dim light I can hardly see them."

"Good, good," Doug said approvingly. "Hit back. You've toughened up, haven't you? You used to cry."

"With rage." Laurie found her arm tucked chummily in his as they walked toward the baggage area. He was tall; the top of her head only reached his chin. Yet somehow their strides seemed to match quite well.

They left the terminal with Laurie's bags, and Doug gestured.

"That's my car."

It was a low-slung sports car, bright red, adorned with extra strips of chrome and waving antennas. Standing by it, his hands on his hips, was a uniformed policeman.

"Yours?" he demanded unnecessarily, as Doug whipped the door open and slung Laurie's suitcases in the back.

"Shore is, suh," Doug replied, with a candid smile. "Part of it, leastways; the bank still owns ever'thing 'cept the fenders."

Bemused by his sudden lapse into a corny Southern accent, Laurie let him shove her into the car.

"Mah li'l sister," he informed the policeman. "Purty as a daisy, ain't she?"

He closed the car door. Laurie promptly rolled down the window. She didn't want to miss a syllable.

"Don't you know you aren't suppsed to park here?" the policeman demanded, indicating a very large, very conspicuous sign that read, "No parking. Driver must not leave vehicle."

Doug's face drooped like that of a disconsolate hound.

"Oh, gee whillikers. Ah shore didn't see that there. Been so long since Ah seen sis, Ah jest run in there. . . . You go 'head and give me a ticket, officer. Ah don't want no special privileges, no, suh."

The officer looked from Doug's sad brown eyes to the Georgia license plate.

"Okay," he said gruffly. "Come on, son, get it out of here."

"Yes, suh! Ah shore thank you, suh!"

The car slid sedately along the ramp toward the exit.

"Of all the con artists," Laurie exclaimed. "You should have been a lawyer instead of an architect."

"Believe me, dear, an architect has to do a certain amount of conning. Good thing I was the star of my college dramatic society."

"Must have been a small college. Even Mother isn't as bad as that."

Doug chuckled complacently.

"Yes, she is. Anna got where she is—wherever that may be—by means of other talents than dramatic ability. Never mind her. Tell me about yourself. What are you doing these days?"

Laurie had learned to be defensive about her specialty, which was domestic life in the Middle Ages. People usually reacted with ill-concealed mirth, or with outrage: "You mean my taxes are paying for somebody to study where they put the privies in medieval castles?"

However, Doug accepted her belligerent, one-sentence statement soberly, and asked several almost-intelligent questions. Only one of the questions was critical, and she had to admit it was a reasonable criticism. "Why Chicago? I don't know much about your field, but I didn't think they had one of the great departments in that subject."

22

"Oh, I have all the material," Laurie explained rapidly. "And I can always get copies of anything I might have missed. What I needed was a computer, and a central library."

"Oh. But why—"

"Tell me about yourself," Laurie suggested.

As she had expected, that subject occupied them for the rest of the drive. The day was overcast, the highway shining with wet; they had passed Frederick before she caught her first glimpse of the mountains, lining the horizon ahead like heavy clouds, mist enshrouding their gently curving flanks. They were soft, low mountains, time-worn and tired, unlike the jagged peaks of the Far West. The spots on the windshield changed from water to small white dots—not the big, threatening snowflakes that had engulfed Chicago, but delicate, secretive. Doug broke a brief silence to say, with obvious satisfaction, "They're predicting a couple of inches of snow tonight." Laurie knew he was thinking of the old house surrounded by sweeping, spun-sugar lawns, the dark pines frosted with white.

Night had fallen by the time they turned off the highway onto the twisting, roller-coaster road that led through the tiny hamlet of Thurbridge to Idlewood. The road was slipery with snow. When they turned into the driveway between the tall stone pillars, Laurie saw the lights of the house shining through the pine branches like scattered yellow fireflies.

"Stop," she said.

"What for?" But he did as she asked. When he switched off the engine the silence was almost deafening—not just the absence of sound, but a quality complete in itself, echoing in ears which had become accustomed to the continual background rumble of a large city. The headlights stabbed into the darkness ahead, but on either side blue-black night pressed against the windows.

It was at this point on the driveway that she had seen the deer, so long ago. Laurie had the feeling that the animals were there now, loitering just beyond the light, in the security of darkness: a ring of unwinking, watching eyes. The thought was not entirely comfortable. She shivered; and Doug, with an uncanny effect of reading her thoughts, said, "Spooky place at night, isn't it? No wonder the old lady is seeing ghosts and goblins."

"Fairies and elves," Laurie corrected. "That's what I wanted to—"

"Same thing. Spooky."

"Come on, now. You can't call elves—"

"Elves are second cousins to ghouls and goblins," Doug insisted. "You and Lizzie used to read those yarns. . . . I remember one night by the fire; it was a rainy, dreary night, and she was telling ghost stories. There was one about a severed hand that crawled around on its fingers, like a spider. Scared me into fits."

"Did it really?" Laurie said, pleased.

"There was another one," Doug went on. "A poem. Funny thing . . ."

"What was funny about it?"

"Funny peculiar, not funny ha-ha. It was about two girls named Laura and Lizzie. Odd coincidence, wouldn't you say?"

"No, I wouldn't. What poem?"

"Don't tell me you've forgotten it. 'We must not look at goblin men, We must not buy their fruit. . . .'"

"'Who knows upon what soil they fed, Their hungry, thirsty roots.' Of course I remember it, but I'm surprised you do. It's called 'Goblin Market.' I had forgotten the names of the little girls, that's all."

"Hard to explain why some things stick in your mind," Doug said. "Compared to the other horrors Lizzie fed us, that was relatively innocuous. But it gave me the cold shivers."

"I don't see why. The theme is common in folklore; ordinary mortals aren't supposed to eat fairy food, it destroys them. But that poem had a happy ending, as I remember. Good little Lizzie saved careless little Laura from the ill effects of the fruit she bought from the goblins. Or was it vice versa?"

"All the same, it gave me the cauld grue," Doug insisted. "Damned unwholesome things, fairy tales. Let's get out of here. I'm starting to see things skulking in the shadows."

"Wait," Laurie said, as he turned the key in the ignition. "I wanted to talk to you about Lizzie."

"What's to talk about? The reason we came was because we didn't know enough about the situation to discuss it."

"Yes, but—"

"I'm starved," Doug said, and put his foot on the gas.

"Chicken," Laurie said. Doug pretended not to hear.

They came out of the trees to see the house ahead, looming high on its small hill. Every window was ablaze with welcome; the carriage lamps on either side of the front door showed the exquisite tracery of the fanlight, which was one of the house's unique features. They also showed a tall figure in boots and plaid jacket, wielding a broom. Uncle Ned, seventy-eight years old, was making sure they wouldn't slip and hurt themselves on the steps.

CHAPTER

2

Doug applied himself to Aunt Lizzie's cooking as if determined to prove that his claim of imminent starvation was not exaggerated. Lizzie had told him he was too thin, but then she always said that; she had told Laurie the same thing, and Laurie was sadly aware that the sedentary, snowed-in winter months had not improved her figure. Oh, well, she told herself, I can't start dieting now; it would hurt Aunt Lizzie's feelings. Besides, Lizzie's chocolate cake, frosted lavishly with whipped cream and decorated with black walnuts and cherries, was too good to resist.

The table was magnificent, set with the old family china and silver. Candles glowed and fresh flowers filled the massive silver bowl in the center of the table. The heavy damask cloth was the one used on major holidays; it had been especially woven in France for Great-grandfather Morton, and it incorporated the family crest amid its pattern of thistles and Stuart roses.

Laurie leaned back in her chair and looked at her brother, who was finishing his second piece of cake under Aunt Lizzie's approving eye. Her certainly was not too thin. A little on the lean side, perhaps, but "a fine figure of a man," as Ida had called him.

The candlelight was kind to the faces of the old people. At first glance they did not seem much changed. As long as Laurie had known them they had been wrinkled and gray-haired. To an eight-year-old, they had seemed as old as Time itself, and it was hard to get any older than that. But as she studied their faces Laurie realized that the years had taken their toll.

Ned had held up well. Leather, once tanned, does not change much until the final disintegration sets in, and a lifetime out of doors, in all weather, had hardened her great-uncle years before. His dark eyes were more sunken and his eyebrows a shade or two lighter than when she had last seen him, but he was still in remarkable physical condition.

Lizzie had gained a few pounds, which wasn't surprising, since she enjoyed her own cooking as much as anyone else. Some years before her hair had turned suddenly from streaked brown to snow white. As always, it was beautifully coifed. She was wearing an astonishing garment—a caftan of crimson sari silk, shot with gold and trimmed along the swooping sleeves with wide rows of gold braid and sequins. She had preened herself like a plump sparrow when Laurie admired the gown, and had whispered in conspiratorial tones, "I got the idea from Miss Taylor. So becoming to those of mature figure, don't you think?"

Ida had always been as gaunt and rigid as her sister was plump and soft. She still carried herself well, despite the arthritis that showed most visibly in her twisted fingers; but the signs of strain were there, in the tightness of her mouth and the purple stains under her eyes. Lizzie might be cracking up mentally—though as yet Laurie had seen no signs of it—but Ida was the one who was suffering physically.

When even Doug had eaten his fill, Lizzie rose grandly to her full five feet height, her crimson draperies billowing.

"We will have coffee in the drawing room," she announced.

"We will if Douglas will be kind enough to carry the tray," Ida said drily. "What possessed you to use that old silver, heavy as lead—"

"We always use Great-grandmother Emily's silver service on festal occasions." Lizzie's pursed lips trembled. "You know that, Ida. You know we always—"

"I'll get the tray," Doug said hastily, as Lizzie's eyes overflowed. "Glad to. I'll even help Laurie clear the table."

"Thanks a heap," said Laurie.

"No need for that," Uncle Ned said. "Jeff does that. In the morning. Leave it."

From under the table, like a second to the motion, came a muffled bark. Ned glanced guilelessly around the room, as if trying to locate the source of the sound.

"I know that dog is under the table," Ida snapped. "And I know you have been slipping it food. Disgusting habit. I am certainly not going to leave food on the table to be gobbled by that creature."

"She's too well trained to do that," Ned said.

Laurie, sitting at her uncle's right, had also been aware of the dog's presence. Its head had weighed warm and heavy on her foot, and occasionally a moist tongue had swabbed her ankle. She lifted the cloth and looked under. The dog, a handsome golden retriever, grinned amiably at her, its plumy tail swishing. Uncle Ned always had a dog, but this was one she had not yet seen. His old Lab, Regina, had died the year before.

"Jeff?" she asked. "He looks as if he'd be happy to clear the table."

"Oh, no, dear, that's Duchess," Lizzie said in shocked

tones; and Laurie remembered that her uncle's dogs were always female. "You know Jefferson. Oh, perhaps you don't. But we have written about him, surely."

"I'd forgotten his name," Laurie said. "Your handyman?"

"Oh, much more than that," Lizzie exclaimed. "Jefferson is one of the family. He's a darling boy, he really is. I don't know how we'd have managed without him the last few years. We feel so fortunate to have found him. Good help is very difficult to get these days. He does everything for us."

"Helps the girls in the house," Ned added. " 'Course I don't need much help with the outside work. Strong as a horse. Nice to have an extra pair of hands for some chores, though."

"I'm looking forward to meeting this paragon," Doug said.

"Oh, well, naturally we expected him to join us this evening," Lizzie said. "But he is so sensitive, so understanding. He *said* he had an appointment, but I know he didn't, he just felt that this first evening we might like to be alone, just the family. Which is absurd, because he is practically one—"

"Hmph," Doug said. He glanced at Laurie and looked hastily away, but not before she had seen, and correctly interpreted, his expression. Jealous. Well, she thought sardonically, so am I. My own fault; if I'd spent more time with them the last few years . . . She turned to Ida.

"I remember, of course," she said. "You've all told me how good he has been. I had forgotten his name." (And, she added silently to herself, we won't ask how I could have forgotten it, mentioned as often as it was.)

If she had hoped for a cool note of criticism, to mitigate the general aura of infatuation that surrounded the absent Jefferson, she was disappointed.

"There is no reason why he should not dine with us on ordinary occasions," Ida explained. "Just the three of us—and he is so helpful about clearing up. In this day and age social distinctions are out of place. And Jefferson is no common person. He is writing a book."

"Is he really," Laurie said. "What about?"

"It is a novel," Ida explained.

"The great American novel?" Doug's tone was sarcastic, but the old lady took the comment seriously.

"Most probably it will be. We must not expect immediate recognition, however. As Jefferson has said so often, modern literature is in a sad state. Critics praise the trash and ignore what is healthy and sound."

"Uh-huh," Doug said.

"With all due deference to Jefferson, I think I will clear the table," Laurie said, pushing her chair back. "You three go into the parlor; Doug and I will deal with this, and bring the coffee."

Once the old people were out of the room—followed, obediently but reluctantly, by Duchess, who cast wistful glances over her furry shoulder as she retreated—Doug began stacking plates with reckless disregard of their age and fragility.

"Who is this creep?" he demanded.

"Jefferson Banes," Laurie said. Strangely enough, the name came quite readily to her now. "Didn't they write you about him? He came just after I was here the last time. It was a relief to me they found him; the Petersons got too old to work, they went to live with their daughter."

"Yeah, they wrote about him. But I thought he was just the usual local man of all work, not some languishing genius."

"He may or may not be a genius, but I don't know why you should assume he languishes."

Doug dumped his stack of plates on the counter.

"They talk about him as if he were a saint. He's wormed his way into their confidence."

"Worming and languishing," Laurie said, in tones

of mock horror. "What other vile habits can this monster exhibit?"

"Jefferson Banes. Silly name. Sounds like a villain in a murder mystery."

"Don't be silly."

"Listen, you don't like it any better than I do. I saw your face when they were raving about him."

"Maybe I don't. But at least I know my attitude is unreasonable. For heaven's sake, don't antagonize the man, will you? If he gets mad and quits, we're in trouble. Lizzie is right; findlng live-in help isn't easy, and they couldn't go on living way out here without someone to keep an eye on them."

"All right, all right. I will be very cool." Doug lowered his voice. "Have you had a chance to talk to Ida?"

"No. You?"

"No, too much general conviviality. Lizzie looks okay, don't you think?"

"Yes. But, you know—"

"Wait a minute. I'd better continue clearing the table or they'll wonder what we're talking about in here."

Doug was back almost at once with a handful of delicate goblets bunched in his hands like beer steins.

"Well?" he demanded. "What were you going to say?"

"Isn't it a little peculiar that Aunt Lizzie hasn't talked about her latest kick? Usually when she has a new hobby she can't think about anything else. And if Ida is right, this one has really grabbed her."

"Hmmm." Doug rubbed his chin. "You're right. I remember the time she went in for spiritualism. I had barely walked in the front door before she had me at the dining-room table with a Ouija board spread out in front of us. She wanted to find out if I was psychic."

"Were you?"

Doug grinned. "She got a couple of fascinating messages."

31

"Doug, you are really the most—"

"Don't leap to conclusions. The spirit of George Washington told her not to have any truck with spiritualism. I—sorry, George—said he was sick and tired of being dragged away from his game of pool to pass on idiotic messages about birds and flowers and love."

"Pool?"

"Well, they had billiards in the eighteenth century," Doug said. "George always struck me as the sporting type. Lizzie didn't bat an eye; she agreed that he had a point."

"Watch out," Laurie said. "Here she comes."

Thanks to her size and her habit of voicing her thoughts aloud, Lizzie's approach was never inaudible. Doug and Laurie were busily at work when she billowed into the kitchen, asking, in somewhat pointed tones, if there was something she could do to help.

The rest of the evening was spent watching television. Ida mentioned that there was an excellent classical-music concert on public TV, but Lizzie refused to miss her favorite sex-and-violence crime show. She squeaked with delighted horror every time one of the "cops" hit one of the bad guys, and although Ida pretended to knit, her aristocratic nose in the air, she watched too, out of the corner of her eye. Ned, his hands folded across his flat stomach, seemed to doze.

Promptly at ten o'clock Ida rolled up her knitting and rose stiffly to her feet.

"Bedtime," she announced. "You two young things may sit up if you like, but we old folks need our sleep."

"Me too." Doug rose, yawning and stretching. "Uncle Ned and I are going out at the crack of dawn to look for beavers or something. I'm bushed. Must be the country air."

"Sleep will be good for you," Ida said fondly. "Laura?"

"You go on," Laurie said. "I'll lock up."

She had hoped her eldest aunt might take this excuse to linger and tell her of the family trouble. But Ida went out with the others, and after a short interval the old house settled drowsily for the night.

Laurie sat staring at the TV screen without hearing a word of the talk show going on. She was conscious of the same warmth and sense of homecoming the house always gave her. But tonight something was different. Under her feeling of drowsy content, an awareness of something obscurely wrong stirred and shifted through the currents of her thought.

Finally she switched off the TV set, checked the doors and the thermostats, and went upstairs. The broad, shallow steps, worn by generations of Morton feet, squeaked faintly as she ascended. The bedroom doors were closed, but when she stopped on the landing she could hear Uncle Ned's lusty snores and a weaker, younger echo from behind the door of Doug's room.

She was about to go on up to the next floor when something soft brushed her ankle, and such was her state of mind that she let out a muffled yelp. Looking down she saw a tawny, sinuous form winding around her feet. Ida's Siamese cat was sixteen years old, and still going strong.

"Sabrina," she whispered. "Why aren't you in bed?"

Sabrina's aristocratic jaws parted. She let out a strident Siamese yowl.

"Sssh!" Laurie cautioned. "Do you want to come upstairs with me? Do you want to go to Aunt Ida?" Sabrina made it clear that she preferred the latter alternative. Carefully Laurie turned the doorknob. As soon as the door was open a few inches Sabrina slid through the gap without so much as a thank you.

Laurie went on up the stairs. Her room was on the third floor. Formerly an attic, it had been remodeled, when she became a regular visitor, into a young girl's dream room. The slope of the roof was so steep that only a very small person could make the most of the space, and even in adolescence it had been necessary for Laurie to roll out of bed instead of sitting up first. She hoped old habits would reassert themselves, so that she wouldn't brain herself in the morning.

Though the room was never used except by her, it was fresh and neat and warm as toast. The house was heated by radiators, which had never been extended to this attic, but registers set in the floor let the heat from below rise, to be trapped under the insulated ceiling. The only windows were at the end, on either side of the huge stone chimney. Their deep sills were piled with cushions. The frilly bedspread, the fluffy rug, and the Peter Rabbit prints had been selected by Aunt Lizzie, years ago. Laurie's tastes had altered, but she would not have removed a single rabbit.

After getting into her nightgown she looked for a book on the shelves that had been set under the eaves. Like the prints, the books were treasures of her childhood, and they suited her nostalgic mood; but she had not realized that so many of them were fairy tales. The Oz books, all twenty-six of them, and the other Baum titles; the Lang fairy books, all the way through the spectrum, from blue to yellow; Japanese fairy tales, African fairy tales, Swedish fairy tales; Andersen and the Brothers Grimm, George MacDonald's Goblin books; *Peter Pan,* of course, and *Pinocchio.* She had always hated Pinocchio. What a little horror he was, sniveling and whining, lying and cheating—a fine hero for a child's book. Monstrous, in fact. . . .

Wind rattled the window frame. Laurie glanced uneasily over her shoulder. Except for the reading lamp by the bed, which she had not yet switched on, the lighting was dim, muffled by ruffly shades and painted globes. One shadow looked like a face with an elongated nose. As she watched it, another strong draft set the curtains to swaying, and the shadow moved.

Why was it that as a child she had never been conscious of the dark, sinister side of the familiar fairy tales? The Grimm stories were retellings of dismal old Teutonic legends. Even the more innocuous stories had terrifying passages—dragons, witches, trolls. Doug was right; elves and ghouls were second cousins, citizens of a world beyond the boundaries of the reasonable universe.

And dear sweet old Aunt Lizzie had fed her on those horrors. Lizzie had selected most of the books, except for a few moral tales contributed by Ida, and if there was a fairy tale Lizzie had missed, her niece couldn't find it. The old lady had kept abreast of the modern contributions to the field too—Lloyd Alexander, C. S. Lewis, Tolkien.

Yes, the collection seemed complete. There were occasional gaps on the shelves, though, and Laurie wondered whether Aunt Lizzie selected her bedtime reading from these books. She wouldn't be surprised. She certainly could not picture the Mortons reading Updike or Saul Bellow. They knew the names of the various parts of the human body, but they were not accustomed to seeing some of those words in print.

Laurie decided she was not in the mood for fairy tales. She shifted position to another section of bookshelves. Here were books of another type—old-fashioned and, in their way, just as unrealistic as the fairy tales; but at least they were not replete with goblins. *Rebecca of Sunnybrook Farm* rubbed shoulders with *Daddy Long Legs* and the masterpieces of Frances Hodgson Burnett. Laurie selected *Little Lord Fauntleroy,* wondering if that angelic small boy was really as revolting as she remembered.

Little Ceddie *was* that revolting. Dearest, his mama, was even worse. Skimming rapidly, and grimacing, Laurie finished the book in record time. Contemptuous as she was of the saintly Cedric, she could understand the appeal of books like this. Virtue was so seldom rewarded in real life that it was nice to read a book in which it not only triumphed, but was endowed with immense wealth, ducal coronets, and the fatuous adoration of everybody in the neighborhood.

She put the book on her bedside table and switched off the light.

Young Cedric's adventures should have been soporific, but Laurie found herself wide awake. For a time she lay staring up at the ceiling, only a few feet above her face. As her pupils expanded, the room seemed to fill with pearly light—reflected moonlight, surely. The snow must have stopped. Sleep continued to elude her, so she got out of bed and went to the window. The view was so lovely that she wrapped her robe around her and climbed up on the window seat.

It had been one of her favorite retreats in childhood. Cocooned in cushions, she had sat there for hours, reading or dreaming. The window looked out over the trees, across the wide gardens toward the woods. Sure enough, the snow had ended. The wind hurried the last straggling clouds along. A remote sliver of moon rode high above the treetops, silvering the blanket of snow on the lawn. The boxwood hedges and sweeping fir boughs were frosted with white, glittering with faint crystalline sparkles. Beyond, like a dark enclosing wall, the trees sheltered the old house as they had done for centuries. There were no other houses visible; no man-made light broke the serenity of the night.

At last Laurie began to feel sleepy. She was about to get into bed when she saw something strange.

It was only a small point of light; but it shone where no light should be, deep among the dark pines. The land was posted. Surely no local hunter would dare to trespass; Uncle Ned's sentiments about hunting were well known, and his influence with local judges was considerable.

As Laurie stared, the light changed color. From a

clear white, it burned rosy red, then flared with blue and emerald green, before turning to a soft ethereal lavender. With each shift of color the light moved, rising and falling like a firefly. But no firefly changed color or position, with such quick, dartling motions. Occasionally the spark of light was momentarily obscured, as if it passed behind a bough or a tree trunk. Finally it soared high and went out.

Laurie continued to look for several minutes, but the light did not reappear. She wrapped the robe closer around her shoulders. The room felt very cold.

She fell asleep immediately, and dreamed that the Tin Woodman, no longer smiling and gentle, but a steel-bodied robot with flailing clublike arms, was chasing her down the Yellow Brick Road. The bricks were crumbling. Grass grew between them. Each green tendril was alive and edged with sharp sawteeth; they lashed at her ankles, uttering tiny wordless screams of mad rage as she fled.

She woke sweating and panting, and lay staring up at the rafters until the reality of waking removed the horror of the dream. She had no trouble falling asleep again; this time she dreamed she had pushed Little Lord Fauntleroy into a mud puddle. His black velvet suit was all nasty and dirty, and his weeping face was that of her brother.

Smiling, Laurie rolled over and sank into profound, satisfying slumber.

CHAPTER

3

The view from her window next morning was even more beautiful than it had been the night before. Fence posts, twigs, and branches were sheathed in a crystal coating of ice that scintillated like diamonds as the sun struck it. Laurie knelt on the window seat, enjoying not only the winter scene but the thought of Doug tramping through the cold in the darkness before dawn. He had not been a nature lover even as a child; the leather jacket and the sports car and a few other unmistakable signs of decadence assured Laurie that he would not find Uncle Ned's frigid vigils any more to his taste now. Leisurely she dressed and went downstairs.

The aunts were in the kitchen. Once the keeping room of the manor house, it retained the stone walls and massive fireplace of its original design. The mantel was a single walnut beam, several feet thick. Lizzie had placed pewter plates and rough pottery along the shelf, and had mounted a musket below.

The musket was not a family heirloom. Lizzie had bought it at an antique shop, to the consternation of Uncle Ned, who saw nothing ornamental, as he put it, about weapons of killing. He had been even madder when he found out the musket was loaded, with ball and black powder. It had not occurred to Lizzie that a spark from the fire below might set the gun off. It was pointed straight at a window—one of those that retained some panes of the precious original glass. But, as Ned sarcastically remarked, chances were that the gun would have exploded first, mangling everyone in the immediate neighborhood. The ball and powder had been removed, but the musket was still in place; a compromise which indicated with some accuracy the relationship between Ned and his younger sister.

Ida was seated at the kitchen table reading the newspaper. She gave Laurie a wintry smile and a stiff "Good morning." Lizzie was puttering around the room, wiping an already immaculate counter. She flung herself at Laurie with a greeting as emotional as if she had not seen her for years, and asked her what she wanted for breakfast. Laurie turned down pancakes, a mushroom omelette, and eggs Benedict; then, as Lizzie's lip began to vibrate ominously, she hastily agreed that baked eggs in cream would be fine, along with toast and jam. The bread would be homemade, she knew, and so would the jam.

Lizzie was wearing jeans that morning—custommade, no doubt, for no store-bought Levi's would have swathed her ample hips so neatly. They were topped by a garment almost as incredible as the one she had worn the night before. It was bright mustard yellow, embroidered from neck to shirttail with violently colored flowers and birds. A belt of heavy silver links studded with cabochon amethysts more or less confined it around the region of what should have been Lizzie's waist. She looked like a giant improbable tropical bird as she trotted from refrig-

39

erator to counter to stove, emitting breathless little bursts of chirping song.

Knowing Lizzie would be preoccupied for a while, Laurie sat down at the table and started on the chilled fruit cup her aunt had had waiting. Ida sipped her coffee. She didn't smoke or drink, but coffee was her vice; she often had ten cups a day. Laurie noticed that her aunt's hand trembled slightly as she lifted the cup; the shadows under her sunken eyes were even more pronounced in the morning light. Too much coffee? Laurie resolved to speak to Ida about it—but not now, with Lizzie listening. The elderly relatives guarded their weaknesses jealously, and resented criticism.

"Are Doug and Uncle Ned still out?" she asked.

"Yes. Heaven knows when they will return. Ned has no sense of time when he is out of doors. Did you sleep well, my dear?"

"Beautifully." Laurie remembered her nightmare, but decided it was not a fit subject for conversation. "Oh, Auntie"—as Lizzie placed a heaped plate before her—"that looks divine, but I can't eat so much!"

"Oh, honey, of course you can. You're pitifully thin! No more than skin and bones!"

"You'll want coffee," Ida said gruffly, and rose to get a cup.

"I'm going to need exercise if I go on eating this way," Laurie said. "Maybe I'll take a walk later. By the way, I saw the strangest light in the woods last night. All colors of the rainbow, moving around—"

A crash interrupted her. Turning, she saw her eldest aunt, gray-faced and rigid, standing over the fragments of one of the cherished Spode cups which had been in the family for six generations.

"How careless of you, Ida," said Lizzie. A frown ruffled her brow briefly, then was replaced by a beaming smile. "I'm so glad you saw them, Laurie. I felt sure you would sooner or later, because you are sensitive to such things, just as I am; but I did not hope they would come for you so soon."

"They? Who? What? No, Aunt, don't do that—let me—"

Laurie started to rise. Ida, gathering crisp shell-like fragments, waved her back into her chair.

"My carelessness, my task," she said, quoting an adage Laurie had heard often in her youth.

Humming, Lizzie went to the cupboard for another cup and saucer.

"Tell me about the light," Laurie said.

"Light? Oh, yes. It must have been Queen Mab herself; her aura is particularly brilliant and colorful. I have not yet been privileged to see her, but several of her lesser ladies-in-waiting have consented to be photographed."

Laurie now had occasion to bless her youthful interest in fairy tales. The speech would have made even less sense than it did without that background.

"The queen of the . . . fairies," she said, gulping over the last word.

"She is sometimes called Titania, but that is erroneous," Lizzie said blithely. She poured coffee with a steady hand. "Her consort, of course, is—"

"Oberon," Laurie said automatically. "Auntie, stop talking for a minute, will you? Did you say photographed? You don't mean you actually have—"

"Oh, dear me, yes. Haven't I mentioned them?"

"No, you have not." Laurie's tone was sharper than she had intended. Her aunt's vague, dithering statements, many of them prefixed by that characteristic, long-drawn-out, meaningless "oooh," had never irritated her more. The sight of Ida, grim and speechless as one of Notre Dame's lesser gargoyles, did not improve her temper.

Lizzie's pink mouth quivered.

"You sound so hard, darling," she murmured.

"I'm sorry. I didn't mean to. I'm just very—*very*—interested." Laurie knew it would not be politic to confess that she had already heard about the fairies. "Do tell me more, Aunt Lizzie."

"Oh, there isn't much to tell," Lizzie said, turning

back to the stove. "I do wish those men would return. Poor Douglas will be starved. Ned is so inconsiderate when he—"

"Auntie. You're teasing me. Tell me about—uh— Queen Mab. And the photographs."

"Oh, I thought I had told you. Dear me, I am becoming forgetful. Old age, perhaps."

"You'll never be old, Auntie," Laurie said. A muffled snort from Ida echoed the sentiment, but Laurie thought her aunt didn't mean it in quite the same way.

Lizzie's sunny smile reappeared.

"You're sweet to say so, darling. I feel that age is in the heart, not in the body, don't you? I did wonder if perhaps this blouse might not be just a teeny bit too youthful. I found it in a little shop in Georgetown; the Indians of Guatemala—or is it Honduras? —they embroider so beautifully, poor souls, and are so poorly paid that one feels guilty, really, in only paying—"

Laurie gave up, but only for the moment. Perhaps Lizzie had changed her mind about talking because of Ida; the older sister's silence fairly vibrated with hostility, and Laurie felt sure she had already expressed herself forcibly on the folly of Lizzie's latest fancy. She would have to try another approach, when she and Lizzie were alone. Toward that end she said slyly,

"I adore the blouse, Auntie. It suits you perfectly. I'll bet you've got lots of pretty new clothes. When can I see them?"

Twice a year, spring and fall, Lizzie made a pilgrimage to Washington, stayed overnight in a hotel, and spent two days shopping at Saks, Neiman-Marcus, Garfinckel's, and the boutiques of Georgetown. On those occasions she went berserk, buying anything that caught her eye, whether it suited her age and figure or not. It usually didn't. Yet there was some truth in Laurie's kindly flattery. Lizzie didn't look as frightful in the youthful garments as one might have expected. She enjoyed them so much that her very joie de vivre made them seem appropriate.

Lizzie's eyes brightened. "I've been dying to show off my new wardrobe, darling. Ida is no fun at all. She has such dull tastes."

"Great. And," Laurie added guilelessly, "you can show me the photographs of . . . the photographs. Did you take them?"

Lizzie looked as if she regretted her moment of candor, but it was too late for her to deny her statement. "Oh, no," she said, with a giggle. "You know how I am about machinery, sweetie."

"Who did take them?" Laurie persisted.

"Not I," said Ida grimly.

"I didn't think so. Who?"

"Ooooh!" Lizzie pounced, her full sleeves flaring; Laurie was reminded of an overweight parrot settling onto its perch. From under the table Lizzie took a limp ball of fluff. Its colors were a gorgeous sable-and-silver blend; its fur was long and soft. It dangled limply from Lizzie's pudgy hands, its green eyes half closed.

"Here's mama's Angel Baby," Lizzie said fondly. "You haven't said hello to Angel Baby, Laura dear."

"I haven't met Angel Baby." Laurie took the cat. It felt as if it had no bones at all. Opening its eyes a trifle wider, it looked at her and began to purr. Laurie was not flattered. The bland contempt in the cat's expression belied the purr. "I thought you had a white cat."

"Sweetums." Lizzie's eyes welled with tears, all in an instant, as if twin spigots had been turned on in her head. "Dear Sweetums passed on last year, Laura. This is her great-granddaughter."

"How is Mrs. Potter?" Mrs. Potter's prize Persians were famous. Lizzie had always gotten her cats from that source.

Before Lizzie could answer, Angel Baby turned suddenly from a hanging, miniature boa to a length of fur-covered muscle. With the agility of a flying

43

squirrel she soared from Laurie's lap to the window-sill, leaving a long bleeding scratch on Laurie's arm.

"Angel Baby always knows when the dog is approaching," Lizzie explained calmly. "She does not get on at all with Duchess."

The door opening onto the stone-floored entryway banged, and after a few moments the men appeared, accompanied by Duchess.

"Get that wet dog out of here," Ida exclaimed, as a friendly but undeniably damp tail swished her calves.

"I dried her," Ned said. "Lie down, Duchess. Lie down, I say!"

Pretending deafness, Duchess considered her options. Laurie was an attraction; but then a movement on the windowsill caught her eye and she leaped toward it. Angel Baby arched her back and spat. Duchess's flailing tail knocked a chair over. Uncle Ned's shouts of "Down, I say!" mingled with Lizzie's agitated shrieks.

The animals' encounter ended with a howl from Duchess and the abrupt departure of Angel Baby, who sailed across the kitchen, cursing, and disappeared into the dining room. Duchess lay down, put one paw over her nose, and moaned.

"Damn cat," said Uncle Ned equably.

"If you would train that ill-bred dog to leave my cat alone she would not get scratched," Lizzie said.

"Just wants to be friends," Ned said. "Your cat's a snob."

"Home sweet home," said Doug, grinning.

"And it's so good to have you home!" Her annoyance forgotten, Lizzie enveloped him in fluttering embroidery. "Now, Douglas, sit down, and I'll have your breakfast in two shakes. You, too, Ned—though you don't deserve it."

She went to the stove. Ned got a bottle and a bit of cotton from a shelf and ministered to the bleeding nose of Duchess, who submitted to the attention with fatuous pleasure. Either the dog was so good-natured she didn't mind the scratch, or else she was so used to such injuries that they had become part of the daily routine.

Taking a chair next to Doug's, Laurie said out of the corner of her mouth, "See any little elves out there?"

"Just Uncle Ned." Doug indicated the old man, who was sitting cross-legged on the floor talking to the dog. Her head cocked, her ears alert, Duchess listened with an appearance of profound interest. Doug grinned and shook his head. "I'm the one who's getting old," he confided, in the same low voice. "Have they always been like this, or am I just more conventional?"

"Both, probably. "We've got to talk."

"Right."

"How about a walk after—whatever the next meal is?"

"Are you kidding?" Doug's voice rose in a howl of outrage. Lizzie and Ned went calmly on with what they were doing, and Doug continued, "I'm going to take a nap. I froze several essential parts of my anatomy and pulled half the muscles in my body this morning. We must have walked twenty miles."

"About four," Ned said, without looking up. "You're out of condition, boy. Stay awhile. I'll get you in shape."

"That's what I'm afraid of."

"Wash your hands and sit down, Ned," Lizzie said, stepping over the dog. "Here you are, Douglas; now eat it up, every bite, and don't dawdle, or it will be time for lunch."

II

Incredible as it might seem, lunch did follow on the heels of that late breakfast; and when it was over Laurie was in no condition to insist on a walk, much as it might have benefited her. The elderly Mortons always rested in the afternoon. Ned, who had long since established squatters' rights to the library, called his siesta "working on my notes," though everyone knew he dozed in the big leather armchair by the fire, with his dog asleep at his feet.

Laurie had planned to follow Lizzie to her room for a cozy chat—and a look at the famous photographs—but, as if she suspected some such plot, Lizzie scuttled out of the kitchen as soon as the meal was over. Laurie would have settled for a confidential chat with her eldest aunt, but Ida also made her escape. Conscious of an uncomfortable cramped feeling in her midsection, Laurie cleared the table and filled the dishwasher. Then she went upstairs, and into Doug's room.

He was lying across the bed, fully dressed. As she entered he lifted his head slightly.

"You could knock," he suggested.

"You wouldn't have answered."

Like her own, Doug's room had not changed since childhood. Uncle Ned's hand was apparent in the decor here; even Lizzie had tacitly conceded that he had a prior right with a boy child. Audubon prints and animal paintings adorned the walls. The wide, low bed had a spread with figures of jungle beasts, lions and tigers and zebras, in colorful profusion. The book shelves contained every book ever written about animals, plus the hearty, innocent boys' books of Uncle Ned's youth. *The Boy Explorers in the Jungles of Africa, The Young Aviators in France. . . .*

Laurie sat down on the bed beside her brother. A muffled voice issued from the head half concealed between Doug's outstretched arms.

"We can't go on like this."

"Like what?"

"Eating." Doug rolled over, moaning faintly. "I'm sick. Lizzie cries if I turn down second helpings."

"I know, I know." Laurie stretched out beside him. "Did you ask Uncle Ned about the Good People?"

"The who?"

"The elves, the pixies, the Men of Peace, the—"

"Oh. Yeah, sure I did."

46

"Well?"

Doug propped himself on one elbow. "God's winged creatures are a far greater wonder than any imaginary elves. Why the hell Lizzie can't concentrate on the miracles of nature instead of fairy tales I do not know, but if that is her interest, why don't you all leave her alone?"

"Is that a quote?"

"Straight from Uncle Ned. He may have a point."

"I'm afraid not." The ache in Laurie's stomach was subsiding. She felt warm and comfortable and drowsy, but conscience would not be quelled. "Aunt Lizzie has pictures, Doug. Photographs."

"Have you seen them?"

"No. You were right, she's acting funny—not funny-weird, as usual. Unusual. She started to tell me about it, and then all of a sudden she clammed up. I spoke a little sharply. Maybe she realized I wasn't going to play this particular game with her. But she did say she has snapshots."

"So?" Doug's voice was slow with encroaching sleep.

"So . . ." Laurie shook off the contagion and forced herself to stay awake. "Lizzie said she didn't take the pictures, and I believe that; you know how she is about what she calls machines. She operates that electric stove, with its dozens of buttons, like a hotshot pilot, but she won't touch anything mechanical outside of the kitchen. Don't you see? Photographs mean a camera. A camera means a human being, taking the pictures. Somebody is playing tricks on Aunt Lizzie."

"Uh-huh . . ." As he lay outstretched, his arms over his head, his shirttail out, his ribs were temptingly exposed. Laurie jabbed her forefinger into his side.

"Wake up. You said it yourself, Doug—this fantasy isn't like Lizzie's usual games. Someone is taking advantage of her. We have to find out who took those pictures."

47

"I know who it was."

Laurie jabbed him again, harder. This time he let out a groan of protest and slapped her hand away.

"What a sadist you are," he mumbled. "I know about the photos. Ned told me. And I know who took them. It was a kid."

"A what?"

"A child, a youth, a young person. As a matter of fact, I'm not sure which of the children took the pictures. There are three of them. Three sweet, adorable little girls. Name of Wilson."

"Wilson. Don't they live near here? I seem to remember a mailbox a few miles down the road."

"Ned said they were neighbors. Around here that means a mile or two away. Do you remember the family?"

"The name is familiar, but I don't remember children. I would, if we had played with them."

"Not likely. They are much younger than we, my aged sib. The youngest just started kindergarten this year. She has," Doug added, "big blue eyes, golden curls, and a lisp."

"A lisp," Laurie repeated blankly.

"Yep. I have heard of lisping villains—didn't Peter Lorre lisp? But not a golden-haired, five-year-old lisping villain."

"But, Doug, that's impossible. A five-year-old couldn't take pictures."

"She could with one of those new cameras designed for the simple-minded. Aim, peer, and push the button." Doug yawned. "I don't know why you're so uptight about this. The snapshots are probably pictures of humming birds or blurry configurations of leaves or—"

A soft tap on the door interrupted him. He called, "Come in."

The door opened, a single tentative inch, and Ida's voice said, "Douglas? Are you asleep?"

Doug winked at Laurie.

"No, Aunt, I'm not asleep. Come in."

"I don't want to disturb you."

"I was just resting," Doug said resignedly. "Struck down by an excess of calories." He drew himself to a sitting position, and Laurie added, "Come in, Aunt. We were just—"

The door, which had been edging coyly open, banged back against the wall. Framed in the doorway like one of Rembrandt's more formidable matrons, her respectable gray hairs bristling, Ida glared.

"Laura! What are you doing there?"

"Nothing." Laurie sat up. "I mean, I was resting and talking to Doug—"

"Get up off that bed immediately."

"Yes, ma'am!" Laurie found herself on her feet without knowing quite how she had gotten there. She met her aunt's eyes. She had nothing to hide, but somehow she felt obscurely guilty.

After a moment Ida's erect frame sagged and her cold eyes softened.

"I beg your pardon, Laura. I did not mean to speak so sharply. I came to ask Douglas if . . . I will speak with you later, Douglas."

The door closed softly.

"Well!" Laurie dropped into a chair. "What was that all about?"

"Can you ask?" Doug fell back into a recumbent position. "Male and female, reclining . . ."

"But you're my brother!"

"That makes it worse."

Laurie leaned forward and peered distrustfully at Doug's averted face. His cheeks were crimson, but she was fairly sure the emotion that warmed them was not embarrassment. More likely suppressed amusement.

"You're disgusting," she said.

"I was hoping you wouldn't find that out right away. Well, I'm awake, damn it. What do you propose to do?"

"That's obvious, isn't it? Interview the Wilson girls and inspect the photographs, not necessarily in that order."

"Want me to do something?"

"You? Do something? Heaven forfend," Laurie said, with awful sarcasm, "that I should intrude upon your congenital laziness. Try to talk to Ida, will you? You always were her favorite."

"Aunt Ida always liked me better than you," jeered Doug, from under the arm he had flung over his face.

"Well, she did. That's okay, I can handle it; she loves me too, but you're the *boy*. Male chauvinism is not restricted to men."

"Um," Doug said sleepily.

"I'm going for a walk," Laurie said.

Out of deference to the elderly sleepers she did not slam the door, but her fingers ached with the desire to do so. She knew Doug had fallen asleep the moment she left the room.

III

One good thing about Chicago winters was that they provided a person with the necessary equipment to survive cold weather. Laurie had brought her boots—heavy, high, hideously expensive. In the silence of the drowsing house she assumed outdoor wear, tied her scarf over her head, and went out. She would not have objected to the company of a large friendly dog, but Duchess was nowhere to be seen. No doubt she was sharing Uncle Ned's blameless slumbers in the library.

Laurie went down the steps and across the lawn, her boots crunching through the thin crust of snow. The sky overhead was translucent blue, the sunlight was brilliant; but it lacked warmth. Following the path, she passed through the gate into the pasture, closing it carefully behind her.

The marks of booted feet preceded her—Uncle

Ned and Doug, no doubt. The woodland paths were kept clear of undergrowth, so she had no difficulty walking, but the tangled boughs overhead cast shadows across the way. Glancing up she saw a hawk hovering lazily. It was looking for carrion. At least in Uncle Ned's domain its prey would not have been trapped or wounded by the hand of man.

Despite the cold air she was warm from exercise when she reached the birch glade and sat down for a rest. This was Uncle Ned's favorite place. He had shaped the fallen trunk of a majestic walnut into a rustic seat. Laurie sat motionless, and slowly the life of the forest, sent into hiding by her approach, timidly reasserted itself. Birds swooped and darted: the brilliant scarlet of a male cardinal, followed by his more subdued mate; a black-and-white red-crested woodpecker; flights of busy brown sparrows and juncos. Ned's bird-feeding station, in the center of the clearing, was soon assaulted by hungry throngs. A brown squirrel, ignoring the tidbits Ned had set aside for his kind, tried to swarm up the post toward the feeder, and was driven away by an indignant blue jay. The jays were rude, aggressive birds, but their beautiful azure plumage pleased Laurie's eye, and she had a certain sympathy with their strutting assertiveness. In a hard world, you had to push to get ahead.

The air was too cold to allow her to become sleepy, but as she sat watching the birds, the peace of the woods surrounded her and she began to relax. Maybe Uncle Ned was right. This brilliant, busy display was as enchanting as any fairy tale, and the wonder of winged flight was a miracle. What was wrong with letting Lizzie seek her own wonders?

Time passed. The early winter twilight was reddening the sky before Laurie felt a change in the atmosphere. A sound somewhere off in the woods scattered the swarming birds. The squirrel vanished with an indignant flip of his tail; two rabbits nibbling at carrots on the edge of the clearing twitched white scuts and disappeared amid a rustle of dry leaves.

Laurie knew the sound had been a natural one—the fall of a clump of snow, perhaps, from a weighted branch. All the same, her heart began to beat a little faster. The silence and the sudden disappearance of life forms was eerie. Twilight gathered along the aisles of the pines. The shadows of the trees stretched out grotesquely across the snow, and the minuscule patterns of small feet seemed suddenly purposeful, a maze outlined by some alien intelligence. A flicker of movement to her left made her start. Her eyes dilated. Surely that shape was . . .

It was only a small snowmound, shaded by dusk and surmounted by a tuft of dried grass, but for an instant it had resembled a dwarfed, semihuman shape, peering with malignant bright eyes over a hump of shoulder.

With a muffled curse at her own unsavory imagination she rose stiffly to her feet. No wonder Lizzie thought she saw fairies in the woods. It didn't take much imagination to shape natural forms into something alien; and if one's eyesight was not quite twenty-twenty and one's perception blurred by age and a lifelong addiction to fantasy . . . The woods were strange places, especially as night drew in. High time she was getting home. She had not intended to stay so long.

She started off across the clearing, slamming her booted feet through the crusted snow with the deliberate intention of making noise. As she lifted one foot to step over a log she heard an echo of her progress somewhere in the distance and paused, boot poised, a prickle running down her back. Something was coming—something heavy and quick. . . .
"Has some survival of an earlier age survived in the deep woods?" she inquired aloud, mocking her own fancies. "Some halfhuman monster men call. . . ."

A dark shape bounded out into the clearing and launched itself at her. Suspended on one foot, Laurie was caught off balance. She toppled over onto her back and the monster nuzzled her throat, emitting hot, panting breaths.

"Oh, get off, will you?" Laurie gasped, pushing at the dog. "You are the worst-trained beast I've ever met, even worse than Ned's usual dogs. Get off!"

"There you are." Laurie saw her uncle standing over her. "Thought you might be lost."

"I'm not lost, I'm prostrate," Laurie said. "Where's the brandy keg?"

Her uncle chuckled appreciatively. Dragging the ecstatic dog from her prey with one hand, he reached into the capacious pocket of his jacket and brought out a flask.

"I carry the brandy. Makes better sense. But don't you tell Ida."

Laurie didn't really want any brandy, but Uncle Ned looked so pleased that she joined him in a swig. She suspected her aunt probably knew about the flask; she knew about everything that went on. But if Uncle Ned liked to think he was putting one over on his strict sister, more power to him. Forbidden fruit always tasted sweeter.

They started for home. The dog ran rings around them, crashed off into the woods and reappeared, her tongue lolling, as if playing hide and seek.

"She doesn't bark much, does she?" Laurie said.

"Not a barkin' dog," Uncle Ned said calmly.

Laurie glanced at him. His craggy profile was reddened by the sunset and the cold air. He was wearing a bright scarlet cap, with an absurd pompom on top; his shaggy brows, lined cheeks, and faint, enigmatic smile made him look like a blown-up version of a gnome or a brownie—some creature totally attuned to its natural environment. Once she would have thought of him as a friendly giant, but now his shoulder was almost on a level with hers.

53

Moved by a sudden rush of affection, she wanted to take his arm, but she knew better. Uncle Ned was as shy of physical contact as the animals he loved. But he must have caught something of her emotion; he turned his head to smile at her, then looked away. They went on in amicable silence, side by side.

4

Lizzie, in the throes of one of her more complex menus, gave Laurie an abstracted greeting and refused her offer of help. Like other creative artists, she preferred to work alone. Shedding boots and coat, Laurie went on stocking feet along the hall and into the parlor.

It was the most formal and, in some ways, the most beautiful room of all. The woodwork and the carved paneling around the mantel were painted a soft blue-green. Curved arches framed the bookshelves that flanked the fireplace. The heavy satin draperies were of a deeper, richer turquoise, and the Aubusson rug repeated this color, complemented by floral designs in navy, rose, and buff. There was no sound in the high-ceilinged room except for the crackle of the fire on the hearth, and at first Laurie thought she was alone. Then she saw that one of the long, high-backed sofas in front of the fireplace had an occupant. Stretched out at full length, his shoes uncouthly displayed against the soft brown leather, Doug slept.

Laurie sat down on the opposite sofa and regarded her brother fixedly. After a moment she realized that her stare was returned. One of Doug's eyes was open.

"Whatever you're thinking of doing, don't do it," he said lazily.

"I'd have dropped something on your stomach if I could have found an object hard enough," Laurie confessed.

Doug chuckled. "Remember the time Aunt Ida sent you to wake me, and you threw her cat at me?"

"Mmmm. It's one of my most satisfying childhood memories."

"I had the scars for years." Doug rubbed his flat stomach thoughtfully.

"So did I, emotionally. Ida gave me a lecture on cruelty to dumb animals."

"Funny, how their pets reflect their personalities. Ida has always favored Siamese, hasn't she?"

"I'm not so sure. About the animals reflecting their personalities, I mean." Laurie stretched her legs and wriggled her toes, basking in the warmth of the fire. "Ned's dogs are big sporting types, but they are always undisciplined and friendly. Siamese cats look aristocratic and aloof, like Ida, but actually they are strident and hammy. Lizzie's Persians are much more snobbish—which she certainly is not."

"All right, but you have to admit her latest is a weirdo. Any cat named Angel Baby has two strikes against it, but this is one spooky feline. It strolled in here a while ago, purring like crazy, and curled up on my stomach, nice as you please. When I reached down to stroke it, it let out a shriek, stuck all its claws in my navel, and took off."

"Angel Baby is weird all right," Laurie agreed. "Maybe it saw the fairies too. . . . Have you talked to Ida?"

"Haven't had a chance."

"You haven't tried hard, have you?"

"Not very. Damn it, I'm relaxing. I've had a hard winter."

"Sure you have."

"Well, how about you? Get any further with your investigation, Mrs. Holmes?"

"Well . . ."

"Not willing to admit we're on a wild-goose chase? Ah, well." Doug sighed, folding his arms under his head. "Who cares? I'm glad I came, anyway. We ought to check in with the old folks now and then."

Laurie was facing the door, so she saw her aunt before Doug did. Stately in garnet velvet, Ida was carrying a tray of hors d'oeuvres. Laurie jumped up to take it from her.

"Thank you, my dear. Where is Douglas?"

"Resting," Laurie said. Doug's face appeared over the back of the sofa.

"Hi," he said. "Sorry, Aunt, I didn't see you."

"That's quite all right." A gleam of affection warmed the stern contours of Ida's face. "You need your rest, working as hard as you do." Unseen by her aunt, Laurie made a rude face at her brother, who widened his eyes and beamed seraphically. Ida turned, and Laurie hastily straightened her countenance. "We are changing for dinner, Laura. There is plenty of time; your uncle is not here yet."

"Plenty of time" meant just the reverse, as Laurie knew.

"I'll hurry," she said and went upstairs at a trot. Admittedly she needed a shower and a change of clothing after her trek through the woods, but she had forgotten that the aunts sometimes went formal for dinner. When one dined solo on tuna-fish salad and crackers, or *á deux* on beer and pizza, one did not don trailing skirts and the family jewels.

Speaking of jewels . . . Having showered and put on the dinner dress she had had the foresight to pack, she reached for the small leather case that held her own jewelry. The only decent pieces she possessed were the ones her aunts and uncle had given her. A pearl ring on her sixteenth birthday—pearls are suitable for young girls—a watch when she graduated from high school, bits of turquoise and coral at intervals.... What had Ida been wearing? Something rather opulent in a subdued way. Garnets? Ida did not deck herself gaudily as her sister did. Everything she wore was in impeccable taste, but it was not cheap.

When Laurie returned to the parlor her mind was still on the subject of jewelry, so she noticed, as she seldom did, the details of what her aunt was wearing. The gleaming burgundy velvet matched the sullen glow of—yes, it was garnets, a collar of intricately inlaid stones with a matching brooch and twin barcelets. Garnets weren't particularly valuable, but these looked old. Maybe the Mortons did have family jewels. Lizzie had never flaunted anything like that; she preferred her gaudy, glittering costume jewelry.

Ida indulged in a glass of wine now and then, for the sake of conviviality. She was drinking port; the deep ruby color of the wine matched the highlights of her dress. As she sat in the firelight glow, her iron-gray hair set in the stiff marcel waves she had always favored, she was the picture of a handsome, dignified old lady, and her usually stern face was softer than usual as she listened to Doug's chatter. She looked up when Laurie came in and smiled approval.

"Very nice, my dear. Sit down. Douglas will fetch you some sherry."

Like pearls, sherry was considered suitable for young girls. Laurie hated it. She noticed that Doug held a tall glass filled with some liquid that was obviously not wine.

"Thank you, Aunt," she said meekly.

Lean and casual in slacks and a sweater, Doug went to the mahogany sideboard where glasses and decanters were set out. Doug was not expected to dress for dinner. Admittedly he would have looked silly in a tuxedo while Uncle Ned, adamantly rural, appeared in his usual overalls. But, Laurie told herself, it was all part and parcel of the tired old mystique of male supremacy. Doug didn't have to get dressed up; Doug could drink Scotch if he preferred it to sherry.

Ah, well, Laurie thought resignedly, taking the glass he offered her, love requires these little sacrifices. She took a sip of the pale amber liquid and gulped, thankful that Doug stood between her and her aunt. The liquid was the right shade, but it was not sherry. His face preternaturally solemn, Doug winked at her and turned away.

"I hope the sherry is not too dry, Laura," her aunt said benignly.

"It's very good." Laurie took another sip. "I feel as if I ought to be helping Aunt Lizzie, though."

"Elizabeth, as you know, prefers to be alone when she is cooking. And," Ida added, magnificently ignoring the contradiction, "Jefferson is helping her."

"Jefferson cooks, too?" Doug asked.

"He is very accomplished. And he will be joining us for dinner. I hope you do not mind. I assure you, he is a presentable young man."

Laurie knew her aunt's anxiety on this score was genuine. In Ida's girlhood, when the house was staffed with bowing servants, none of them would have been allowed to sit down with the family.

"My dear aunt," she said with a smile, "if it doesn't bother you, it certainly isn't going to bother us. After all, I worked as a waitress last summer."

A spasm of pain crossed Ida's face.

"I know that dear. If I had been told in advance of your intention I would have taken steps to see that no such indignity was necessary. The very idea of a Morton being subjected to the rude jokes and pecuniary insults of lower-class persons—"

"They weren't all lower class," Laurie protested.

"And it was honest work. I thought Great-Grandfather Angus believed in the ennobling effect of hard work."

Doug crossed the room to take Laurie's empty glass and administer a gentle kick in the shins. *Don't argue with her,* the kick said.

"I am not criticizing your motives," her aunt said. "Only your judgment. You are too young to realize that some persons—that certain men may assume—er—"

"I won't do it again," Laurie said.

"I am relieved to hear you say so."

Uncle Ned's entrance ended the lecture. Booted and overalled, his gray hair standing out around his face, he was as out of place in the stately room as a cow in a boudoir. Pausing only to smile at Laurie and nod at his sister, he made straight for the sideboard and poured himself his customary libation—four fingers of Scotch. He drank it without stopping, his Adam's apple bobbing up and down; then he drew a long breath of satisfaction and put the empty glass on the tray. He had done this every evening of his life, as long as Laurie could remember.

"When do we eat?" he inquired, wiping his mouth on a huge red bandanna handkerchief.

Crudities which would have produced a freezing criticism if someone else had committed them failed to rouse Ida when her brother was the culprit. Probably, Laurie thought with an inner chuckle, she had long since given up hope of reforming him.

"You know Elizabeth always takes a glass of sherry before we dine," she replied. "She should be joining us shortly."

Ned nodded. Hands in his pockets, feet wide apart, he took up a stance in front of the fireplace and looked around the room.

"Where's Duchess?"

"Shut in the porch. I will not have that uncouth animal in here knocking over glasses with her tail and nibbling at the food."

"What food?" Ned looked mutinous. "Got any of those little crackers? I'm hungry."

Silently Ida indicated the table. Ned crossed the room in three clumping strides, swept up a handful of canapés, and crammed them into his mouth.

"Good," he mumbled. "Can't see why Duchess has to be excluded. She wouldn't touch anything."

Ida replied acrimoniously. Laurie leaned back and let her thoughts wander. She knew the argument would go on, unresolved and unresolvable, until someone interrupted it. On the sofa opposite, Doug was smiling, his eyes half closed. Time had turned back; it was as if they were ten years in the past, hearing the same voices saying the same things, surrounded by the familiar objects.

But things weren't the same. No doubt, Laurie thought, it was her perceptions rather than the facts themselves that had altered. She had changed a great deal in the two years that had elapsed since her last visit. Her fondness for and gratitude toward the old people had not lessened in the slightest, but she was aware of practical points she had never considered before.

Ida and Ned were still arguing about Duchess when Lizzie came in. Her costume that night was the most bizarre she had worn yet, which was saying a good deal—a solid glitter of gold cloth trimmed with huge fake emeralds and rubies. The crimson and green sparks flared along the front of her flowing robes and weighted down the long sleeves.

But on this occasion Lizzie's costume failed to hold her niece's attention. Lizzie was not alone. Following her at a respectful distance was the handsomest man Laurie had seen for years. (She had never, even at the height of her infatuation, considered Bob good-looking.)

He was as dark as Bob was fair. His high cheekbones and thin, expressive mouth, his olive complexion, suggested Spanish or Italian blood. His proportions were so perfect that he looked taller than he actually was, and the casual, open-necked blue cotton shirt set off his broad shoulders and strong throat. His black hair was cut neatly but inexpertly, so that waving locks fell casually across his high forehead. More remarkable even than his physical handsomeness was the sheer animal vitality that set his black eyes snapping; a wave of almost palpable electricity filled the room when he entered it.

". . . will certainly be overdone if we don't eat soon," Lizzie was saying.

"You've plenty of time for a little nip, ma'am," the beautiful man told her. "Sit down and let us bask in the light of your gorgeousness."

Lizzie giggled and obeyed.

"You forget yourself, Elizabeth," Ida said. "You have not performed introductions."

"No need." Doug rose to his feet. Laurie noticed that he was holding himself erect, making the most of his height. Childish, she thought; he was half a head taller than the newcomer, but what did mere inches matter?

"You're Jefferson, of course," Doug went on. "I'm Douglas Wright. My sister, Miss . . . Carlton."

Laurie was probably the only one who noticed the stammer before her last name. No wonder Doug had trouble with it; Anna's habit of changing husbands had made it difficult for her children to remember what name they should answer to in any given year.

Doug's attempt at a young-lord-of-the-manor condescension was a failure. Jefferson's dark eyes moved in Laurie's direction and went straight back to Doug.

"Hi, Doug," he said. His voice was low and rich—black velvet, Laurie thought idiotically—but with an underlying roughness.

Without further courtesies Jefferson moved with the grace of a cat toward the decanters and poured Lizzie's wine. He handed it to her with a bow and a twisted smile.

"Here you are, luv. Drink up."

"Thank you." Lizzie giggled.

Jefferson turned to Uncle Ned. "I checked out that sound in the car you were complaining about, sir. Just a loose rod. It's okay now."

His manner had changed, subtly but perceptibly; it was bluff, man-to-man talk, with a tinge of respect that held no shadow of subservience.

"Good." Ned nodded amiably. "I quit driving a few years back," he explained to Laurie. "Perfectly capable still, you understand; eyes are as good as ever. But you never can tell. Shouldn't take chances. Might hurt something."

Laurie knew he was talking about animals rather than people; once, when a squirrel had dashed out under the wheels, he had been unable to avoid it and had mourned for days.

"So Jefferson acts as your chauffeur?" she asked.

"Jefferson does everything," Lizzie said fondly.

"Except cook," Jefferson said. "But I'm learning—from the best." He smiled at her. Lizzie simpered.

"Oh, one of the first lessons is not to let things get over-cooked. Come along, Jeff. We'll serve."

"I'll serve, you just sit." Jefferson took her hand and heaved her to her feet. He did it nicely, with no suggestion of effort, which was no small trick, considering Lizzie's size. "I know how to do it with style. You taught me, didn't you?"

As the youngest woman present, by quite a few years, Laurie did not rate an escort. She had to pull out her own chair, while Uncle Ned performed that service for Ida and Doug assisted the younger aunt. Jefferson had vanished into the kitchen. As soon as they were seated the door swung open and he appeared, effortlessly balancing a big tray. He served soup. Placing Laurie's bowl before her, he gave her a quick sidelong look. He did not speak, or smile.

Laurie ate her soup. However, she never had the slightest recollection of how it tasted.

Doug insisted on helping clear away the first course, and after that things were more relaxed. He and Jefferson wove a complex pattern through the swinging doors, letting out warning shouts as they approached the barriers, and turning the remainder of the meal into a game. Laurie supposed that the food was excellent, as Lizzie's cooking always was, but her taste buds appeared to be paralyzed.

After that first penetrating, smileless stare Jefferson did not look at her. He served the food, he ate, he complimented the aunts and teased Lizzie, he exchanged comments with Uncle Ned, without seeming effort. He even broke through Doug's wary hostility with a compliment about Doug's car, and they talked about engines and tachometers and other technicalities.

Laurie ate tasteless food and speculated. Whom did he remind her of? But it wasn't difficult to trace his fictional antecedents—he resembled all the dark, brooding heroes she had ever read about. Heathcliffe, Rochester, Max ... whatever his name was, the hero of *Rebecca*.

And still he refused to look at her.

Laurie was sure it was deliberate, and by the time the meal was over she was quite annoyed. They went back to the parlor for coffee. When Jefferson had served them and taken a modest place a little outside the circle around the fire, she turned to him.

"Aunt Ida tells me you write, Mr. Banes," she said.

He stared at her for a moment, his dark eyebrows lowering. Then he grinned broadly, white teeth flashing like a toothpaste commercial.

"How well you put it Ms. Carlton."

Against her will Laurie felt her lips curve in an answering smile. He had caught the sarcasm in her question. Score one for him. No—score two. He had not taken offense. His voice had been amused, not malicious.

"What are you writing, exactly?" she asked.

"A book."

"She means," Aunt Lizzie explained, "what kind of book, Jefferson. Fiction, poetry, essays—"

"Oh, I see." Jefferson pondered, his eyes downcast. He had very thick lashes. Miniature brushes, they shadowed his cheeks. "Well, now, I could synopsize the plot, but that doesn't really give one the flavor of a book, does it? Rather like those trots one buys to get through English-lit. courses. Besides, I haven't figured out the ending yet."

"It is a novel, then?" Laurie persisted.

"Yes. A historical novel. Set in fourteenth-century France."

"But that's my field," Laurie exclaimed. "Medieval history."

"I know." The firelight set red sparks dancing in his eyes. "You have some devoted fans here, Ms. Carlton; they talk about you and your brother all the time."

"How boring," said Doug.

"Not at all. One of the reasons why the book is progressing so slowly is that I've had to do a lot of research. I feel," Jefferson said earnestly, "that a historical novel should be true to fact, insofar as the facts are known."

"Absolutely," Laurie agreed.

"Maybe you can give me some tips, then. Seeing as it's your field."

"I'd be glad to."

"Great." Jefferson put his cup down and rose. Muscles rippled; Laurie tried not to stare. "If you'll excuse me, I'll get to my chores now."

"Oh, don't go just yet," Lizzie said.

"Temptress." Jefferson snatched her plump hand and raised it to his lips. "Get thee behind me, Miss Lizzie. Work before play. That was a super meal, by the way."

He kissed her hand enthusiastically, restored it to its owner, swept the circle with an ingratiating smile, and went out.

"I'll help him," Laurie said.

"Oh, no." Lizzie lifted a warning hand. "That is one of the little tasks Jefferson prides himself on doing. He won't allow anyone to assist him."

"But he has so much else to do."

"Oh, and he does it all so well. Isn't he sweet?"

"Nice fella." Uncle Ned, in his favorite position before the fire, nodded solemnly. He leaned toward Laurie and said in confidential tones, which were clearly audible to everyone in the room, "He talks that silly way to Lizzie 'cause she likes it. But he's sound otherwise. Good with his hands."

There was a pause. Laurie realized that three pairs of eyes were fixed on her. They were waiting for her comment. Was it so important to them that an outsider should admire Jefferson? She said cautiously, "He seems like a treasure." She knew she had said the right thing when three pairs of lungs emitted a long, blended sigh. And, she told herself, if Jefferson had happened to overhear, that patronizing comment would annoy him very much.

"He certainly is," Ida said. "Without wishing to sound selfish, I must say that I hope his novel will prove to be very long."

Laurie tried to catch Doug's eye, and failed. He was slouched on the sofa, his hands in his pockets, his legs stretched out, his eyes focused on the tips of his shoes. She turned to Ida, who had taken out her knitting. Her busy needles flashed in the firelight.

"What are you making, Aunt? That's pretty wool; such a lovely pale pink."

"Pink for girls," Ida said. "One of the neighbor children."

Silence descended. Uncle Ned rocked back and forth, whistling softly under his breath. Doug sulked. Laurie had no doubt that he was sulking, though she was not sure why he was in a bad mood. Part of it was probably jealousy. He was accustomed to being the family pet, and now Jefferson seemed to have supplanted him. Well, the man has earned it, Laurie thought.

She looked at Lizzie, who was fussing with the cups on the coffee tray.

"Auntie, how about showing me your wardrobe? You promised you would."

"No fair." Jefferson had returned. Smiling, he took the cup Lizzie held out to him. "You can't take my opponent away, Ms. Carlton. I owe her a million and a half already, and I insist on my revenge."

"A million and a half what?" Laurie asked.

Lizzie chuckled. "Matchsticks. Isn't that quaint? We play for matchsticks. Of course Jefferson is exaggerating the amount. But he will wager so wildly!"

Jefferson had taken a gameboard from the cupboard under the bookshelves. He opened it on the table in front of Lizzie and sank gracefully to a sitting position, his legs crossed.

"Checkers?" Laurie said in surprise.

"Most sophisticated game in the world," Jefferson said blandly, setting out the pieces. "Okay, Miss Lizzie—black or red?"

"Oh, dear, it's so difficult to decide . . ."

Doug rose. "I think I will run into town."

"Of course, dear," Ida said graciously.

"I'll lock up when I get back. Now don't you wait up for me."

"I know better than to do that." His aunt gave him a glance which, for her, might almost be described as roguish. "But don't be too late, Douglas."

"No, ma'am." He leaned over and kissed her wrinkled cheek. "Good night, all."

Laurie followed him into the hall.

"What's the idea of running out on me?" she demanded.

"Want to come along?"

"What for? The night life of Frederick is not exactly uproarious, as I recall."

"You never knew anything about the night life of Frederick, you innocent creature. I'll find something to do, don't worry."

"I'll just bet you will. Why can't you spend a quiet evening with the old folks?"

"I refuse to watch Jefferson play checkers. I mean, there are limits."

"You mean, you don't want to watch him ingratiating himself. You can't stand being in second place, can you?"

Doug smiled smugly.

"Aunt Ida still likes *me* the best."

"So far. She won't be so crazy about you if you sneak off to the fleshpots of Frederick every chance you get."

"You don't understand. Aunt Ida expects a young man to sow a few wild oats. Listen, sweetie, I have carefully maintained relations with a few old buddies in town; Ida accepts that. But it wouldn't do for you. Your suitors will have to call at the house, hat in one hand, corsage in the other."

"Like Hermann Schott," Laurie said gloomily. "Ida thought he was just the type."

"Good old chubby Hermann. I remember him well."

Laurie shied back as Doug made a gesture that might have ended in a hearty brotherly smack on the bottom. Doug started up the stairs.

"I don't know what your gripe is," he said. "You're obviously having a sensational time. Go back in there and continue drooling over Mr. Rochester."

"You've got your Brontë heroes mixed," Laurie said. "You mean Heathcliffe."

"Aha. You noticed."

Laurie made a rude face at Doug's retreating back and returned to the parlor.

Jefferson had lost another ten thousand imaginary matchsticks by the time the clock on the mantel chimed ten. Laurie had to admit he lost very cleverly—and it is not easy to cheat at checkers. He finished the final game and rose to his feet, shaking his head ruefully.

"Time I got back to my high-born heroine. Thanks,

Miss Lizzie. Shall I leave the board? Maybe Ms. Carlton would care to give you a game."

"I can't afford to lose any matchsticks," Laurie said.

"I don't know why you are being so formal," Lizzie said, shaking her head in playful reproof. "I'm sure Jefferson won't mind if you call him by his first name."

"You may call me Laura," said Laurie, as Jefferson turned toward her. "Prefaced, of course, by Miss."

"She's joking," Lizzie explained.

"I see," Jefferson said seriously.

"On the other hand," Laurie went on, "I can hardly call you Mr. Jefferson."

Jefferson grinned. "Make it Jeff."

He held out his hand. After a moment, Laurie took it.

All the same, he was a little too good to be true. Hunched over the dressing table—which had surely not been that low a few years ago—Laurie brushed her hair and scowled at her reflection in the mirror. She had checked the kitchen before coming upstairs; it was immaculate, every surface shining like the mirror in front of her. What the hell, she asked herself, was a man like that doing out here in the country catering to the needs of three old people?

Well . . . maybe he *was* writing a book. She was in no position to sneer at the eccentricities of literary types, not when her thesis topic caused raised eyebrows or guffaws of hearty laughter. Jefferson was getting room and board—and what board!—in exchange for the chores he did. Lizzie had mentioned other help, including a professional cleaning team, so there wasn't all that much to do. With a minimum of organization—and Jefferson looked capable of organizing his life well enough—errands and shopping and chauffeuring could be kept to a minimum. No doubt he had plenty of time for his great American novel.

He seemed genuinely fond of the old people. Some men were like that, Laurie assured herself—nice, kind to others. Perhaps he had lost his mother or grandmother early in his life and was giving the Mortons the sort of cherishing he would have given them. Perhaps he was an orphan and was enjoying the pleasures of family life.

Anyway, it was none of her business. So long as he did his job, his motives were his own affair.

Laurie decided she had better find an engrossing book and stop thinking about Jefferson. It was barely eleven o'clock—the shank of the evening—but she was in no mood to work, although she had dutifully brought some of her notes. She yawned. It must be the fresh air. She was tired, and she felt no envy of Doug, on the loose in Frederick.

Squatting down before the bookshleves, she looked with more favor on the collections of fairy tales. Maybe Doug was right; they had gotten too worked up about Lizzie's latest kick. If Ida had been really worried about it she would have said something by now. After all, Ida was no spring chicken. Probably she had lost her temper with Lizzie one day and had dashed off those two letters . . . had told Jeff to make sure they were mailed . . . and he, misunderstanding her urgency, had sent them special delivery.

Laurie decided to start on the Oz books. She could read all the early volumes, the ones written by Baum himself, in a couple of weeks. It would be relaxing to read about a world removed in every way from the grim period of history she had been studying—a world without sex or violence or torture or betrayal. Even the Wicked Witch wasn't particularly violent. She talked a lot, but she didn't do much.

Her hand was on the spine of *The Wizard of Oz* when she noticed the book next to it. Her eye had passed over it the night before, noting only the word "fairies" in the title; now she realized that this was not one of the worn, familiar books of her childhood. Curious, she drew it out.

An Encyclopedia of Fairies. The back cover quoted a review from the *Southern Folklore Quarterly,* and other comments, such as, "a valuable reference book." Not fiction, then. The book was new, its paper cover bright and unworn.

Opening it at random she saw that the entries were arranged alphabetically. "Grey Neighbors"—one of the euphemistic names for the fairies—was followed by "Grig," which, the author remarked primly, was "rather a debatable fairy. The *Oxford Dictionary* gives the word as meaning a dwarf, or something small. . . ."

Laurie raised amused eyebrows. No, not fiction. She turned over a few pages at random and, more and more intrigued, took the book to bed with her. She now remembered having read a review of this volume, or of one like it. The "little people" had always been a legitimate subject for folklore, of course. No doubt Lizzie had bought the book because of its title and had squirreled it away among the children's library in order to hide it from Ida's critical eye.

Laurie leafed through the book, finding some of her old favorites neatly classified and labeled. One that particularly delighted her was a version of the Rumpelstiltskin story. In this case the uncouth dwarf that saved the girl from her boastful folly was named Tom Tit Tot, and it was "a little black thing with a long tail, that looked at her right kewrious." It twirled its tail rapturously every time the girl guessed its name wrong. It wasn't Bill, or Sammle, or Methusalem. " 'Well, is that Zebedee?' says she agin."

" 'Noo, 'tain't,' said the impet. An' then that laughed an' twirled that's tail till yew cou'n't hardly see it."

" 'Take time, woman,' that says; 'next guess an' you're mine.' An' that stretched out that's black hands at her."

"Wow," Laurie said under her breath.

The girl got the name right next time, and the impet shriveled up and blew away.

Laurie went on to learn about "Trooping Fairies," and the Pwca, a Welsh version of Puck, and "Queen Mab," who was, as she had surmised, the queen of the fairies in the sixteenth and seventeenth-century stories. Then she came upon the Love Talker.

His other name was Ganconer. He appeared to maidens in lonely valleys and made love to them before fading away and leaving them to pine to death.

I met the Love Talker one evening in the glen,
He was handsomer than any of our handsome young men,
His eyes were blacker than the sloe, his voice sweeter
far. . . .

"Oh, bah," Laurie said, and closed the book. "Blacker than the sloe. . . ." She wondered what a sloe was. It sounded very poetic. Probably a bug.

She did not want to read any more about fascinating supernatural male creatures with black eyes and sweet voices. Turning out the light, she went to open the window.

The night was so beautiful that she lingered, though the cold air made her shiver. Clouds had gathered in again while they sat in the drawing room, and now snow was falling, softly, silently, out of a sky like dark-gray silk. Already it had covered the scars made earlier on the lawn by booted feet, and the dim, soft snow blanket reflected the gray of the sky. Rather apprehensively Laurie looked at the enclosing circle of trees, but though she strained her eyes for several minutes there was no sign of the strange light she had seen the night before. She got into bed and pulled the covers up to her chin.

Snug in her nest of blankets she soon grew warm, but sleep did not come. Her mind flickered from one subject to another as her hands had flipped through the pages of the book. "Black as a sloe ..." A vegetable? Like an eggplant, perhaps? Checkers was a stupid game. Black pieces, like round empty black eyes. The fleshpots of Frederick ... roadside taverns, with neon jukeboxes and bars made of glass blocks, and bored high-school girls in tight skirts. ... "I met the Love Walker. ..."

She was drifting off when a sound penetrated the last crack of consciousness in her mind. At first it blended with her final waking thoughts—jukeboxes, fairy pipes in lonely glens. Laurie sat bolt upright, straining her ears. She had not been dreaming. There was music out in the cold white night—thin, ethereal music, bell-like single notes repeating a theme over and over.

The blankets had become twisted around her legs. She untangled herself and ran to the window.

The music was faint and far away, but surely the sound could not carry so clearly all the way from the distant woods. Yet the wide stretch of lawn appeared to be unmarked. The curtain of falling snow blurred objects, but she would have seen anything that moved.

The floor under the open window felt like ice. Laurie hopped from one foot to the other. She couldn't decide what to do. She had no desire to go out into that chilly emptiness alone. Even if some human agency was producing the unearthly music ...

She stopped herself in the middle of that thought. Of course it was a human agency. The sound could not have been made by wind or water; it was too regular. The repeated motif was a tune, of sorts. So the musician must be human. Maybe Jefferson was a flautist and tootled himself to sleep after his arduous labors, like Sherlock Holmes playing the violin. Maybe Uncle Ned had taken up the recorder. Maybe Aunt Lizzie ...

She was about to say the hell with it and get back into bed when she heard another sound. This one did not come from outside. It was closer at hand—inside the house.

The first thump and rustle were followed by a series of soft noises, some of them unmistakably the patter of unshod feet. Laurie's scalp prickled. The sounds were so close, almost as if they were right in the room. Something invisible, padding softly on bare feet . . .

Then she remembered the register in the floor.

The room below hers belonged to Aunt Lizzie. She had never noticed noises before, but that was to be expected; the old lady went to bed before she did, and apparently she was a quiet sleeper. Laurie dropped to the floor and pressed her ear to the register just in time to hear Lizzie's door open. It did not close.

This time Laurie did not hesitate, at least not mentally. She knew what she had to do, but she was shivering, and she had no intention of pursuing her aunt through the night-cooled house without a robe. It took her a while to find hers, thanks to her slovenly habit of dropping it on the floor when she retired, and she was still groping for her slippers when the silence belowstairs erupted into pandemonium—shouts, crashes, the barking of a dog. She abandoned the slippers and ran.

The upper hall was dark, but she knew every inch of the way. She had crept down to the kitchen often enough for a midnight snack. A light which had been left burning in the hall below, no doubt in anticipation of Doug's return, shed a faint glow on the stairs. Laurie went faster. The battle was still in progress. As she reached the landing, someone let out a high-pitched shout. Though falsetto with pain or fury, it was a man's voice.

She followed the sounds to the kitchen. By the back door a large dark mass writhed and moaned. Her rational mind knew that it was a group of intertwined bodies, two or more, but it looked perfectly ghastly. "Does some strange survival of the ice ages . . ." That same rational mind told her to stand still and get some light on the subject.

A number of fantastic theories had flashed through

her brain as she ran, but none of them was as wild as the tableau that met her astonished eyes. Doug leaned against the wall, his hand covering the lower part of his face. Crimson dripped from between his fingers. The door was wide open. Snowflakes and a chilly breeze blew in. In the doorway stood Jefferson, snow frosting his disheveled black hair. Hanging over one of his outstretched arms was the limp body of Aunt Lizzie. Her feet were bare, her white hair bristled with curlers, and she was enveloped in an enormous flannel nightgown printed with puce roses and green leaves. Lace formed a frill around her face and fell from the wrists of the gown over her dangling hands. Her eyes were wide open.

Laurie's horrified gaze registered one last incongruous detail—a long, feathery golden tail sticking out from under the kitchen table.

Before her heart had missed more than three beats Aunt Lizzie, still dangling, remarked querulously, "What on earth am I doing here?"

"If you don't know . . ." Laurie began. Her voice failed. Lizzie frowned. "I do think," she said, "that I might be allowed to stand. This is a most uncomfortable position."

Jeff let out a long breath. Laurie saw that he appeared to be as thunderstruck as she was. Tentatively he moved his free arm and shifted Lizzie to a more decorous position.

"Are you all right?" he asked anxiously. "You scared the living daylights out of me, Miss Lizzie."

"Yes, dear, I'm quite all right," Lizzie said placidly. "But I do wish you would put me down. And close the door, please. No sense heating up all outdoors."

Handling her as if she were made of glass, Jeff sat her down in the nearest chair. He turned to close the door and saw Doug, who was still dripping blood. His eyes widened.

"Good God," he said.

Doug lowered his hand. The blood, as Laurie had suspected, came from his nose. As a child he had been susceptible to nosebleed, an infirmity she had often taken advantage of.

"Is that all you can say?" he demanded thickly. "I owe you one, you son of a—"

"Douglas!"

Ida stood in the doorway, her severe navy wool robe clutched tightly around her. She had spoken out of instinct, to save Doug from uttering a vulgarity; but although she was as straight and dignified as ever her face was so ghastly that Laurie started toward her. She looked sicker than either Doug or Lizzie, who was now humming quietly to herself and swinging her feet in time to the music.

"I am quite all right," Ida said, answering the question implicit in Laurie's outstretched hands and worried face. "Though it is a wonder, considering the frightful outburst that awoke me. What is going on? Douglas, you are bleeding onto the floor."

"Sorry." Doug reached for a handful of paper towels. He applied them to his nose and said in a voice whose outrage was scarcely muffled by the paper, "That—uh—guy hit me! I was coming in the back door when somebody ran into me and then that—"

"Just a minute." Jeff, relaxed, his hands in his pockets, surveyed the others with a faint smile. "I think I know what happened. Let me talk, okay?"

"Urgh," Doug said, through the paper towels.

"Please do so," Ida said. She went to the sink and dampened a towel, which she handed to Doug. Laurie took off her robe and tucked it around Lizzie's bare ankles.

"Oh, my dear," Lizzie said in a shocked voice. "You mustn't appear in your nightgown in front of young men."

"Be still," Ida said.

"Well, I think it isn't proper. And that gown is really quite . . . it is rather. . . . Where did you get it, darling? The color isn't right for me, but perhaps in a pale green or blue instead of that dark amber shade—"

"Elizabeth!"

"Oh, goodness gracious, a person can't breathe around here," Lizzie said crossly. "Why don't you put on the kettle, Laura dear. So long as we are all here, we might as well have—"

"Right. I will." Laurie looked significantly at Ida, whose face had turned from gray to scarlet. The easiest way of shutting Lizzie up was to do as she suggested.

"Now then, Jefferson," Ida said with a martyred sigh.

"Yes, ma'am." Jeff was trying not to smile. His casual air aggravated Laurie. She was still breathing quickly from shock.

"I heard Doug drive in and thought I had better check to make sure he closed the gate," Jeff explained. "It was a nice night. I like to walk in the snow. I was coming back along the drive when I heard bloody Cain break loose in here. Thought maybe Doug had run into a burglar or something. I came along as fast as I could. Found the two of them"—his gesture indicated Doug and Lizzie—"kind of mixing it up in here. The door was wide open; I recognized them in the light from outside. I grabbed Miss Lizzie and she went limp. Scared me, like I said. Sorry, old chap, but it wasn't me that slugged you. Must have been Miss Lizzie."

"Oh, Jefferson." Lizzie's mouth formed into a tremulous circle. "Oh, I would never do such a thing as strike Douglas. Oh, I can't imagine why you are telling such lies."

"I was just kidding." With the feline grace so characteristic of him, Jeff dropped to one knee and took the old lady's hands. "I'm sorry, Miss Lizzie; I didn't mean it. He probably ran into the door. You know how men are when they get in late, after a night in town."

The knowing twinkle in his eyes won a smile from Lizzie.

"Oh, naughty," she said. "I'm sure Douglas would never . . . Would you, Douglas?"

"Never," Doug said. "Aunt Lizzie, you had better get back to bed before you catch cold. Let me carry you."

"Oh, you needn't carry me," Lizzie said, her good humor quite restored. "You'd have a hard time of it, darling boy, strong as you are. I can walk perfectly well. But I think a nice hot cup of tea before—"

"No tea, it is full of caffeine," Ida said firmly. "You won't sleep a wink. Come along, Elizabeth."

"Oh, very well . . . spoilsport!"

But she took her sister's extended arm. Ida glanced over her shoulder at the others.

"Be sure you lock up, Douglas," she said. "Good night to all of you."

The three who were left maintained silence until the sound of the old ladies' feet on the stairs had died away. Then Jeff picked up Laurie's discarded robe and held it for her.

"I hate to be instrumental in covering up that nightgown Miss Lizzie rightly admired," he said. "But you'll catch cold if you don't put this on."

Eyes black as sloes—whatever they were—met hers with a candid, friendly gravity. Laurie let him help her into the robe. She dropped limply into the chair Lizzie had vacated, and Jeff turned his attention to Doug.

"You okay? Want an ice cube down your back?"

"No, thanks." Doug dabbed at his nose. The bleeding had stopped, but he looked terrible. Laurie was reminded of certain medieval paintings that depicted, with bloody accuracy, victims of massacre, murder, and assault.

"We may as well have that cup of tea," Jeff said. He reached the kettle just before it started to shriek and made the tea with quick efficiency. After he had served it he lifted the cloth and peered under the table.

"It's okay, you can come out now," he told the dog.

Duchess emerged, her wary eyes sweeping the room. When she saw only friends she erupted into exuberance, jumping up and down and waving her tail.

"Sit down," Jeff said. The dog instantly obeyed, her eyes fixed adoringly on Jeff's face.

Duchess's response was the last straw for Doug.

"You listen to me," he began.

"That's what I plan to do." Jeff turned to him. "Don't get me wrong, Doug; I'm just doing the job I get paid to do. I'm fond of the old folks. They've been damned nice to me and I'm one of those peculiar people who appreciates a favor. I guess maybe I . . . Well, as I said, I like them. But even if I wanted to, I couldn't take your place in their affections." Then he added, with a flash of pride Laurie found even more attractive than his humility, "If you want to move in and take over my job, that's fine with me. You've got a better right, but you've got no obligation. I do."

"Okay," Doug said quietly. "I can't argue with that."

"Then let's sit down and talk. What happened tonight worries me, and I'm sure it worries you too. Has Miss Lizzie ever walked in her sleep before?"

"Not that I know of." Doug pulled up a chair. "You think that's what happened?"

"I don't see what else it could have been. She wouldn't go out on a night like this—undressed, in bare feet."

"My God," Laurie said, appalled at the idea, "she'd catch pneumonia in five minutes. Or if she fell, and lay there unconscious for any length of time . . ."

Doug's face lost some of its healthy color.

"She was starting out the door," he admitted. "I didn't know who it was; I just saw a dark shape and grabbed it. I suppose I scared her. She started to scream and wave her arms. . . ." His hand went to his nose. "She must have been the one who slugged me, at that. It hurt like hell."

"I read somewhere you aren't supposed to wake a

sleepwalker," Jeff said. "It's a shock to their nervous system. She didn't know where she was or who you were." He smiled rather maliciously at Doug, who was gingerly testing the afflicted member. "I have to admit I swung at you before I saw who you were. Don't know whether I connected or not. If I did, I'm sorry."

"My jaw hurts too," Doug muttered. "But I guess it's a good thing you came along when you did." Needing some vent for his irritation he turned a hostile eye on Duchess, who was still sitting at attention. "You were a helluva lot of help," he told her. "Some watchdog!"

Duchess wagged her tail.

"Let's get back to the subject," Laurie said. She was pleased—of course she was; why shouldn't she be?—that the two men seemed to be getting along more amicably, but the futile exchange of courtesies designed to salve one male ego or the other irked her. "If Aunt Lizzie is walking in her sleep, something has to be done about it. It could be dangerous."

"I bet Ida knows," Doug said. "She was upset, but she wasn't surprised now was she? If this had come as a shock to her she'd have talked it over with us instead of saying good night in that final way. She's avoiding questions."

"But why would she do that? This is serious. Wouldn't she want us to help?"

Jeff shrugged. "She's a proud woman," he said slowly. "And people of her generation are funny about . . . well, about anything that suggests . . ."

"Mental illness?" Laurie supplied.

Jeff looked at her gravely. "You wouldn't be so quick to say that if you didn't know something, Laurie."

"Don't you know about the fairies?" Laurie asked, and then blushed as she realized how idiotically she had phrased the question.

"Hey," Doug began. Laurie turned to him.

"We have to tell him, Doug. He's right; this is his

responsibility as well as ours. He can't help if he doesn't know the facts."

"Fairies?" Jeff's face was a blend of bewilderment and amusement. "You mean *fairies*—with transparent wings, like that?"

"There wouldn't be any other kind around here," Doug said sourly.

"Thanks." Jeff made him a mocking bow.

"Stop being so cute," Laurie snapped. "Aunt Lizzie probably doesn't know the slang meaning of the word, or what it implies. And as a long-time reader of Andrew Lang, let me say I personally resent that use of a perfectly good old Anglo-Saxon word."

"French, I think," Jeff said gravely.

"Oh, go to hell."

"Naughty, naughty. Your Aunt Ida wouldn't like that." Jeff's smile disappeared. "I guess it isn't funny. Seems to me I do remember Miss Lizzie chattering on about elves or something. . . . I've got to admit I don't always listen to what she says. Do you really think she was on her way out to search for fairies on a snowy winter night?"

"She was . . ." Laurie hesitated. Then, in a rush, she finished the sentence. "She was called out by the music. I heard it too."

The men stared at her, and then at one another. Then they looked back at Laurie.

"I did hear it," she insisted. "Far-off piping, like a flute or recorder, or something. I was standing by the window trying to figure out where it came from when I heard Lizzie get out of bed. Her room is right under mine, and there is a register in the floor."

"So there is." Doug nodded. "You sure you weren't half asleep?"

"Standing up? It would be something of a coincidence, surely, if two of us started sleepwalking on the same night. I tell you, I heard it; and there was nobody out here. Nobody at all."

CHAPTER

5

You were imagining things," Doug said feebly.

"I suppose I imagined this!" Laurie's agitated gesture included the kitchen door and his battered nose.

"Wait a minute." Jeff frowned, his dark brows meeting in the center of his forehead. "It could have been a bird, Laurie."

"It wasn't any bird I ever heard. It played a tune."

"A tune? Can you repeat it?"

"No, I've no musical sense whatever. And it wasn't much of a tune; just four or five notes, repeated endlessly."

"Anyhow," Doug objected, "birds don't sing at night."

"Nightingales do."

"Oh, come off it," Doug said. "Nightingales in Maryland, in the winter?"

"It's unlikely, but it's not impossible. And the other alternatives are." Jeff pondered. "I'm not insisting on a nightingale. I wouldn't know one if I heard it. But suppose an exotic bird had escaped from a zoo or an aviary and had somehow managed to survive. It could be something like that, couldn't it? And if Miss Lizzie had heard it before, it might have stimulated her—uh—peculiar ideas about fairies."

"It's possible," Laurie admitted. She couldn't help contrasting the reactions of the two men. Jeff had believed her statement, without question or doubt. Using it, he had formulated a very sensible theory—almost the only sensible theory. Whereas Doug . . . She scowled at him. He scowled back.

"I still say you were imagining things."

"Well, thanks a lot for—"

"That's really not the point," Jeff interrupted. "Don't you see, it doesn't matter why Miss Lizzie went rambling in the middle of the night; the problem is to keep her from doing it again. There's no 'could be' about it; it is damned dangerous. She could kill herself."

"So what do you propose?" Doug asked sarcastically. "You seem to have all the answers."

Jeff refused to take offense. "I haven't got any answers. I could sit up all night and watch; but I couldn't cover all the exits. And I can't lock the doors from the outside; not only have I no authority to do such a thing, but if there were a fire you'd be roasted in your beds." He looked at Laurie, his dark eyes somber. "I've no authority to do anything. This is up to you two."

"Hmph," Doug said more amiably. "You're right. I think the first step is to quiz Aunt Ida, don't you, Laurie?"

"Definitely. She knows, or at least she has suspicions. That's your job, Doug. She's more apt to confide in you—the big strong stalwart man of the house."

Doug made a rude face at her. "And what's your job?" he inquired.

"To talk Aunt Lizzie into showing me the photos of the fairies," Laurie said.

It took her until the middle of the following after-noon to corner Lizzie.

When she came down that morning she found only Doug, brooding over a cup of coffee.

"They've gone grocery shopping," he explained, as she surveyed the silent, spotless kitchen. "The big expedition of the week."

"Uncle Ned didn't drive, did he?" Laurie poured herself a cup of coffee and sat down.

"No, Jeff took the girls. Ned is out bird watching or badger watching, or whatever."

"So you weren't able to talk to Ida?"

"No. They were bustling around getting ready to leave when I came down."

"Did Aunt Lizzie say anything about last night?"

"She asked me how I hurt my nose."

Laurie studied that feature. It did show signs of wear and tear.

"A reasonable question," she said.

"But don't you see? She's forgotten the whole incident—or is pretending she has. Poor Aunt Ida looked like hell warmed over." Doug's sympathetic tone softened the comment, which would certainly have horrified his aunt. "No wonder she's haggard; I bet this has happened before."

"So you noticed."

"The bags under her eyes? Sure I did."

"What are we going to do?"

"We've got to do something." Doug stared moodily into his cup. "If we don't, that Jefferson character will. He's practically running the place now."

"Why don't you like him?"

"Who says I don't? Oh, hell, I guess I'm jealous. He sounds like a decent guy, doesn't he?"

"Yes," Laurie said.

"I guess we should be glad there's somebody like that around to watch over them."

"Yes," Laurie said.

"He talks as if he really cares about them. If," Doug added, "you say 'yes' again, I'll slug you."

"You and who else? Okay, I see your point. We'll take action today—if we can pin the old darlings down."

But the shopping trip to town was the big excitement of the week, and the shoppers did not return until almost noon. By the time the groceries had been put away and Aunt Lizzie had delightedly displayed the fashion magazines she had bought, it was time for lunch. And after lunch it was time for naps. And after the naps . . .

"We are dining with the Schotts this evening," Ida said, pausing on her way upstairs. "I'm sure you will be glad to see them again, Laura."

"The Schotts," Laurie repeated.

"Hermann is now with a bank in Hagerstown," Ida said. "Quite a personable young man. You need not dress formally, Laura, but I hope you have a pretty frock."

"Pretty frock," Laurie said stupidly. Doug, standing next to her, placed his foot over hers and bore down. She yelped.

"Ow! I mean, yes, Aunt, I'll wear . . . something."

"I certainly hope so," said Ida, and proceeded on up the stairs.

Laurie turned to her brother, who had covered his face with both hands in an unsuccessful attempt to muffle his unseemly laughter.

"Stop that, you ghoul. Don't they ever give up?"

Tears of amusement seeped from Doug's eyes.

"They want you to settle down," he gurgled. "Right here in the old neighborhood, safe from the wiles of the wicked world. You ought to be flattered."

"You wouldn't say that if you remembered Hermann as well as I do," Laurie groaned. "Doug, you've got to talk to Ida. Grab her the minute she comes out of her room. She's avoiding us."

"Fair enough, if you do the same thing to Lizzie."

Laurie spent the next hour lying on the floor by the register. She was stiff and disgusted by the time she heard the bedsprings creak, and the long exhalation of Lizzie's yawn.

"Now where did I put that box?"

Laurie went downstairs and tapped on the door.

"Are you awake, Auntie? Can I come in?"

"Oh . . . just a minute, darling. Just a . . ."

There was a delay before the door opened. Lizzie's topmost chin showed a suspicious smudge, which might have been chocolate. Laurie did not comment.

"I stopped by for a sneak preview," she said, smiling. "What are you going to wear tonight? Something gorgeous, I'll bet."

Lizzie, who had been eyeing her warily, relaxed a trifle.

"I wanted it to be a surprise," she said.

"You'll dazzle the men, whatever you wear. But I couldn't wait."

"Well . . ."

"Dazzle," Laurie decided, was the right word. Her aunt had a childish fascination for garments that shone and twinkled and glittered. Sequins, gold braid, fake gems trimmed the flowing garments she took from her closet. Only their obvious expensiveness saved them from bad taste, and in some cases even the fancy labels didn't do the trick. Laurie admired and exclaimed and asked Lizzie to try on some of the clothes. And Lizzie, with touching generosity, tried to give a few to Laurie.

". . . if we fastened the sash tightly . . ."

"Oh, Auntie, I couldn't."

But as she studied herself in the full-length mirror Laurie was surprised to find herself weakening. As an adult she had never been able to afford expensive clothing, and this bejeweled, fur-trimmed, golden garment was the last thing she would have selected, even if she had been given carte blanche. It was pretty, though, in a barbaric way. The heavy brocade dropped straight from a gathered yoke, so the differences in their girths didn't really matter. The robe was too short, though. It barely reached her ankles.

"All I need is a horned headdress and I'd look like Isabeau of France," she said aloud. She twirled.

"Wear it tonight," her aunt urged. "It looks adorable on you, sweetheart."

Laurie came back from the fourteenth century. So that was in Lizzie's mind, was it? She was supposed to lure Hermann with her new finery.

"No, I'm not going to get dressed up tonight," she said shortly.

"Well, take it anyway. It looks—"

"Adorable?" Softening, Laurie bent down to give her aunt a kiss. "Honey, I couldn't look adorable unless I chopped off my feet. I'm too tall. Tell you what; if I have a heavy date, I'll borrow this."

Turning to restore the robe to Lizzie's closet she realized that dusk was gathering in. The snow had subsided to a few vagrant flakes. It had been necessary to lull Lizzie into a state of relaxation so that she would be more amenable to questioning, but time was getting on and she had not yet come to the purpose of her visit.

"Did you hear the music last night?" she asked.

As she had hoped, her shock tactics were effective.

"You heard it too?" Lizzie asked.

"Uh-huh." Laurie's voice was casual. "It was so pretty. I've never heard anything like it."

"You're the only one besides me who has heard it," Lizzie said. "Ida says I'm making it up."

"I certainly heard it. You were not making it up. Shall I tell Aunt Ida?"

"No. She's hopeless. She only hears what she wants to hear."

Laurie had to admit there was some truth in that. If Aunt Lizzie was losing her marbles, she still had a few left. The innocent old face, surrounded by a halo of white hair, disarranged by the trying-on, almost made her ashamed of her sneaky tactics; but she reminded herself that it was for Lizzie's own good.

"Maybe you and I are more sensitive to such influences," she suggested.

"Oh, I do think that is so true! You always were sensitive as a child; such a delicate, wistful, dreamy little girl."

Privately Laurie questioned this evaluation. She didn't remember being particularly sensitive—pudgy was more like it, thanks to Aunt Lizzie's cookies—and she had vivid recollections of tomboy pranks for which her aunt had gently scolded her. However, it was not for her to question such a convenient lead.

"I loved fairy tales," she said, with a sigh. "I was looking over the collection last night; such nice memories. I don't think you missed a single one, Aunt Lizzie."

"I tried not to."

"It was such a thrill to see the light the other evening, and hear the music," Laurie gushed. "Now you must show me the photographs, Auntie. I'm dying to see them."

Lizzie gave her a suspicious look. "Ida is so nasty about it," she said querulously.

Laurie threw her oldest aunt to the wolves without a qualm.

"You know how she is. A wonderful woman, but no imagination."

"Well . . ."

"Please, Auntie."

"Well . . ."

Laurie had to hide her eyes and promise not to peak while Lizzie disinterred the photos from a secret cache. Her hands obediently over her eyes (she was later to regret this scrupulousness, but at the time she had no idea it would be important), Laurie wondered what else the old lady kept among her treasures. A box of chocolates, certainly, though why she would bother to hide it when no one tried to curtail her eating, Laurie could not imagine. Perhaps it was like Uncle Ned's flask—forbidden fruit, or an unreasonable facsimile thereof.

After much scrabbling and gasping Lizzie told her she could look. Shyly, like a child offering to share a prize, she held out a few colored snapshots.

When Laurie asked to see the photographs she was not sure how she meant to deal with them. She knew it was futile to point out the falsity of an image to a true believer, but she hoped the pictures would be so bad—blatantly blurred or conspicuously unrecognizable—that carefully expressed skepticism would dim her aunt's enthusiasm. She was in no way prepared for what she saw.

There were four pictures. All seemed to have been taken by an ordinary cheap camera, like the popular Instamatics. The first showed an unidentifiable patch of coarse grass and a rock—an ordinary rock. Sitting on the rock was a fairy.

It was not a hummingbird or a queer configuration of a natural object. It was a small winged creature wearing tights, or else its own scaly hide. It was green—not only its limbs and paler, transparent wings, but its face and . . . hands? Tentacles was more like it. The fingers, surely more than five of them, were inordinately long and flexible. The face was half hidden, as if the creature were looking over its shoulder, but what Laurie could see of its features made her catch her breath. They were human, in a way, but the eyes were too large, almost insectlike, and the nose came to a sharp point. Most disturbing of all was the malicious half-smile that crooked the corners of the creature's mouth.

Laurie knew Aunt Lizzie was waiting for comment, but she was incapable of speech. She turned to the next photo.

This fairy was perched on the branch of a fir tree. A pine cone, nearby, gave a good idea of its size. It had wings and long hair and was unquestionably female. Its face was even more unpleasant than that of the first creature. The hair was Medusalike, resembling strands of thick wool or multitudinous antennae. Some of the strands were blurry, as if they had been moving when the picture was taken. Hair, hide, and face were pale lavender.

Hastily Laurie flipped through the remaining photos. One had turned out badly; the creature had moved and would not have been identifiable if she had not seen the other pictures. The last of the collection was the best—or the worst; a whole bevy or band or pride of the creatures in what appeared to be animated conversation on a maple branch. Their bodies were partially concealed by the brilliant scarlet and gold leaves, and Laurie was glad she didn't know what they were talking about.

The pictures had been taken several months before. The autumnal leaves and green grass proved that.

It was with some reluctance that Laurie forced herself to meet her aunt's waiting eyes. Lizzie looked apprehensive and triumphant at the same time. She did not need Laurie's verbal comment to know that she was impressed; her face must have shown her shock and surprise.

"Amazing," Laurie muttered.

"Aren't they? If Conan Doyle could have seen these!" Lizzie's eyes sparkled. "I met him once, you know. A man of great sensitivity, but . . ." She lowered her voice as if about to impart a great secret. "But I suspect just a teeny bit gullible. His pictures were nothing like these. I hate to say it, but I think he was taken in. Cutouts, my dear; obviously paper cutouts."

"Really?" Laurie scarcely heard what she was saying. Her mind was in a whirl. She looked through the pictures again and found them even more disturbing the second time. "Auntie, can I borrow these?"

"No!" Lizzie snatched, so quickly that one of the snapshots bent in her hands. "No, you promised. They are very rare. I can't take a chance of their being mislaid."

"I understand." Humor them, Laurie told herself. You are supposed to humor crazy . . . Crazy, my eye, she thought. If she's having hallucinations, so am I.

"Well, then, couldn't you get copies of them? I promise I won't publish them or—"

"Oh, you couldn't do anything like that! It would be dreadful. I promised to keep them a secret."

"Whom did you promise? Who took these?"

In her urgency she forgot to guard her voice, and Lizzie retreated, clutching her photos, with an exaggerated expression of terror on her wrinkled face.

"Now stop that, Auntie," Laurie exclaimed. "You know I'd never do anything you didn't want me to. I'm sorry I spoke so brusquely, but I'm very interested."

"Well, perhaps I can get copies of them."

"I would appreciate that."

"I'll try. You can see, can't you," Lizzie said, rather pitiably, "why I was so interested?"

"Yes," Laurie said. "I can see."

III

She left Lizzie rummaging in her wardrobe and went down the hall to Doug's room. He was not there. A tap on Ida's door received a rather grumpy response.

"I am dressing, Laura. We are leaving shortly. Are you ready?"

"I will be."

Laurie went downstairs. The family inhabited only the central portion of the house; the west wing was not used, though its antique-filled rooms were meticulously cleaned at regular intervals. The heat was kept to a minimum in that area, however, and Laurie hoped she wouldn't have to track Doug through the chilly corridors. She found him in the parlor, in his favorite position on the sofa. A half-empty glass stood on the floor by his trailing hand; his eyes were closed and he was breathing heavily through his nose.

Hands on her hips, Laurie stood looking down at him. He was her mother's son, her half-brother; but the traditional blood tie did not color her feelings toward him. He was virtually a stranger. A good-looking man, certainly, but it wasn't the Morton brand of good looks. He didn't in the least resemble their delicate, fine-boned mother. Maybe he looked like his father. Laurie had no way of knowing. There were no pictures of Mr. Wright in Anna's house. Perhaps Anna had slashed them to bits; such was her engaging habit whenever she shed a husband.

Laurie wished she could draw. It would be fun to do a caricature of Doug as a modern knight, recumbent on his tombstone. The casual modern clothing would be a funny contrast to the stiff position, ankles crossed like a dead Crusader's, arms folded on his chest.

Doug's eyes opened. They were a bright, clear brown with little flecks of gold, not the dark Morton brown.

"I was not asleep," he said.

"Of course not." Laurie pushed his feet off the couch and sat down. "Did you talk to Ida?"

"Yep."

"Well?"

Doug reached for his glass. How he could drink without spilling when he was practically prone Laurie did not know, but he managed it.

"Lizzie used to walk in her sleep when she was a kid," he said. "Then the habit stopped—until a few months ago. Ida caught her one night, heading out the kitchen door. She didn't think too much of it until last week. Lizzie got out again and they didn't find her until the next morning."

"My God," Laurie gasped. "But she looks all right— didn't she get sick?"

"The Lord looks after fools and children," Doug answered. "It had rained earlier that evening, but after midnight the rain stopped and the temperature rose. That's one of the reasons why she didn't even catch cold. That, and the fact that Duchess had gone with her. They found the two of them curled up under a tree, warm as toast."

"My God," Laurie repeated helplessly.

"Uncle Ned usually leaves Duchess loose in the house at night," Doug went on. "Under the fond delusion that she's a watchdog. She is insatiably curious—and Lizzie left the back door wide open when she went out. Duchess went along for the walk."

"That must have been when Ida wrote us," Laurie said. "I'll bet the poor old dear has been sitting up nights watching Lizzie. Why didn't she tell us about it?"

"You know how she is—tough as rock. She was ashamed of her panic after she had written. I think she was trying to make herself confide in us, but it's hard for her to admit there is a situation she can't handle—or that one of the marvelous Mortons has become senile."

Laurie shook her head. "It's more than that, Doug. Lizzie isn't seeing things. Or, if she is, I'm seeing them too."

"The photographs?"

"Yes. I tried to get them away from her so I could show you, but she's like a child with a favorite toy. Doug, I've never seen anything like them."

"Not hummingbirds, or shadows?"

"Not by a damned sight." Laurie went on to describe the snapshots, aware that she was not doing them justice. "It was their faces," she ended. "Half human, half . . . something else. And filled with malice. They were disturbing, Doug."

"I've got to see them."

"I asked Lizzie if she could get copies. She said she'd try. Doug, no child took those photos. Either they were faked by someone a lot smarter than I am, or—"

"Come on. You don't really believe that."

"I don't believe in fairies, not after seeing those snapshots," Laurie said vehemently. "Goblins, gnomes, evil spirits, maybe."

"Aren't there bad fairies as well as good ones?"

"Fairies are soulless," Laurie said. "Neither good nor bad. Some are benevolently disposed toward mortals, however, while others are definitely malicious. The book I was reading last night talked about a group called the Unseelie Court—"

"Un-sealy?"

Laurie spelled the word. "It comes from an old Celtic word meaning 'holy.' The Seelie Court was the good guys, and the Unseelie—"

"I get it. I guess I should have a look at those pictures. They must be remarkable to shake you up this badly."

"What are we going to do now?"

"Get ready to go out to dinner," Doug said. "You better hurry."

"But I can't—"

"Of course you can. Tomorrow we'll pay a call on the Wilsons. I'd like to talk to those remarkable children; they seem to be at the bottom of this in some way. But we can't do it tonight; nice little kiddies spend the evening doing homework and go to bed early. We'll take turns watching Lizzie's door after she goes to bed, to make sure she doesn't go for another late stroll. I told Ida we'd take on that job."

"Of course."

"Then what else is there to do right now?"

"Nothing, I guess. Why don't we ask Jeff to share the watch?"

"No."

"Why not?"

"Because he's a suspect."

"A . . ." Laurie's voice failed her. "What are you talking about?"

"It follows, doesn't it? If somebody faked those photos, then Jeff is an obvious candidate."

"But why would he—

"Why would anybody? Since there is no sensible motive immediately apparent, Jeff is as good a prospect as anyone."

"But . . ." Laurie stopped. "You're jealous," she said.

"Of whom?" Doug cocked a lazy eyebrow at her. "You or Lizzie?"

IV

The Schotts' home was not far away. Doug drove the family Lincoln; as he pointed out, it was ridiculous to ask Jeff to take them and come back for them when he was quite capable of handling the car. The night was cold and overcast. As they descended the steps their breaths made meeting patches of whiteness in the air.

Doug stowed his ladies carefully in the back seat. Even Laurie did not disdain his helping hand; she was wearing the highest, most tottery high-heeled shoes in her possession, for reasons known only to herself. Uncle Ned, in his duffel coat and red knit cap, got in the front beside Doug and helped him drive.

"Watch out for the bridge. It always freezes before the road. Fifteen miles an hour is plenty fast enough. Make sure you look both ways when we come to the intersection. The trees block your vision. This next curve, there's a family of raccoons that crosses the road sometimes. I always make Jeff slow down when we come to . . ."

Laurie had to admire Doug's patience. He followed Ned's instructions to the letter, without so much as a snarl.

Like the Mortons, the Schotts were "old family." The area had been settled by two different national groups, the Scots and the Germans. If they had ever been antagonistic, their enmities had long since been forgotten as the "old families" drew together against the newcomers. Mary Schott had been a MacGregor. Though she was younger than Lizzie by about ten years, they were good friends. She greeted them all with cheerful cries.

"So good to see you two children again! Hermann was thrilled when he heard you were back, Laurie. And Doug, how you have grown!"

"People do," Doug said moderately, surrendering his jacket to George Schott, who slapped him on the back with such hearty goodwill that he staggered.

"Sure does make a fella feel old," George said. "Seems like only yesterday you and Hermann were fishing in the creek down there, playing ball—"

"And trying to gouge each other's eyes out," Doug said. "We fought a lot, as I recall."

George threw his head back and roared with laughter.

"You sure did. Boys will be boys. Best thing in the world, learn to defend themselves."

"Balderdash," said Uncle Ned distinctly. "Fighting never makes any sense."

"Good old Ned." George let out another shout of laughter. "Always the peacemaker, eh? Remember the time you came down and wanted me to thrash Hermann because he gave Doug a bloody nose?"

From the contemplative expression on Doug's face Laurie thought he remembered the occasion quite well. She didn't; but she did recall that Hermann was three years older than Doug, and that he had always been heavy for his age. Doug had been wiry and slim.

Balancing on the unaccustomed stilt heels, she swayed, and Doug caught her arm.

"What are you wearing those stupid things for?" he whispered. Thanks to her added three inches, his mouth was now on a level with her ear.

"Never mind."

When the visitors' outdoor clothing had been carried away by the maid, the Schotts led them into the living room. The house, like that of the Mortons, was very old. The gracious room, with its wide carved moldings, was furnished in impeccable taste. Every piece looked as if it had been selected by the editorial staff of a "beautiful house" magazine, and Laurie had a feeling that if a single object had been moved so much as an inch from its designated place, the Schotts would have called in a decorator to replace it.

Hermann was busy with ice and bottles. The gilt buttons of his tartan waistcoat strained across his rotund tummy. Laurie was happy to see that her guess had been correct; in her high heels she was a full inch taller than Hermann.

"Excuse me for not greeting you right away," Hermann said. "But I always say the best hospitality is to have the drinks ready, isn't that right? And . . . here . . . we . . . go! Sit yourselves down, folks, and the waiter will pass among you."

He was even worse than she had anticipated. Laurie was ready for a drink—perhaps alochol would numb her critical faculties—and she was annoyed to observe that Hermann had not bothered to consult her tastes. The Schotts drank Old-Fashioneds, so everybody drank Old-Fashioneds. There were a few glasses of sherry for the ladies, who were served in strict order of age, so one glass of wine was left on the tray when Hermann came to Laurie. Bending with some difficulty from the region of his waist—that feature could not be more closely defined—he proffered the tray and grinned horribly.

"It's been too long, my dear," he whispered.

"Since what?" Laurie hesitated for only a moment. She did not like Old-Fashioneds, but anything was better than sherry. She took one of the fat, squat glasses with some difficulty. It was so draped with bits of fruit she could scarcely get a grip on it.

Hermann's smile wavered, then reappeared broader than ever.

"Little devil," he whispered, winked, and moved on.

Laurie saw that Doug had been watching. The muscles in his thin cheeks twitched. He was trying not to laugh. She took a firm grip on her glass and of course did not throw the contents at him.

Laurie was sitting on a loveseat. Now that it was too late, she realized she had been maneuvered into this position, and she had a strong hunch that when Hermann finished serving the drinks, he was going to occupy the place next to her. She grimaced at Doug and jerked her head sideways, hoping he would get the hint and sit beside her. He gave her a blank stare. She suspected he knew quite well what she was trying to convey.

However, retribution was about to fall on Doug's unsuspecting head. The pitter-patter of dainty feet was heard without. As one man the Schotts stopped what they were doing and turned, like well-trained extras, to stare at the open archway. The Emperor comes, Laurie thought. His Majesty approaches. . . . And then, as she saw who it was: Here she is, Miss America!

The newcomer wore a long taffeta gown of a bilious shade of green. It was exceedingly low cut and quite inappropriate for a quiet family evening, particularly since none of the others were in evening dress. The contours displayed by the low-cut neckline were worth the display—if, Laurie thought, you liked lots of pink, plump, healthy flesh. The girl's face was pretty—if, thought the same critic, you didn't mind a complete absence of intelligence, humor, and amiability.

George Schott rose ponderously from his chair.

"Here she is," he boomed. "Our little Sherri. You all remember Sherri, I'm sure. Grown, hasn't she?"

Sherri pouted prettily.

"Oh, Daddy!" she said.

She whirled into the room, nodded at the Morton ladies, and snatched Laurie's limp hands. "I bet you don't remember me," she said.

"You were twelve," Laurie said. "Always . . ." She

stopped just in time and substituted "busy with Four-H or something," for what she had started to say: ". . . always whining and following me around."

Laurie had not forgotten that Hermann had a younger sister, but since the subject of Sherri Schott interested her less than almost any other conceivable subject in the world, she had not thought about the girl for years. Maybe she had assumed the little brat would not live to grow up. But she had; she certainly had. Laurie turned a benign smile on Doug and purred.

"Just look at Sherri, Doug. Hasn't she gotten to be a big girl!"

Caught off guard, Doug had the look of a man with one leg in a bear trap, and the bear advancing rapidly toward him.

"Oh, yes, she has," he said feebly.

Sherri plumped herself down on the arm of his chair, obliterating him in green taffeta. He fought his way out of the rustling folds.

"I bet you wouldn't have recognized me," Sherri said.

"No, indeed," Doug said.

"Coke for my baby sister," Hermann said, offering a glass. "She doesn't drink, Doug. Or smoke."

Doug's fascinated gaze was riveted on Sherri's bosom, which, to be honest, was the most conspicuous object in his field of vision.

"Or go out with boys?" Laurie asked sweetly.

Hermann took the question seriously.

"Not much, no. She's pretty fussy. And I'm even fussier, aren't I, honey?"

"You mean you okay her dates?" Laurie demanded.

"Why, sure. That's what a big brother is for, eh, Doug?"

"Isn't it nice," said Mrs. Schott loudly, "to see four young people so handsome and so well matched."

The hideous evening dragged on. Laurie was too annoyed by Hermann's ponderous advances to enjoy the spectacle of Doug being pursued by Sherri. Surely, she thought, none of the elders really believed any romantic—much less matrimonial—alliances were going to come of this! Probably they figured it was worth a try. When Hermann wasn't hinting broadly at his hopes of advancement in the bank, and his intention of building a nice new split level, with all the modern conveniences, as soon as he got another couple of thousand saved, he was telling Doug of Sherri's virtues. Most of these seemed to be negative. She didn't drink, she didn't smoke, she didn't drive a car or believe in Women's Lib or allow her Pekingese to sleep on her bed. Hermann didn't mention her most conspicuous asset, but Doug scarcely removed his dazzled eyes from it. Well, be fair, Laurie told herself; it's all the girl has got.

After about a million years Ida decided they had better be getting home. Ned nodded agreement.

"There's that one bad patch on the hill," he remarked. "You know where I mean, George; solid ice by now, solid ice."

The Schotts tried to dissuade them, but to no avail. As they drove away, Laurie looked back. Sherri was framed in the doorway, her hair lit from behind, her wide skirts carefully arranged.

"Wave bye-bye to Sherri," she said to Doug.

"Funny," said Doug.

"Hasn't she grown into a pretty girl," Laurie murmured.

"She's a perfect idiot," Ida said crisply.

"Aunt Ida," Doug sighed, "I love you."

"But Hermann is an up-and-coming young businessman," Ida went on. "And of a good family, too. The Schotts are not the most intelligent people of our acquaintance, but the character of the family is unexceptionable."

Laurie thought of several comments she might have made, but she did not make them. Sherri wasn't good enough for the young heir, the last scion of the Mortons, but for a mere female, Hermann was quite a catch. She couldn't really be angry at her aunt, though. In the old days, a girl's family knew all about her beaux—their families, their financial status, even their medical histories. Such knowledge was no guarantee of finding a suitable mate, but it did eliminate some of the dangers. Like all parents, and parent-substitutes, the aunts were appalled at the modern world, and they had some right to feel that way. It was a dangerous place. Hermann's family was wealthy, healthy, and, if not wise, at least free of mental and emotional disorders. A girl could do worse. And Laurie devoutly hoped she would.

It was almost eleven o'clock when they reached home, and the aunts and uncle were yawning, exhausted by the unaccustomed late hours. Doug dropped them at the front door and took the car on around to the garage. Laurie managed to get a word with Ida as they dispersed to their rooms.

"Doug and I will take turns watching," she murmured.

"I appreciate that." Perhaps Ida would have said more, but Lizzie, ahead of them on the stairs, turned to inquire, "Are you coming up now, Ida?"

"Yes, of course. Good night, Laura dear."

Laurie went to the kitchen, arriving just as Doug came in the back door.

"All quiet?" she asked.

"No pixies, if that's what you mean. Your hero is burning the midnight oil. I could see him pacing back and forth, past his window. Apparently the muse is not active tonight."

"I've done a certain amount of pacing myself when I was trying to finish a paper," Laurie said.

"Really? Now me, I always found a brief nap restored the old brain and gave me strength to type a few more lines."

"Do you want a cup of tea, or a sandwich, or something?"

"Not now. I may yearn for sustenance in the small hours. Want me to take the first watch?"

"I don't care?"

"You take it, then. Wake me about three."

He left. Laurie, who had hoped to get in a few pointed remarks about green taffeta and voluptuous bosoms, felt frustrated and restless. There was no way of working off steam by means of cleaning or washing dishes; the kitchen was as spotless as any kitchen could be. She made herself tea and cut a few chicken sandwiches, which she wrapped in wax paper and put in the refrigerator. Then she checked the doors and turned out the lights. She would sit in her room, right next to the register; she couldn't miss hearing Lizzie if the latter should get out of bed.

She made herself comfortable, dragging an easy chair into position and placing a lamp by it. She started to change into a robe, then selected jeans and a sweater instead. Funny, how slowly the time was going. The antique French clock ticking on the mantel told her it was just past midnight. Fortunately she wasn't sleepy. If she began to feel drowsy she would go downstairs and pace the hall.

She was tempted to select a nice soothing book, but knew that would be a mistake; she needed something to keep her awake, and mentally alert. With a wry smile she took out the *Encyclopedia of Fairies*. That should do the trick. Since she had seen the photographs, her attitude toward fairies had changed radically. A ghost story could have been no more disturbing to her nerves.

This time, instead of turning aimlessly through the book, she searched for information, even though the sane part of her mind jeered at her for trying to be rational about an irrational subject.

As she had thought, the Unseelie Court was a collection of malevolent spirits. She had not known there were so many. They came in all sizes and shapes and all degrees of wickedness. Half-forgotten childhood stories came back to her, reinforcing the unpleasantness of what she read. George MacDonald's goblins, misshapen and malicious, working to steal

102

the Princess as a bride for their horrible dwarfish prince. Andersen's Ice Queen, cold as that frozen substance itself, chilling little what's-his-name to death as she stole him from mortal life. The goblins in Christina Rossetti's poem, "clucking and gobbling, mopping and mowing," as they harassed poor Laura.

Laurie got up and turned on the overhead lights. The shadows retreated, but they were still there, biding their time, waiting till her vigilance relaxed so they could slink out again. . . . "This is ridiculous," Laurie said, and started at the sound of her own voice.

She returned the book of fairies to the shelf. Thoughts like those weren't keeping her awake, they were scaring her half to death. What she needed now was something solid and normal and matter-of-fact—Louisa May Alcott, or *Rebecca of Sunnybrook Farm*. As her eye ran along the books—with occasional breaks, while she glanced nervously over her shoulder—a name caught her attention. Conan Doyle. What was Doyle doing among the fairy tales? *Sherlock Holmes* and several of the historical romances were in the other bookcase.

She ran her finger back along the spines of the books and located Doyle again. Memory stirred: Aunt Lizzie had mentioned Conan Doyle when they were talking about the photographs. What had she said? His pictures weren't anything like hers. . . . Cutouts. Paper cutouts. Something like that.

The title of the book was *The Coming of the Fairies*. No wonder she hadn't noticed it before. Doyle's name was in small print, the title much larger. The key word would have been noted and the book dismissed as just another work of fiction.

The picture on the cover—a pair of rather sexy lady fairies sitting on a flower—suited this assumption. But the first sentence of the preface told Laurie that she had found a significant addition to her knowledge.

"This book contains reproductions of the famous

Cottingley photographs, and gives the whole of the evidence in connection with them. The diligent reader is in almost as good a position as I am to form a judgment...."

Laurie decided she was definitely a diligent reader. She took the book to her chair—pausing to listen at the grille and hearing only silence. Before long she was deeply engrossed, shadowy terrors forgotten, in the mingled fascination and pathos of the situation Doyle described.

The "famous photographs" had been taken by two little girls—cousins—and, Laurie discovered as she read, not all that little. One had been fourteen, the other sixteen. Doyle went into laborious detail about how he was drawn into the case, under the commonly held but illusory conviction that detail constitutes scholarly proof. After a while Laurie became impatient. She flipped through the book and found the photos themselves.

They were, of course, in black and white. The first showed one of the girls, "little Elsie," wearing a pointed pixielike hat and a gown with long, full sleeves. Her hair flowed virginally over her shoulders. She sat on the ground, one hand extended; and at her knee, mincing along, was a gnome. He was about a foot high. His hat was a miniature version of the one the girl was wearing, he had striped wings and a beard, or perhaps a ruff around his neck.

Paper cutout. That was what Lizzie had said, and that was the first thought that came into Laurie's mind. The gnome was as flat as a piece of cardboard, and not well drawn. When she looked more closely Laurie thought there was something rather suspicious about little Elsie's hand, the one extended toward the dwarf and, in fact, touching him. It was too long and too large for the rest of her body. Was Elsie's real hand behind this peculiar construction, holding the "gnome" upright? Laurie thought it probably was.

The second photo was of the other girl, Frances.

An angelic-looking young lady, with flowing curls and an enormous white bow, she seemed to be shying back, as well she might, for the fairy fluttering in midair before her had its knee practically up her nose. This was a conventional, gauzy-winged fairy wearing an exceedingly skimpy garment. The fairy in the next picture was similarly attired. She (her contours, in the semitransparent dress, were decidedly female) had a modish " 'twenties bob," and a profile that might have come out of one of the fashion magazines of that period.

"Oh, Lord," Laurie murmured. "Poor old Conan Doyle."

She remembered that he had been drawn to spiritualism after the untimely death of his son. A good man, an intelligent man—an example of how intelligence bows to a driving emotional need. He had taken the fairies as seriously as he had taken the idea of communication from beyond the grave, and it was pathetic to observe his struggles to produce "evidence." He made much of the fact that various photographic experts had testified that the negatives had not been tampered with. But why should they be? Laurie thought pityingly. It was so obvious how it had been managed. The girls—one of whom had studied drawing, even if she had not learned to do it well—had taken the photos themselves, with no one around. "The little people won't appear to adults, only to those for whom the bloom of childhood is yet untarnished."

Laurie's lip curled. Doyle had lived into the twentieth century, but he was a Victorian at heart; and when he babbled on about the bloom of childhood, he really meant virginity. It was an old theme in folklore. Only a virgin could catch a unicorn. Witches often lost their powers after sexual intercourse. And only an innocent child could see the fairies. Just another example of the value men placed on that wholly meaningless physical feature. Women knew better; but in most periods of history they soon learned to pretend that it was equally important to them. If they didn't, their husbands and brothers and fathers beat the tar out of them.

Laurie studied the photos again. Yes, in each case there was a convenient branch nearby to which the fairy could be attached. In the first case, either the gnome was propped up in an erect position—a stick or stone behind him would have done the job—or he was held up by that weird-looking hand of Elsie's. No doubt the "little girls" had found the whole business highly entertaining, and in a way Laurie didn't blame them. Fooling the grave, bearded adults must have given them great satisfaction. Children of that period had so few acceptable vents for their hatred of the grown-up world. They weren't allowed to beat up old ladies, or sprinkle their conversation with Anglo-Saxon ejaculations.

Laurie finished the book. It told her little she did not know, except to reinforce her conviction that half the world was nuts. Not crazy, not stupid—just nuts. Ready to believe anything they wanted to believe and ignore all contradictory evidence. And yet ... A troubled frown replaced Laurie's contemptuous smile. Conan Doyle's pictures were obviously cutouts, just as Lizzie had said. But what were Lizzie's? Two-dimensional they certainly were not.

The time lacked a quarter of an hour to three, but she decided to wake Doug anyway. She was getting sleepy. She tiptoed downstairs, pausing to listen at Lizzie's door. Doug's door was open. She pitied any girl he slept with. You couldn't exactly call it snoring, but it came close.

She took him by the shoulder and shook him. He responded with a series of hideous snorts and finally woke.

"Wha's time?" he inquired, rubbing his eyes.

"Three o'clock," Laurie said mendaciously. "Aren't you cold?"

"I wasn't, till you messed up the covers." Doug sat up. The blankets, now around his waist, displayed a hairless, rather pallid chest, but well-developed muscles rippled as he stretched. "Hand me my shirt, will you?"

It was draped over a chair next to the bed. Laurie obliged.

"All quiet?" Doug asked.

"So far." Laurie brandished *The Coming of the Fairies*. "Here's something for you to read while you keep your lonely vigil."

"Since when have you been selecting my reading material? I'm right in the middle of a fascinating tale; got it at my favorite adult bookstore in Atlanta. I keep it locked in my suitcase so the aunts won't come across it by accident and have—"

He broke off with a pained grunt as Laurie dropped the book, with deadly accuracy, onto his lap.

"You'll find this more engrossing than any X-rated novel," she promised, and left him.

CHAPTER

6

Laurie slept late again next morning. She would have slept even later if Lizzie had not tiptoed noisily into the room and rearranged her bedclothes. The twitching and patting finally roused her, and she opened her eyes to find Lizzie's anxious face close to hers.

"Well," said her aunt, with a prolonged sigh of relief, "I was beginning to worry about you, darling. It's almost noon. Don't you feel well?"

"I'm fine. I sat up late last night . . . reading."

"Oh, you shouldn't do that." Lizzie settled down in a chair and folded her hands. "It isn't good for you. Early to bed and early to rise—"

"I know. You look healthy, I must say. Did you sleep well?"

"Beautifully." Lizzie's face was innocently serene, which was no proof that she had had a quiet night. But Laurie assumed Doug would have awakened her if anything had happened. "It's a lovely day," Lizzie went on. "You missed breakfast, so I have prepared an extra large lunch. And Hermann called. Twice. I told him you had gone out."

"Why did you tell him that?"

"Oh, but I didn't want him to think you slept so late. It isn't . . . I mean, it doesn't look . . ."

Laurie suppressed a desire to pull the covers over her head and go back to sleep.

"What did he want?"

"Well, he didn't tell me, naturally, but I suppose—"

"Never mind. Forget I asked. I'll be down in a few minutes, Auntie."

"I'll just get lunch on the table."

Lizzie trotted out. Laurie muffled her mouth with the covers and swore. Hermann certainly wasted no time. What lie could she tell him, to get him off her back? She couldn't say she was engaged or married; the word would get back to the aunts and they would be all a-twitter. Some undesirable trait—perhaps a hereditary disease? How about insanity in the family? Laurie grinned unwillingly. That was too close to the bone.

She went down to one of Lizzie's mammoth lunches. Doug and Uncle Ned had not yet returned from their morning walk. Laurie allowed herself a malicious grin when she heard that. Ned would whip Doug into shape if he stayed long enough. He probably had not gotten back to bed last night.

The aunts kept her company while she ate, chatting about this and that. Didn't she think it would be a good idea to have a quiet family evening, after the dissipations of last night? Unless she had a previous engagement . . . Oh. She didn't. Well, then, they could look at some pictures of the good old days, when Laurie and Doug were children. Doug would have to operate the projector; Ned always broke it.

Ordinarily Laurie would have objected to this nauseating suggestion, but she merely murmured faintly, being absorbed with the more serious problem of inventing an excuse for Hermann. How about alcoholism? No, that *would* get the aunts in a tizzy.

No use hoping Hermann could be sworn to secrecy; as a child he had been the worst tattletale in the neighborhood, and there was no reason to suppose he had changed. A hint—just a hint—that her mother and father had not been married?

Fortunately for her she had finished eating before the telephone rang again. She leaped to her feet as if the sound had engendered an electric shock, and snatched at her coat.

"Walk," she babbled. "I think I'll run out and see if I can find Doug and—"

"You had better wait, darling, it might be for you," Lizzie said, with a giggle and a meaningful glance. Ida had gone to answer the telephone. Her measured stride, and the length of the hall, made it unlikely that she would reach the instrument quickly, but Laurie was taking no chances.

"No, no, Auntie, I've got to—need some fresh air—walk . . ."

As she bolted out the door she heard Ida calling her name; but since Ida never succumbed to the crudity of shouting, Laurie was able to pretend she hadn't heard.

She didn't stop running until she had crossed the garden and was safely hidden behind the boxwood hedge. Then she paused to catch her breath.

It was cold and sunny. The garden looked forlorn under its cover of slushy snow, spiked with the dead brown branches of rosebushes. Hands in her pockets—she had forgotten her gloves, as she always did—Laurie started along the path between the high green hedges. The box was Ned's pride—over a hundred years old, most of it. Its thick, healthy growth made a rather dismal shade, which had kept the snow on the gravel path from melting. It was crusted hard. Laurie took a few quick running steps and slid. It was glorious. She did it again, throwing her arms out for balance.

She saw Jeff long before she ran into him, but there was nothing she could do except yell a warning.

Clinging to one another, they swayed back and forth until they had attained a precarious balance. Laurie was whooping with laughter. The sight of Jeff's anxious face, as they tottered, only made her laugh louder.

She was unaware of what an attractive picture she made as she stood there, cheeks red with cold, dark curls wind-blown; but she was too experienced to miss the change in Jeff's expression as he looked down at her. His arms tightened.

"Sorry," she gasped.

"I'm not."

The words were trite enough, but Jeff's deep baritone invested them with glamour. He drew her closer.

A romantic moment would certainly have ensued if Laurie had not remembered something. "I met the Love Talker . . ." Nonsensical, meaningless memory—but her smiling lips tightened and her body stiffened. Jeff's arms released their hold.

"What were you running from?" he asked lightly.

"How did you know I was running from something?"

"Male intuition. Weren't you?"

"The telephone," Laurie admitted.

"Ah. The worthy Mr. Schott?"

Laurie shoved her hands in her pockets and turned away.

"Do you know everything that goes on around here?" she asked. She meant it as a joke, but her tone was petulant.

"Hey, don't get mad. You know what small towns are like—gossip, nothing but gossip. Shall I challenge him to a duel, or waylay him in a dark alley?"

Laurie's momentary annoyance evaporated.

"No need to go that far," she answered, smiling. "But you could help me to think of a good excuse to get rid of him. I had already considered insanity and alcoholism."

"Not nearly good enough." Jeff wrinkled his forehead and appeared to ponder deeply. "Tell him you've been converted to Buddhism or some other eastern sect. Stare into space and talk about the Light."

"Not bad."

"You're cold," Jeff said, as she blew on her fingers. "Come on to my place, if you're still on the lam."

Laurie eyed him askance. He shook his head, his eyes twinkling.

"There's no spot on earth where you'd be safer from my advances, lady. I took a girl there once; every time I—er—started making progress, my guilty mind conjured up an image of your aunt, staring at me in frozen disapproval. The thought paralyzed every muscle in my body."

"I'd like to see your pad," Laurie said with a smile. He took her arm—to keep her from slipping—and they walked on.

"Or," Jeff said suddenly, "you could tell him you'd expect him to adopt your illegitimate baby."

"What illegitimate—"

"I see your problem," Jeff said thoughtfully. "You're too literal-minded. If you could just dismiss the feeling that your remarks to Hermann have to have even the slightest foundation in fact—"

"But he'd tell his mother and she'd tell the aunts," Laurie protested. "Ida would have a heart attack."

"You've got a point."

He continued to produce increasingly absurd "excuses for Hermann" as they crossed the yard. They finally decided that the best was a vague, unfounded accusation. "I know about you, Hermann; you don't suppose I could ever be serious about a man who has done what you've done?"

"That's perfect," Jeff said gleefully. "How can he disprove something that never happened? Although," he added, after a moment of thought, "I wouldn't be surprised if he turned pale and ran. He must have something nasty on his conscience."

The little cottage where Jeff lived had once been one of the slave quarters. The small stone buildings had stood in a line behind the stables, on a tiny street of their own. All but three had tumbled into ruin years before. Jeff's was the largest of the lot. Built of the same pale stone as the main house, it had two small windows, one on either side of the door, and an even smaller window above. Jeff flung the door open with a flourish and stood back.

Laurie had expected something small and low-ceilinged and dark. The glare of light that met her eyes made her blink.

The whole lower floor was one large room. The back half of the roof had been replaced by glass, like a skylight. Stairs led up to a loft, open at one end. The furniture was sparse: only a low bed, covered with a bright modern spread, a few chairs, a table, a desk, and a typewriter. Cupboards lined the end wall, which also had a tiny sink, stove, and refrigerator.

Laurie's first impression was one of austerity and cold. The plain plastered walls had been whitewashed; the floor was bare except for a few scatter rugs. But the rugs were lovely handwoven blends of brilliant color and the spread on the bed was a print of savagely vibrant reds and emeralds and blues.

"I like it," she said, and then blushed, thinking what a stupid, patronizing thing it was to say. But Jeff's voice was warm when he answered. "Thanks. I fixed it up myself; your folks paid for the materials, but I did the work."

Laurie went toward the desk. It was covered with papers. A thick sheaf of them stood beside the typewriter. Before she could get close enough to see what was written on the pages Jeff was beside her.

"No fair peeking," he said.

"Okay," Laurie said meekly. "I don't blame you; I hate having people look at my stuff before the final draft. Do you ever let anyone read any of it?"

"No. I take my motto from Sir Walter Scott: 'I neither give nor take criticism.'"

"Well, okay; I was just asking."

"Fair enough," Jeff said. "It's just a phobia of

mine, I guess. When I was living in New York—" He broke off suddenly, and Laurie asked, "Is that where you're from?"

"I was born in the Midwest. But I worked in New York for a while; some of my friends were would-be writers. I got bloody sick and tired of those arty sessions where everybody sits around drinking wine and reading bits of their work. None of it ever amounted to anything. They didn't really want to write, they just wanted to talk about writing."

"The same thing happens in the academic world," Laurie said. "Some of my friends have been working on their doctorates for years and years. Me, I just want to get it over with."

"Sit down and tell me about the Middle Ages," Jeff said, gesturing toward the bed. "I'll make some coffee."

"Where shall I start?" Laurie sat down. The bed was very low and very soft. It was almost impossible to sit primly on it, so she kicked off her shoes and curled up, feet tucked under her. She wondered as she did so if she was acting wisely; not that she would have been averse to what her aunt would have called. . . . Good God, what would she call it? She couldn't imagine Ida referring to the subject at all, no matter how obliquely. As for Laurie's own instincts, they were under complete control. The very idea of being caught in a compromising position (yes, Ida might put it that way) by one of the aunts, or Uncle Ned, made her break out in a gentle sweat.

Yet, perversely, she was mildly put out when Jeff handed her a mug of coffe and promptly retreated to a chair clear across the room. He hadn't been kidding when he asked her to talk about the Middle Ages; he started firing questions at her. They were good questions, specific and detailed.

After admitting ignorance on two points in a row, Laurie said ruefully, "There's quite a difference between a scholar's approach and a novelist's, isn't there? I'm stupider than I thought."

"It's a different approach," Jeff said. "I need such tiny details. It's hard to find them in history books. I want women to read this, so I've got to have stuff about clothes and jewelry and makeup. Even the men's clothing—did they wear underwear? If so, what was it like?"

"Oh, it's that kind of book, is it?"

Jeff grinned. "That's what sells, honey. And if Sir Godfrey rips the clothes off Lady Isabeau I can't describe her buttons popping unless they had buttons back then."

"It would be fun to do a take-off," Laurie said. "Have Lady Isabeau's buttons pop, then break off for a long pedantic discussion of buttons. When they were introduced, what kinds of buttons they were. Quote your authorities—"

"Invent authorities," Jeff interrupted. "The learned Professor Doctor Hermann Von Schott, *Die Buttongeschlüpfer der Mittelalten über den Hauptglobber—*"

Laurie started to laugh. "It wouldn't sell, I'm afraid."

"I could do it in odd moments, as comic relief," Jeff said, his eyes gleaming. "Come on, give me some more authorities."

"Edward Hightower-Smythe," Laurie suggested. "*Clasps, Buttons, Buckles, and Other Methods of Joining Together Garments During the Period between 1415 and 1418.*"

They had composed a lengthy bibliography—including a journal entitled *Zeitschrift für Studien der Untergarmenten*—when the mood was broken by a prolonged howling without. Laurie recognized her own name.

"What the hell is that?" she demanded.

"Sounds like your brother," Jeff replied calmly.

"My . . . Oh. Doug."

"He is your brother, isn't he?" Jeff inquired. "Hey, there's one for Hermann. Tell him you and Doug—"

"That's not nice." The frigidity of Laurie's tone

surprised her as much as it did Jeff. She added, "I don't even like him."

Jeff tried to keep a straight face, but his lips twitched violently, and after a moment Laurie broke down.

"I just meant," Jeff explained, "that you could tell Hermann he was your lover, masquerading as your brother. If Hermann tattled that one to the aunts, they'd think he had flipped and they'd stop pushing him at you."

Doug's bellows were getting louder. Laurie rose reluctantly to her feet.

"I'll consider it," she promised. "Thanks for the coffee, Jeff. I enjoyed this."

"Me too. Seriously, can I pump you some more? I've got a lot of unanswered questions."

"Any time." Laurie peeked out the window. "I think I'll just wait a minute. . . ."

"Scared of him?" Jeff's voice was scornful.

"Certainly not!" Laurie grabbed her coat with one hand and the doorknob with the other. She plunged out of the house straight into Doug, who was standing on the doorstep. He promptly fell over and Laurie fell on top of him.

It took him a few moments to get his breath back. Laurie was in better shape, her fall having been cushioned by his body; her elbows on either side of his face, she watched with mild concern while he gasped and wheezed. The door of the house had closed quietly behind her, as if Jeff had decided it would not be tactful to volunteer assistance. A wise decision, Laurie thought.

"This is ridiculous," Doug said, after a time. "Get up. If Ida saw us . . ."

Laurie scrambled to her feet and offered a hand which Doug coldly ignored.

"Were you looking for me?" she asked.

"Yes, I was looking for you. The aunts are dithering. They said you walked out two hours ago and disappeared. Lizzie thinks the elves kidnapped you. Ida thinks a bear ate you—"

"And you thought I had gotten lost? How nice of you to be so concerned."

Her brother told her what he had thought. "And I was right, too," he concluded, with a malevolent glance at the door of the cottage.

Laurie gasped indignantly. "You have a dirty mind."

"*You* have a dirty mind, if you think that's dirty. Look, I don't give a damn what you and Heathcliffe do in your spare time, but don't do it here, will you? It would shock the aunts out of their socks if they got wind of it; they'd fire Jeff and then we'd be up the creek with no resident caretaker."

"Practical, aren't you?"

"Always. There's a fairly decent motel in Thurbridge, called the—"

"Oh, shut up."

Doug rubbed his bruised shoulder.

"Actually," he said, in a more conciliatory tone, "I was looking for you because I thought we had a date. To see the Wilsons."

"Oh. I forgot."

"I bet you did," Doug muttered. "All right, all right. Let's go, shall we? Better tell the aunts you're safe first; then they can take their nice naps."

Laurie refused to go into the house, in case there had been further messages from Hermann, so Doug went to announce her return and then joined her at his car.

"You're supposed to call Herrman," he announced, rolling the *r*'s viciously.

Laurie said a bad word. Doug grinned.

"You can't avoid it," he said smugly.

"Oh, yes, I can. And," Laurie added, "you'd better help me. He'll be throwing out not so subtle hints about you calling Sherri and setting up double dates, once he gets a foothold."

"Hmmm." Doug rubbed his chin. "Maybe you're right at that. I think I'll tell Herrrrman I'm married."

"Oh, no, you don't. I may need to use that one myself. I'm in a much more vulnerable position than you are."

The car slid between the stone pillars and out onto the main road. Doug said in a changed voice. "Have you thought about what we're going to say to these people?"

"No," Laurie admitted. "Not in detail. I was just going to tell them the truth."

Doug gave her a quizzical glance.

"Innocent creature. Well, maybe that's the best line after all. I certainly can't think of any sensible lie."

"Do you know where we're going?"

"Not exactly. It's down this way, I think; I seem to remember a mailbox. Look for the name."

Two miles down the road they found the mailbox. There was no house in sight, only an unpaved side road thickly enclosed by brambly bushes, formidable even in their winter barrenness.

"That's it," Laurie said. "Wilson."

"Pray we don't meet anybody," Doug said, and turned cautiously into the road.

There was reason for his concern. The track was only wide enough for one car, and it went up and around in blind curves. Fortunately it was not long. After about three quarters of a mile the track divided. One branch led into the woods; the other turned sharply and plunged into a hollow, where a single house stood. It had to be the Wilson house; there was no other habitation in sight. At a distance it appeared to be a singularly ugly version of the typical farmhouse of the area: two-storied, with a high, pointed gable in the center of the steep-pitched roof, and double-decker wooden porches along one side. It had been painted a depressing brown; except for a few scrawny bare-branched trees there were no shrubs or plants visible around the rough, mud-splashed foundation. By contrast, the barn behind the house was brilliant with fresh red paint.

Doug pulled up in front of the house, next to an old Jeep stationwagon. On close inspection the place was even more depressing. Paint was flaking off the wooden pillars of the porch, and one of the steps sagged, rusty nails protruding threateningly. The front windows were blank eyes, the shades within closely drawn.

"Maybe nobody's home," Laurie said hopefully.

"We can but try." Doug got out of the car and climbed the steps. Laurie followed.

There was no doorbell or knocker. A wooden screen door drooped on its hinges; the screen was torn in several places. After searching in vain for a piece of solid wood on which to knock, Doug opened the screen and banged on the door itself.

Hands in her pockets, shoulders hunched, Laurie shivered. It was chilly in the shade of the porch, but the temperature was only partially responsible for her feeling of cold. The house was forbidding—not sinister, just withdrawn and unwelcoming. She saw no animals, heard no birds. But as the silence descended again, after the reverberation of Doug's knocking had died away, she was aware of sounds within the house—music, muffled but somehow lugubrious, even though faintly heard.

Doug raised an eyebrow and prepared for another assault on the door. Before he could knock they heard footsteps—solid, slow, ponderous. Laurie's scalp prickled. Then there was a sound of rattling. A key turned, a bolt was drawn back; the door creaked, stuck, then opened.

Laurie would not have been surprised to see any monstrous version of humanity, from a withered crone to a cretinous giant in overalls. Instead she found herself facing a comfortably plump, smiling country housewife. Mrs. Wilson wore a dark print dress with a white bibbed apron over it. Apron and dress were both spotless and starched till they crackled. Her graying hair was wrapped in a braid around her head. It looked varnished. Not a hair was out of place. The unmistakable, unforgettable smell of fresh-baked bread accompanied this vision of old-fashioned domestic comfort.

Doug introduced them. Mrs. Wilson nodded, her chins wobbling.

"Well, it's nice to see you. I heard you was home. Come in. Sorry I took so long to answer, but most folks come to the back. I don't suppose I open this door onct a year."

The inside of the house was as neat as the outside was bleak and neglected. However, it could not be called cheerful. The hall floor was covered with drab-brown matting. The only piece of furniture in sight was a huge, hideous hall tree, with a box at its base and several coats hanging from the pegs. Through a door to the left Laurie caught a glimpse of the parlor. The furniture was lined up along the walls, and there was not a picture to be seen.

"Come on back to the kitchen," Mrs Wilson said hospitably. "We'd set in the parlor, only I'm jest in the middle of baking. Hope you'll excuse me."

If Laurie had been given her choice she would certainly have preferred the kitchen. It was equally lacking in ornamentation. The oilcloth on the table was plain blue-and-white check, the curtains were an even plainer solid navy. But any well-scrubbed kitchen is bound to look pleasant, and this one was no exception. The wooden chairs and cabinets were old enough to look quaint, and although the dishes in the corner cupboard were heavy country ware, they shone with cleanliness.

The music came from a small radio on the counter top. An unctuous, oily man's voice was crooning about the arms of Jesus. Mrs. Wilson switched it off, but it had given Laurie the clue she needed. The Wilsons must belong to some fundamentalist sect that frowned on vain adornment. The dark print dress, the absence of even the cheapest pictures . . .

Anyway, Mrs. Wilson looked pleasant. Laurie transferred her instinctive dislike of the house to the unknown, as yet unseen Mr. Wilson.

"You'll hev coffee and a roll, I hope," Mrs. Wilson said. She opened the oven door and skillfully transferred four crusty brown loaves onto the counter beside a row of others already cooling there. Into the oven went two lattice-topped pies and a pan of biscuits. Another mass of dough waited to be rolled out. Pallid white and shapeless, it sprawled obscenely on the top of the counter. Laurie saw a mouth-watering assortment of baked goods already done: corn muffins, buns glistening with caramel topping and bristling with nuts, whole-wheat and white bread, a row of pies. She eyed Mrs. Wilson's immaculate apron with awe.

"Do you have a pastry shop?"

Mrs. Wilson chuckled. "No, Mr. Wilson wouldn't stand for me to go out to work. I sell to a bakery in town, and to the neighbors. But Mr. Wilson is a good hearty eater himself, praise the Lord."

She poured coffee from a pot sitting on the back of the stove. Laurie accepted her cup with a murmured "thank you." When Mrs. Wilson offered a plate of sticky buns she shook her head.

"They look delicious, but I couldn't eat a bite."

"I could," Doug said greedily. "My great-aunt is no slouch as a cook, Mrs. Wilson, but it would be a sin to pass up anything as good as this."

Mrs. Wilson looked pleased. Clearly she approved of men with hearty appetites. But after a moment Laurie saw that although the woman continued to smile, her eyes had narrowed slightly, as if something in Doug's speech or appearance had disturbed her.

Certainly he was out of place in that prim kitchen. The leather jacket, the slightly too long hair, the expensive shirt with its pale stripes and tiny gold flowers . . . Her own tight jeans and T-shirt were just as incongruous. Not extreme, by modern standards, just incongruous. But Mrs. Wilson wasn't staring at her.

The woman turned away and waddled to the counter. Plunging her hands into the mass of dough she kneaded it briskly and then began to pat it out into a thick rectangle.

"Yes," she said, in response to Doug's comment. "Miz Lizzie is sure a good cook, but she don't bake much. How is she these days?"

Doug glanced at Laurie. She shrugged. This was a perfect opening, but she was damned if she was going to take the initiative. Let the young heir, the favored male, ask the first question.

"Fine," Doug said weakly. Mrs. Wilson's back was still turned. Laurie grimaced violently at her brother. Doug licked his sticky fingers. Then he said, "Actually, she isn't all that fine. The reason we dropped in, Mrs. Wilson, is—though your cooking is reason enough!—is—uh—we wanted to talk to your daughters about Aunt Lizzie's latest hobby. About— uh—er—um—"

"Fairies," Laurie said disgustedly. "Fairies in the woods."

Mrs. Wilson stood motionless for a moment. Then her hands came down on the dough with a loud smack. It sounded as if she had spanked a large, bare-bottomed baby. She turned.

"Don't tell me that foolishness is still going on! I told that child when she first come in here talking like that, it was a sin against Scripture. Her daddy is going to be real mad. He don't hold with such things."

"Wait," Doug said quickly. "I'm not accusing the girls of anything. I'm sure they obeyed—er—their daddy. We just want to find out how this business started."

"Oh, well," Mrs. Wilson said. "It was Baby that started it, I guess. Mind, I'm not blaming Miss Lizzie, but it was her that put it into the child's head, all them fairy tales and suchlike lies she told her."

Laurie was only too well aware of the fact that few people can relate a coherent narrative. Mrs. Wilson was not the most intelligent woman in the world—and, to be fair, she probably didn't know what they were driving at.

"Let me get this straight," she said. "Aunt Lizzie was telling—reading?—fairy tales to . . . Baby? What is her name?"

"Betsy," Mrs. Wilson answered. "She's the baby, only five."

Betsy, Baby, Lizzie, . . . The diminutives were beginning to grate on Laurie's nerves. She decided that from now on she would only answer to Laura.

"Her and Miss Lizzie got to be friendly last summer," Mrs. Wilson went on. "Miss Lizzie is a good soul, I don't say she's not, even if the grace of the Lord isn't in her. She's soft about children. And the girls was always sneaking away from their chores, playing in the woods. Miss Lizzie used to run into them there. Betsy'd come home talking about little people, with wings an' all. I never paid her much mind, she's quite a one to talk, Betsy is. But one night at supper she started on about elves or whatever, and her daddy got real upset. He licked Mary Ella and Rachel real good."

"Wait," Laurie said again. "Wait. I don't understand, Mrs. Wilson. If Betsy was the culprit . . . I mean, the one who was talking about elves—why did her father punish the older girls?"

"Why, they was supposed to be watching over Betsy. They ought to know better."

Laurie and Doug exchanged glances. Mrs. Wilson went on, "None of them has said a word about it since."

"I'll bet," Doug muttered.

"What about the photographs?" Laurie asked.

"What photographs?"

"Aunt Lizzie has some snapshots. Of—well—they

look like . . . She doesn't have a camera. We were under the impression that one of your daughters had taken them."

Mrs. Wilson shook her head. "I don't know about no photographs."

Laurie gritted her teeth. Talking to Mrs. Wilson was like trying to run through her bread dough—slow and sticky.

"Do the girls own cameras?"

"Cameras? No. Their daddy don't hold with such things. Now what did I do with that biscuit cutter?"

"I wonder if we could talk to the girls," Laurie said desperately, wondering if Mrs. Wilson's children would be as slow-witted as their mother.

"No reason why not. They'll be home from school pretty soon." Mrs. Wilson found the missing implement and began cutting out biscuits. "Only don't get 'em started on that silly business again. Their daddy won't like it."

Doug had eaten three buns and was obviously fed up, in every sense of the word. He signaled to Laurie, suggesting retreat. She shook her head. He hadn't seen the photographs. She had.

Mrs. Wilson began to sing. She had a low, rather pleasant voice.

> "When I see His holy blood
> Then happiness does flood
> Into my joyful heart when day is o'er;
> When I see His grievous wounds
> Then my loving spirit swoons—"

Laurie never learned the last line of this gem; the back door swung open and Mrs. Wilson broke off.

"Well, here she is," she said. "Here's Baby. You can talk to her if you want."

Laurie stared.

Baby Betsy could have doubled for Baby Shirley Temple in her youthful prime; but Shirley's early movies had not been in living color. Betsy had bounc-

124

ing taffy-blond curls, dancing blue eyes, dimples—
the works. She wore a snowsuit of a vivid robins'-egg
blue and matching cap lined with bunny fur. The top
of her curly head—Laurie calculated—would just
about reach her own hipbone.

"This here is Miss Lizzie's great-niece and -nephew,"
Mrs. Wilson said precisely. "Say hello, Baby."

"Hello," said Baby. She examined them and then,
with the unerring instinct of the female, young or
old, trotted over to Doug. "Help me take off my
snowpants," she said, putting a soft, mittened hand
on his knee.

"Oh. Sure." Doug looked blankly at her. "How?"

Baby Betsy giggled. "Funny man."

"Come here, Baby," Laurie said. "I'll help you."

Betsy shook her head. Taffy-colored curls bounced.

"No. Betsy wants nice man to he'p her."

Doug was looking fatuous, if helpless. Laurie seized
the infant charmer and had her out of her snowsuit
before she could protest.

"There," she said, returning Betsy's hostile stare.

"Thank the lady," said Mrs. Wilson. "Betsy, have
you been—"

Before she could finish the question they heard
footsteps on the back porch.

"Here's the girls," Mrs. Wilson said. "You can talk
to all of 'em at onct."

Of course, Laurie realized—the older girls would
take a different school bus. Betsy, though not as
babyish as she liked to appear, was probably in
kindergarten. The others . . .

Junior high school—at least. No wonder Betsy
was so spoiled. There must be seven or eight years
between her and her closest sister.

They stood in the doorway staring shyly at the
strangers. Unlike their little sister they wore dark,
drab clothing and ugly, home-knit stocking caps.
Their faces were bare of the slightest hint of makeup.
The younger of the two, sallow-skinned and pimply,

had long dark braids and a heavy face. The older was a miracle.

Even the shapeless coat could not hide her grace. Masses of tumbled curls, the color of primroses or pale scrambled eggs, spilled out from under the knit cap. Her eyes were blue and long-lashed, her mouth a soft pink.

Laurie glanced sideways at her brother. He looked like a feeble-minded owl. His eyes bulged and his mouth hung open. It dropped even farther when the golden-haired maiden removed her coat. Her long-sleeved blouse and simple dark skirt somehow managed to display a figure which was, to say the least, precocious.

Laurie kicked Doug. He continued to stare.

"Hang your coats up, girls," Mrs. Wilson ordered, in a brisk tone quite unlike the softer voice she had used to Betsy. "Then get back in here. These is Miss Lizzie's folks, that you've heard her talk about. They want to ask you some questions."

The golden-haired beauty—Cinderella in a cheap dark skirt—looked apprehensive. The other girl glowered. Neither spoke. They went obediently into the hall and did as they were told. Betsy leaned across Doug's knee and reached for a bun.

"I wanna glass of milk, Momma," she whined.

Mrs. Wilson produced the milk. The older girls returned. Betsy leaned more heavily.

"Can I sit on your lap?" she asked Doug, batting her lashes at him.

"Why, sure, you can," Doug said. He lifted her up. An expression of pain crossed his face as Betsy's sticky fingers clutched his jacket.

"Go ahead," Mrs. Wilson said. "They got homework to do, so if you wouldn't mind—"

"Wead Betsy a stowy." Betsy picked up a battered book and shoved it against Doug's nose.

"Maybe later," Doug said.

"Wead a stowy now!"

"*Not* now," Laurie said.

126

Betsy, who had long since recognized her as an enemy, not to be seduced by dimples, pouted, but shut up.

"Now, girls." Laurie turned her attention to the older children. They stood side by side, hands clasped; their stiff poses and wide, apprehensive eyes made Laurie feel obscurely guilty. "Look, there's nothing to worry about," she assured them.

Her smile won no response from the girls. She tried again.

"My name is Laurie. You are—Rachel?"

A nod from Cinderella.

"Then you must be Mary Ella," Laurie said to the dark, sallow child. "We just wanted to ask you how Miss Lizzie got interested in ... in ..." (Weird! She would have found a four-letter obscenity as easy to pronounce.)

"Fairies," Doug said jerkily. Betsy was wriggling on his lap and he was beginning to look disenchanted. "You girls know Miss Lizzie; you like her, don't you?"

Mary Ella mumbled, shuffling her feet; but Rachel, after a long survey of Doug from under preposterously long lashes, smiled shyly and suddenly. Her pretty white teeth were just a little crooked. The disharmony gave her smile an elfin enchantment.

"Yes, sir, we sure do. She's a nice old lady."

"She likes you too, I'm sure."

"I hope so, sir," Rachel said modestly.

"Well ..."

(How can I put this? his eyes asked Laurie. She shrugged. The girl isn't a baby or a moron, her eyes replied. Doug looked outraged.)

"Well," he went on, "you know old people sometimes get funny ideas."

"Oh, yes, sir." Rachel had relaxed; her blue eyes were fixed trustingly on Doug's face. "Granny was like that, before she died. She thought she was a little girl. She called us by her sisters' names."

"Miss Lizzie is not like that," Laurie said. For

some reason she felt outraged at the child's calm description of senility, and at her assumption that Lizzie was in that state. "She has photographs, Rachel. Do you know anything about them?"

"No, ma'am."

Rachel's rose-petal lips imprisoned her smile. Her lashes dropped, hiding her eyes.

"Do you have a camera?"

"No, ma'am."

"Their daddy doesn't hold with buying expensive toys for kids," Mrs. Wilson added. "Rachel, you tell the lady the truth, now. You didn't try to fool poor old Miss Lizzie, did you?"

"No, Momma."

Doug, torn between Betsy's squirming and the fascination of that exquisite, flowerlike face, said quickly, "Rachel, don't be upset. We believe you. We're just trying to figure out how Miss Lizzie got these notions about elves."

The girl's wistful face brightened a she looked at him. Before she could speak, Betsy, who sensed she was loosing Doug's attention, announced, "Betsy saw the faiwies. Miss Lizzie showed her."

"Betsy!" Mrs. Wilson frowned. "You know what your daddy told you. That's lies, that is, and you know what our sweet Jesus does to bad children who tell lies."

It was clear that sweet Jesus had a heavy hand with liars. Rachel flinched, as if at some unpleasant memory, and even Betsy looked daunted.

"It's not a lie, Momma," she said quickly. "Just a stowy. Miss Lizzie told me stowies. She tells lies, Momma, not Betsy."

"You didn't see no such thing, did you?"

"No Momma. Miss Lizzie told Betsy."

Laurie bit back an impatient exclamation. They weren't getting anywhere, except deeper into a morass of confusion. The girls were obviously afraid; and she had not helped the situation. Rachel didn't care much for her, and the other child, Mary Ella, might have been a block of wood for all the response they had gotten from her. It was as if her older sister had taken her portion of beauty and sensitivity, leaving Mary Ella none.

"We'd better go, Doug," she said.

"Just a minute. Tell me something, Rachel. When was it that Betsy came home talking about fairies? How long ago?"

"Last summer," Rachel said promptly. "August. She was—"

Mrs. Wilson made a sudden violent movement, so out of keeping with her usual slow style that they all jumped.

"Here comes your daddy," she said.

She might have been announcing the arrival of Beelzebub. The animation left Rachel's face. Mary Ella did not move, but she seemed to shrink, becoming at once smaller and more solid. Betsy slid down off Doug's knees and ran to the door. When it opened she flung herself at the man who came in and wound her arms around his knees.

"Daddy's home! Hello, Daddy. I was vewy good in school today. I got a gold star."

Mr. Wilson filled the doorway from side to side. Laurie was not surprised at his bulk—she had seen how his wife cooked—but she realized it was not all fat. His shoulders were heavy with muscle and the hand he placed on Betsy's golden head looked like that of a gorilla, thick-fingered and sprouting black hairs. The brief caress was his only expression of affection or of greeting. Laurie wondered from what source Rachel had gained her delicate beauty. There was no trace of it in Mrs. Wilson's doughy, complacent face, or in her husband's heavy features. His eyes were a muddy, inexpressive brown, his mouth both fleshy and pinched. He needed a shave.

"You're home early," Mrs. Wilson said.

"It's raining." Wilson's growl made the simple statement into an accusation. "Had to quit. Now I've gotta finish the job tomorrow. Means I can't get to the Shotwells till Saturday."

"That's too bad."

"Who's this?"

"This is the Mortons' great-niece and -nephew," Mrs. Wilson began. Doug rose.

"My name is Wright, Mr. Wilson. This is my sister. Glad to meet you."

Wilson eyed the extended hand as if it were a dead fish but finally took it grudgingly and let it go almost at once. He did not greet, or look at, Laurie.

"What are you girls doing, standing around here?" he demanded, turning on his daughters. "If you ain't got no work to do I'll find you some in a hurry."

"These folks wanted to talk to them," Mrs. Wilson explained. "Set down, Poppa, do, and I'll get you something to eat."

Wilson hung his damp jacket on a peg and thumped his ample posterior into a chair. He turned an inimical eye on Doug, who was still standing.

"What do you wanna talk about? They been in trouble?"

"No," Doug said. "No trouble. We just—"

"It's about them elves again," Mrs. Wilson said.

Taken in isolation the statement might have sounded funny, Mrs. Wilson's flat, matter-of-fact voice contrasted so oddly with the key word. Laurie had no desire to laugh, however. Wilson's face could hardly have been more forbidding; its normal expression was a dark frown; but now his eyes narrowed and an angry flush rose in his cheeks.

"Again? I thought I fixed that the first time. Guess I didn't make it hard enough, huh? You, Rachel, you come over here and—"

"Wait a minute," Doug interrupted. "Rachel hasn't done anything. Nor have the other girls. It's our aunt who has this idea, and we just wanted to ask your children how it all started. No reason for you to punish them."

The speech would have had the desired effect if

Doug had not added the last sentence. Laurie knew he was, in fact, controlling himself considerably. The pallor of Rachel's face had aroused all his knight-errantry. All the same, the direct defense was a mistake. Wilson's flush of anger had started to subside. Now the dark blood returned to his face.

"I don't need nobody to tell me when I should chastise my children, mister. The Scripture says 'Spare not the rod,' and I don't, neither. The female is a vessel of iniquity. Lyin' is a abomination unto the Lord. A man is master in his own house, an'—"

"Hev some coffee, Poppa." Mrs. Wilson put a cup and a plate of rolls in front of her husband. He crammed one of the pastries into his mouth and glowered at Doug.

"I wouldn't presume to interfere with your outré notions of discipline," Doug said coldly. "All I said was—"

Wilson didn't know what outré meant, but he knew he was being insulted. He swallowed, with a repulsive gulping sound, and banged his fist down on the table. The veins in his neck bulged. High blood pressure, Laurie thought. No wonder. All that hating is a strain on the system.

"I heard what you said, mister," he shouted. "An' you heard what I said."

Laurie stood up and took Doug's arm. It felt like stone.

"We must be going," she said. "Thank you for the snack, Mrs. Wilson. It was delicious."

"I'm gonna give you a couple loaves of bread for the old ladies," Mrs. Wilson said placidly. "Like I said, Miss Lizzie's no hand at baking. But they're good neighbors."

She glanced casually at her husband. Having engulfed another roll, he had been about to burst out again; but as his piggy little eyes met those of his wife he closed his mouth.

"Thank you." Laurie accepted the neatly wrapped

loaves. They were still warm. "Sorry to have bothered you."

"Yeah," Wilson growled. "Folks who don't have to work for a living stick their noses into other folks' business . . . You girls still here? Git." The girls got. Mary Ella didn't seem capable of quick movement, but it was amazing how suddenly she left the room. Rachel followed, her eyes downcast. Wilson turned his beady eyes back to Doug. "An' you, better go home an' tend to your own business. That crazy old lady is your business. Lock her up."

Doug appeared to have been rooted to the spot. Laurie held the bread in one arm; the other hand, on Doug's sleeve, felt his muscles quiver and knot. She nudged him with her shoulder. Finally, he moved.

CHAPTER

7

It was raining hard. They had to circle the house to reach the car. Laurie had propelled her infuriated brother through the nearest door rather than remain in the house a moment longer. Oh, well, she thought; maybe the rain will cool him off.

Doug didn't speak until they were in the car. His lean face had remained calm and expressionless throughout the conversation with Wilson. It was still impassive when he raised his fist and brought it down on the steering wheel with a crash.

"Feel better?" Laurie inquired.

"Not much. My God! That monster ought to be locked up. He's sick!"

"He's probably a hard worker and a pious member of the church."

"He's a monster. What he is doing to those kids—"

"Vessels of iniquity, you mean."

"I guess that's why he's so much tougher on Rachel than on the others," Doug said, in a calmer voice.

"I guess. Oh, he's sick all right, by your definitions and mine. In Puritan New England he'd have burned witches. In biblical times, he'd have been a bosom buddy of Saint Paul's. Some men feel threatened by women. And Rachel is a woman, physically, if not legally. That's why people like Wilson turn to religion; it's so nice to be able to justify your neuroses by means of Scripture."

"You can justify almost anything by means of Scripture," Doug said. "It is a compilation, after all. He sure has those women beaten down "

"He seems to have a sneaking fondness for Betsy."

"God, what a revolting child! The way she fawned on him—"

"I agree, she's awful; but you can't blame her for buttering up to Daddy. It's a defensive strategy. Mary Ella defends herself by becoming a lump. Sadists don't enjoy torturing victims unless they respond. And Mrs. Wilson—"

"Thoroughly cowed," Doug said.

"I'm not so sure. She's got more control over that gorilla than even he realizes. Did you notice how he shut up when she made that remark about what good neighbors the Mortons were?"

"Hey, that's right. Wilson wouldn't shut his big mouth to keep on good terms with neighbors; there must be some other factor. Do you suppose Mrs. Wilson meant 'landlords'?"

"I wouldn't be surprised." Laurie glanced uneasily out the window. "Let's go, Doug, before we get trapped by floodwaters. I'd hate to spend any more time here."

"Okay." The car swung in a circle, skidding in the mud. "I hope Wilson doesn't beat those kids."

"Why use the plural? You're worried about Rachel."

"I wonder how old she is," Doug muttered.

"Young enough so you could get arrested for what you're thinking."

"I do not know which is worse, your grammar or your low, vicious, evil—"

"I'm sorry." Laurie slid down in the seat. The dismal, soggy, gray landscape matched her mood. "She *is* lovely, and she *is* pathetic. I feel very sorry for her. I'm depressed. Do you realize we didn't learn anything? What a waste of time."

"I wouldn't say that."

"You mean that Rachel denied taking the pictures?"

Doug's face was still bedazzled. Laurie chose her words with care. "I wouldn't blame her for lying, Doug. She's terrified of her father. Where are you going? The house is—"

"I know where the house is. We're overdue for a conference, and it's impossible to have a private conversation in that place."

"Where are we going?"

"There's a little place down the road—"

"It's too early for a drink," Laurie said.

"Never too early for a beer, my dear. Vi's will be empty this time of day; the good buddies don't come in till after work."

As Laurie had surmised, the "little place" was a tavern—a tacky-looking, gaudily painted cinderblock structure on the outskirts of the small town that was the nearest metropolis to Idlewood. The interior was a decorator's nightmare of cheap plastic and outhouse-humor posters; but at least it looked fairly clean and was, as Doug had promised, virtually empty. Vi, a big, gray-haired woman with a prominent red nose, greeted Doug by name.

"Early for you, isn't it? And who's your friend?" She winked.

"My sister," Doug said quickly.

"Your . . . Oh—oh, yeah. I heard you was here on a visit, Miss—uh—"

"Make it Laurie. Good to meet you, Vi."

"Likewise," Vi said heartily. "I remember you, from years back; my dad owned the grocery store in town, and your Uncle Ned used to bring you with him sometimes. I sure wouldn't have known you."

They had to chat for a few minutes before Vi let

them retire to a booth. The only other patron was at the far end of the room, in a semirecumbent position. His eyes and mouth were open, but it was obvious that he was totally disinterested in the outside world.

"Good beer," Doug said, after a moment.

"Not bad. What do you want to talk about?"

"Aunt Lizzie, of course. I'm beginning to think we got on our horses and rode off in all directions on a wild-goose chase."

"Talk about mixing your metaphors—"

"Oh, you know what I mean. What have we got, really? A sweet little old lady, who has never been known for her logical mind, showing signs of senility. At her age that's not surprising. The only problem I can see is what steps we ought to take to make sure she doesn't hurt herself wandering—"

"No," Laurie said.

"No what?"

"No, that isn't all we have." Laurie ticked the points off on her fingers. "One, the lights I saw in the woods. Two, the music. Three, the photographs. When you talk about senility you're talking about subjective hallucinations. Those are three separate, objective phenomena—witnessed by an outside observer. . . ." She broke off with a gasp as an outrageous idea occurred to her. Doug was staring intently at the dregs of his beer and refused to meet her eyes. "By me," Laurie said, controlling her voice with an effort. "Is that what you think? I'm the only one who has seen those things—"

"Hey—hey, take it easy, will you? I never suggested—"

"It was implicit in what you said."

Doug's eyebrows soared till they all but vanished amid the tumbled hair on his forehead.

"I guess it was at that," he said, mildly surprised. "But I didn't mean it that way—honest. Damn it, this is the most peculiar situation I've ever been involved in. There's nothing solid. Every time I try to grab hold of a fact it turns to smoke and melts away."

"I know what you mean. Any outsider would react just as you did. On the face of it, it's just a case of a crazy old lady and an impressionable female who doesn't want her auntie put away. Look, I'd be willing to discount the lights and the music, either or both. I can invent logical explanations for them, if I must. But those snapshots were something else."

"Then who took them?"

"Rachel," Laurie said.

She expected Doug to look outraged or skeptical. Instead he nodded thoughtfully. "I agree, we can't take her denial literally. But you've overlooked a suspect."

"Who?"

"Mary Ella."

"Mary Ella! Why, she didn't even . . ." Laurie considered the idea. "How old do you suppose she is? Thirteen, fourteen? Yes, I guess she could be a dark horse. She doesn't react, but that doesn't mean she isn't feeling emotion."

"Let's have another beer," Doug said.

"Don' min' iffah dew," came a sepulchral echo from the far end of the room.

"Good Lord," Laurie exclaimed, peering around the edge of the high partition that formed the back of the seat. All she could see was an arm waving high in the air. Thanks to her current overdose of fantasy, she was reminded of Arthurian legend— though this arm was clad in faded denim instead of white samite, and it brandished a beer stein in lieu of a magic sword. King Arthur a la Monty Python.

"Never mind him," Doug said. "He's programmed to respond to only one word. Where's Vi? I want—"

"Don't say it. And don't call her, not yet. There are one or two other points I want to make, while we've got some privacy. First, I—well, I don't blame you for being somewhat skeptical about my evidence. You haven't seen me for years. You don't really

137

know me. I might be one of those emotional types who imagine things."

His arms folded on the table, Doug listened intently.

"You might be," he said, when she paused.

Laurie had expected him to deny the charge, if only out of politeness. Oddly enough, his candor pleased her.

"Let me point out, however, that my room is directly over Lizzie's, on the same side of the house; and that you are a heavy sleeper. If the lights and the music are aimed at Lizzie, I'm the only other person in the house who is in a physical position to see and hear them."

Doug nodded. "Good point. Go on."

"The pivotal evidence is the photos," Laurie said. "I knew when I was describing them to you that I wasn't conveying the shock they gave me. All I can say is that they were *not* photographs of any natural phenomenon, and that they were clear and unmistakable. They prove that something other than Lizzie's admittedly wild imagination is responsible for her belief in pixies."

"I read that book of Doyle's you gave me," Doug said.

It took Laurie a few seconds to understand the pertinence of this comment. Then the meaning, with all its permutations, flooded into her mind, and in spite of her resolution to remain calm she felt her cheeks burn.

"Doug, the pictures were nothing like those! I mean, I am not a complete moron. Do you think I'd be taken in by—"

"I don't know. As you just said, I don't know you very well."

"All right." Laurie applied herself to her beer stein; unlike Doug's, it was still half full. The interval gave her time to compose herself. "Look," she said, "part of our problem is that we haven't had time to talk. I wanted to discuss that book with you because it seemed to me there are certain parallels in the two cases. But Doyle's photographs are obvious frauds."

"Why couldn't he see that? The man who wrote *Sherlock Holmes* and *The White Company* wasn't stupid."

Laurie shrugged. "Brighter men than Doyle have fallen for obvious psychic tricks. I guess most people have a—well, a weak spot or two in their mental fabric. They can be perfectly logical about most things, but they throw logic out the window when you hit them where it counts."

"True, O pearl of wisdom. Hey," Doug said awkwardly. "I didn't mean—"

"I know. Let's not go on apologizing. What I'm trying to say is that Aunt Lizzie's pictures are as different from the ones in that book as a dime-store plastic rose is from the real article. In the first place, hers are in color. In the second place, her elves are three-dimensional; not flat, cardboard silhouettes. The grass was flattened by their feet. They were moving. And finally—the little ladies in Doyle's photos are *dated*. I mean, the hair styles and figures and so on are the sort of thing a child of the nineteen twenties would draw. Like a paper doll. Lizzie's fairies are far out—alien. If I met one of them in a dark alley I'd scream and run."

"Humph. Obviously," Doug said, "I've got to sneak a peek at those pictures."

"She's got some sort of hidey-hole in her room. Believe me, I'd burgle it if I could. I've reached that point. Why don't you work your wiles on her?"

"I'll try," said Doug unenthusiastically. "But you were always her pet. Listen, I really do want another beer, and it's getting late, and—"

"Okay, okay, call your girl friend, but don't—"

The warning came too late. Doug's shout of "Hey, Vi, how about a refill?" aroused not only Vi but the drunk in the far booth.

"Thanks, pal, don' min' iffah dew."

"Go back to sleep, Sam," Vi yelled. "You've had enough already. You want another one, Laurie?"

"No, thanks. Too fattening."

Vi put Doug's drink on the table and gave Laurie a critical glance. "You don't have to worry, honey."

Laurie discounted the compliment. Next to Vi's ample inches she looked like a sylph.

"Turned into a right pretty girl, you have," Vi went on. "You were all skin and bones and big eyes when you used to come to town." She turned her attention to Doug. "Now you, you were always skinny and homely. Can't say you've changed none."

"Ha ha," Doug said. "Thanks, Vi."

"Don't know where you get your looks. Sure ain't no Morton in you. Look at Laurie, she's got the high cheekbones, and her eyes are set wide, like her aunts'. But you—"

"Changeling," Laurie said. "The fairies stole the real baby and left him."

Doug's sense fo humor did not seem broad enough to encompass this badinage. He scowled impartially at Laurie and Vi.

"What's this I hear about Miss Lizzie seeing fairies?" Vi asked.

The question hit her audience like a bomb. Both stared.

"Where did you hear that?" Doug demanded.

Vi shrugged. The gesture set off a chain reaction of fleshy ripples that ran clear down to her feet.

"Oh, you know; people talk. Miss Lizzie is sure a queer one. Good soul, but queer. Always has been."

Laurie decided that since the subject had already become neighborhood gossip, there was no reason to be reticent—or strictly truthful.

"She got the idea from the little Wilson girl," she said. "Who are the Wilsons, Vi?"

"Oh . . . them." Vi pulled a cloth from her pocket and began wiping the table. "They rent that farm from your folks. Been there . . . oh, I guess it must be ten, fifteen years."

"And they're still renting?" Doug, surprisingly attuned to the nuances of rural life, pounced on this. "How come Mr. Wilson hasn't bought a place of his own?"

"He's a contractor, not a farmer. Runs a few cows and chickens back in there, that's all. Hard worker, too. Problem is, he tithes."

Doug looked blankly at Laurie.

"That means he gives part of his income to his church," she explained smugly. "Ten percent—"

"Not him," Vi snorted. "Twenty-five percent."

"What church does he belong to?" Laurie asked.

"One of them strange sects—not a regular Methodist or Presbyterian. He's an elder."

"He would be," Doug said.

"Comes in here every Saturday," Vi said. "Reads the Bible and lectures my patrons."

"You're kidding," Laurie exclaimed.

"No." Vi chuckled tolerantly. "Well, maybe not every Saturday; he goes other places too. But this is the closest. Makes a good show; my customers kind of enjoy it."

"We met his daughters today," Laurie said.

"Them poor kids! My niece goes to school with one of 'em. Bright as can be, all three, and hardworking; the old buzzard has the two oldest out earning already, cleaning and babysitting and the like. They sure lead dogs' lives. Only place they go is to school and to church."

"I guess they aren't old enough to date," Laurie said, aware of Doug's interest.

"He won't let anything in pants come near those girls," Vi said dourly. "Wouldn't surprise me if he contracted 'em in marriage, the way they used to do in the old days. And they say the oldest, what's her name?—Rachel—is a real beauty. He run one boy off the place with a pitchfork, if you can believe it, just for walking the girl home from the school bus."

"So that's why—" Doug began.

"Why he was so nasty to you," Laurie agreed. She

explained to Vi, "We stopped by the house today, and he treated Doug like Jack the Ripper."

"I'm not surprised," Vi said. "Watch yourself, Doug; no fooling around there."

"She's just a child," Doug said stiffly.

"Uh-huh. All the more reason to leave her be. Want another beer?"

"No, thanks. We'd better be going. Want any help with the old sot down there before I leave?"

"Oh, he's no problem. Comes in here every day when I open, gets soused, and falls asleep. His boys pick him up when they get through with work. Come by again, you two. And leave Rachel alone, you devil, you."

Laughing uproariously she waddled off.

The rain had slowed to drizzle when they left, and darkness had crept in, trailing a cloak of fog.

"One more thing," Laurie said, as Doug started the car. "I'm tired of all the secrecy and tact. I move we get this out in the open tonight."

"Okay."

"What's the matter?" Laurie studied his gloomy profile, illuminated in all its lean austerity by the dashboard lights. "Are you dreaming of Rachel?"

"Cut it out, will you?"

"I'm not being sarcastic. I can see her appeal, I really can. She's Cinderella, with a wicked father instead of a mean stepmother. I think we ought to try once more to talk to her."

"How? Mrs. Wilson is as bad as the old man, in a different way. Rachel won't say anything in front of her mother."

"I wonder if we could catch her when she leaves school," Laurie suggested. "If you drove her home she'd not be late; that school bus must go a round-about route. And I'd be with you, as chaperone, in case her mother did find out."

"Not a bad idea." Doug's face brightened.

The short drive home was an uncanny experience.

Every foot of the terrain was familiar to Laurie, yet in the drifting fog it took on the vague dimensions of a strange landscape. The dark shapes looming up beside the road might have been elongated Martian monsters instead of trees; they seemed to lunge out at the car, bony arms waving, as the headlights picked them out of the mist.

Laurie felt as if her mental landscape had undergone a similar transformation. She had been trained to marshal facts, and she had, under pressure, produced a convincing structure of evidence for Doug. Yet she had failed to mention the real reason for her concern, because it was irrational. Doug would have dismissed it with a patronizing smile or a raised eyebrow. But she had been convinced, from the day the whole thing began, on a snowy afternoon in Chicago, that Lizzie's most recent fantasy was different from all the others. The facts she had learned confirmed that feeling, but they had not produced it. Furthermore, in their discussion they had both delicately skirted around the most important question of all. If, as she believed, an active, malicious intelligence had produced the phenomena that fed poor Lizzie's delusion, then the burning question was: why? At that point Laurie's reason and imagination both came to a dead stop. To think that someone would want to harm the innocent, amiable old woman was almost as preposterous as little green elves in the woods.

After the uncanny darkness without, the house was so warm and normal that Laurie's theories seemed even more absurd. Lizzie was bustling around the kitchen as usual, humming loudly to herself and tripping over her long skirt; Uncle Ned was in his chair at the kitchen table, whittling. He never actually made anything, he just whittled till he had chipped the wood away, and the aunts had become so accustomed to this performance that their complaints were stilted and perfunctory. Ida was her normal

143

self too. She gave Laurie a lecture on being out so late, and sent her upstairs to shower and change for dinner.

Instead of going to her own room, Laurie opened Lizzie's door and slipped inside. If I'm caught, she told herself, I'll say I wanted to try on that ridiculous robe she tried to give me. It was hateful, thinking of lies, sneaking and prying; but it had to be done.

She did not anticipate any problem in finding Lizzie's secret hiding place, although the wide, random-width floor planks and the extensive use of wood paneling offered only too many possibilities. Yet it had to be fairly accessible or the old lady wouldn't have been able to get to it. Not too high, then—and probably not too low down. Aunt Lizzie didn't bend easily. The sunken, rectangular panels framing the fireplace were likely prospects, as were the strips lining the deep window embrasures. But push and prod and poke as she would, Laurie could not move any of them. She was finally forced to give up the search. Lizzie would have to be bullied into producing the pictures.

Laurie came downstairs to find the rest of the family assembled in the parlor enjoying their before-dinner wine. She had worked herself up to a pitch of forthright efficiency, determined to proceed with or without Doug's cooperation; and the first sentence of her speech had already formed itself in her mind when she marched into the room. Then she saw Jeff.

She couldn't talk frankly in front of Jeff—not without strenuous opposition from Doug, at any rate. How could she have forgotten he would be there? He was not the sort of person one easily forgot.

He greeted her casually, but his dark eyes met hers with such warmth and pleasure that Laurie came perilously close to blushing like a schoolgirl. She took the sherry he offered her—it was sherry, not Doug's substitute—and sat down.

144

Why not talk in front of Jeff? She argued with herself while the others chatted. The Mortons regarded him as one of the family, and he seemed not only fond of them but sensible of his obligations. The responsibility was his, after all. He had been hired to look after the old people while their relatives went their selfish separate ways. She sat up a little straighter and cleared her throat. Then she realized that Doug had been watching her like a scientist examining a particularly disgusting germ. He caught her eye and made a slight but unmistakable sideways motion of his head. Laurie signaled back: why not? Doug's reply was a grimace. Laurie had anticipated a negative response, and would have debated longer, but Ida saw Doug's face and demanded to know if something was hurting him.

When they went in to dinner Laurie managed to get a word with her recalcitrant brother.

"I thought we agreed to get this out in the open," she whispered.

"Not in front of him. After dinner."

Conversation at the table would have dragged if it had been up to Doug and Laurie. Jeff kept the ball rolling—teasing Lizzie, discussing spring crops with Ned, listening deferentially to Ida's occasional comments. It was almost as if she and Doug weren't there, Laurie thought. It did not appear that they were much missed, and the credit—or blame—for that had to go to Jeff. He had added years to the old peoples' lives, not only by helping them with the chores but by injecting his young, vital personality into their world. More and more Laurie felt that Jeff had a right to be involved in their problem.

She avoided Doug's glance, but he watched her like a hawk, prepared to swoop down and silence her if she spoke out of turn. After dinner Jeff withdrew to the kitchen. When the others had returned to the parlor Doug took the bull by the horns.

"Now that we're alone," he began, somewhat pompously, "there is a family matter we must discuss."

Aunt Lizzie beamed at him. "Oh, darling boy, are you going to be married?"

"Married?" Doug looked horrified. "What on earth gave you that idea, Aunt?"

"Well, it is certainly high time. You aren't getting any younger, Douglas. Marriage and children give a young man stability. And I would love to have a new baby in—"

"Aunt Lizzie!" Lizzie's lip began to quiver, and Doug moderated his voice. "I'm sorry, I didn't mean to yell. But I want to talk to you about something a lot more important than my love life—such as it is—and you keep getting off the track."

"Well, I'm sorry, dear, but—"

"And don't go quivering your lip at me, either. I'm on to your tricks."

He smiled, but his tone was stern. Lizzie eyed him for a moment, her head tipped to one side. She looked like a little white-headed bird, and Laurie could have sworn her bright, sparkling eyes held a glint of hidden amusement.

"I don't know what you mean, Douglas. And I can't imagine what family matter you have in mind. We have no problems."

"You!" Doug said sharply. "You're the problem, Aunt Lizzie. You and your habit of wandering out of the house in the middle of the night."

"Oh, dear." Lizzie sighed. "I'm afraid you are right, Douglas. I really am sorry about that. I won't do it again. Would you like more coffee?"

"No, I would not. And if you think that settles it—"

"Well, I don't really see why not. I admit it was thoughtless of me. In the future I will be more careful. Do you know, Ida, this coffee is really not very hot. I think I'll just run out to the kitchen and—"

Doug pounded at the air with his fists, as if trying to knock down the words that pelted him.

"You aren't doing very well, Doug," Laurie said. "Let me have a crack at it. Auntie, what Doug is trying to say is that we want to know *why* you've been going out. I want you to show him those snapshots."

"What snapshots, darling?" Aunt Lizzie transferred her bright, empty smile to Laurie.

"You know which ones. The fairies."

"Oh, those."

Doug continued to claw at the air. Laurie was tempted to join him, but plowed doggedly on through the smoke screen.

"Yes, those. You go up right now and get them, Auntie."

"You promised me you wouldn't tell anyone about them."

The effect of the big dark eyes swimming with tears, the quivering voice, the soft, pouting lips, was so overwhelming that Laurie almost failed to see the flaw in the argument.

"I didn't promise any such thing," she said firmly. "Now you stop that, Aunt Lizzie. We're only doing this for your own good."

The tears vanished like dew in the sun. The pouting lips became sullen instead of pathetic.

"I don't want to," Lizzie said.

"You have to."

"Elizabeth." Ida spoke. "Go upstairs immediately and do as Laura says."

Lizzie glanced desperately at her brother. She got no help from that direction either.

"Pack of nonsense," Ned grumbled. "Go along, Liz, and let's get this silly business settled. It's taken up too much time already."

"You're all horrid to me." Lizzie wept. Crystalline tears trickled down her cheeks.

Laurie felt like the lowest crawling form of life. She might have been tempted to weaken if she had not glanced at Doug and seen the same repentant self-hatred in his face.

"Scat," she said. "Right this minute."

Lizzie got up and trudged toward the door. She dragged her feet instead of scampering happily as she usually did; the droop of her shoulders and her forlorn shuffle were exquisite expressions of a breaking heart. A little too exquisite, perhaps. Laurie wondered how much of Aunt Lizzie was for real. Had the sweet innocent old lady been putting them on for years?

It seemed to take Lizzie forever to reach the doorway, while the others sat in uncomfortable silence. Then—as Lizzie had probably calculated—a last forlorn hope appeared, in the person of Jeff. One look at Lizzie and his smile vanished.

"What's the matter?"

"You keep out of this," Doug said rudely.

"Oh, Jefferson!" Lizzie clutched at him, her wet face turned up trustingly. "They are being so mean to me. Make them stop!"

For once Lizzie's histrionic talents played her false. She was unaware of the depth of the jealousy Doug felt for the other man, and her appeal set off all Doug's worst instincts.

"It's none of his business," he snapped.

"No." Ida had been sitting like a carved image, her only comment so far the direct order to her sister. Now she shifted position and spoke with her usual authority. "I am afraid that it is Jefferson's business, Douglas. I had intended suggesting that he be invited to join us. However, he has no authority to prevent us from insisting that Elizabeth produce those photographs. Nor, when he has learned the truth, will he have any desire to do so."

Jeff looked bewildered, as well he might, but it didn't take him long to see where the path of duty led.

"Miss Lizzie, you know I'd do anything in the world for you, but if the rest of the family agrees, I'm certainly not in any position to argue with them.

You know they love you and want whatever is best for you. So do I."

"Oh—bah!" Lizzie stamped her foot.

"Bah?" Jeff repeated, trying to keep his face straight.

"Bah and pooh on all of you! All right, I'll do it, but I will hate all of you forever!"

She stormed out of the room, her draperies flying.

"She won't, really," Laurie said. "Don't look so worried, Jeff."

"I sure don't like to hurt her feelings," Jeff said. "Miss Ida, would you care to tell me what the—what is going on? If you don't want to let me in on this I understand, but if I can help—"

"Oh, you can," Laurie said. "I've been wanting to talk to you about it, Jeff, but . . ."

"I see." Jeff's glance at Doug was so quick only Laurie observed it. "I wondered if something wasn't going on," he said. "You know I've been worried about her sleepwalking. Are these photos the same ones you mentioned the other night?"

Laurie had to search her memory. "I guess I did mention them," she said. "But I didn't see them until the other day. They are really something."

"Preposterous frauds," Ida said.

"You saw them, Aunt?" Doug asked.

"No. I have no patience with such nonsense."

"How about you, Uncle Ned?"

"Me?" Ned roused himself from a reverie. "Now what the hades would I be doing with pictures of fairies?"

Laurie had to admit that the idea was ridiculous.

"There aren't any such things," Ned explained seriously. "So if Lizzie thinks she has pictures of 'em, why, she's wrong, that's all."

"She's taking an awfully long time about finding them," Laurie said uneasily.

Doug started to his feet. "Damn! Excuse me, Aunt Ida . . . We shouldn't have let her go up there alone. What if—"

His speculation was interrupted by a long, wavering cry. Before any of them could move, they heard Lizzie's feet pounding down the stairs. She appeared in the doorway, her eyes wide, her hair disheveled. "They aren't there! They are gone!"

CHAPTER

8

They *were* gone.

Lizzie's distress appeared to be genuine. She even allowed them to examine her hiding place, which was behind one of the panels on the right of the fireplace. A false knothole in the wood proved to be a spring which, when pushed, released a catch within.

The only objects in the hiding place were baby pictures of Doug and Laurie. Since the latter could think of no sensible reason why Lizzie should hide these, she was forced to the conclusion that Lizzie had removed her real treasure before sounding the alarm. A forgotten, crumpled candy wrapper indicated the nature of one of these treasures. About the others Laurie could only speculate. But it was certainly possible that Lizzie herself had hidden the photos. Laurie was beginning to suspect that her aunt was a consummate actress. By comparison, Anna was a mere amateur.

They returned to the parlor and Jeff went to get

fresh coffee. The discussion continued; but Laurie was painfully aware of the fact that she now had no real case. The photographs were the only solid evidence she had had, and she and Lizzie were the only ones who had seen them.

Lizzie was maddeningly indirect in her responses to the questions they hurled at her.

Had she taken the photographs?

Lizzie went on at some length about her inability to manipulate "machines," and was finally stopped by Doug.

"Who did take them, Auntie?"

"One of the girls," Lizzie said sullenly.

"The Wilson girls?"

"Well, of course. The other children don't come to visit the way they used to. Years ago," Lizzie said pensively, "they walked to school. I made cookies. Chocolate-chip. You remember, Laura, that recipe I got from—"

The scene took on the atmosphere of a police interrogation. Uncle Ned left, muttering disgustedly. Ida sat on one side of Lizzie, Laurie on the other; their captive cowered, her elbows pressed to her sides. Doug paced the room, turning from time to time to hurl a question at his aunt. Jeff leaned against the mantel, watching. He said nothing.

Lizzie finally admitted that she didn't know which of the Wilson girls had taken the pictures. Betsy had given them to her. She had read fairy tales to Betsy, last summer. She had lent books to the other girls.

"The second girl, Mary Ella, is quite intelligent," she added helpfully. "But her father will not purchase story books for her. He considers them works of the devil. The man is surely an anachronism in this day and age. He should have lived in old Salem. I felt it was my duty to encourage—"

Laurie began to feel like a stormtrooper, with a monocle and a whip. Lizzie fought her every step of the way, rambling off into one idiotic discursus after another. No, she had not seen the fairies herself. That was ridiculous! Only a child . . .

They interrupted her in the middle of this lecture and pressed on. Well, yes; once she had caught a glimpse of iridescent wings, moving so fast they were a rainbow blur, and Baby Betsy had said . . . Yes, of course she had heard the music. What else could it be but a fairy piper? No one in the house played a musical instrument, except for those piano lessons she herself had been forced to endure, years before. Really, she did not believe in forcing a child to study music against its will. Didn't they agree? The only possible result—

It was at this point that Doug said in a very loud, very firm voice, "I am going to scream."

"Me, too," Laurie said wearily. "Auntie, don't you realize we're only trying to protect you? You could be seriously hurt if you keep going out at night."

Lizzie opened her big brown eyes even wider. They were perfectly dry. She had given up crying some time back, when it proved to move none of her inquisitors.

"Oh, but darling, that's absurd. What possible reason could anyone have for wanting to hurt me?"

Laurie was about to protest when she realized that the statement was not a non sequitur. It was simply the conclusion she herself had reluctantly faced that afternoon. Aunt Lizzie had leaped blithely over the intervening steps in the reasoning process, but she knew what they were. She might be crazy, but she wasn't stupid.

Laurie was groping for an answer when she happened to see something that robbed her of speech. Ida was a lean, thin woman, and her recent worries had made the term "haggard" not entirely inappropriate; now she looked worse than haggard. She looked ghastly. The color had drained from her cheeks and the purple rings around her eyes stood out like fresh paint.

In the ensuing silence Laurie heard footsteps approaching. Ned peered into the room.

"Telephone," he said. "For you, Laura."

"If it's Hermann," Laurie began. Her uncle smiled at her.

"He called once before," he said calmly. "Told him you weren't here. This is a woman. Sounds upset."

"Thanks," Laurie said. "You can go back to—er—work in the library, Uncle Ned."

"All right," Ned said amiably. "Fat men never make good husbands," he added, and ambled off.

There were telephone extensions all over the house; Laurie herself had insisted on this, some years before, when she realized that the old people were becoming less and less capable of taking care of themselves. Ida had grudgingly accended to the necessity, but had refused to allow one of the instruments in the parlor. That chamber, at least, should preserve its dignity, without shrill bells ringing and people wanting to sell you cemetery lots.

Laurie went to the phone in the hall, hidden in a cubicle under the stairs. She wondered who it could be. Mrs. Schott, indignant because she refused to date Hermann? Bless Uncle Ned, he was on her side anyway.

She picked up the telephone.

"Miss Carlson? Thank goodness I found you, what took you so long? I'm in a terrible hurry. It's your mother, there was an accident and she's in the hospital. The doctor says you'd better hurry."

Laurie felt as if her tongue had swollen into a huge unmanageable mass that filled her mouth and made speech impossible. She and Anna had never been close, not as mothers and daughters were supposed to be, but she had a certain affection . . . Greater than she had known, until this moment.

"How—how serious is it?" she managed to say.

"Not good, I'm afraid. They say you better come right away. They don't know how long . . . Well, I'm sure glad I reached you. Good-bye."

"Wait. Wait, who is this?"

It was too late. The click at the other end of the wire was distinct.

Laurie stood holding the telephone. Stupid woman, she thought. Why do people get so excited they can't make sense? But she knew she was being unreasonable; the caller must be a neighbor or friend of Anna's; naturally she was upset, and breaking the bad news had not been a pleasant task. She returned the phone to its cradle and turned to face Doug.

"What's wrong?" he asked.

"How did you know?"

"Heard you ask if it was serious. Someone you know well?"

"You know her too. . . . Doug, I'm sorry. It's Anna. She's still . . . alive, but they think—"

Doug's face went white, but his voice was calm.

"They? Who? Who called?"

"Some woman. A friend of Anna's, I guess. She was so upset she forgot to give me her name."

"See if we can get plane reservations," Doug muttered, reaching for the phone. "How soon can you leave?"

"Right now. I'll just—"

"Wait a minute."

Laurie, halfway up the stairs, turned. Doug stood holding the phone, a foolish expression on his face. "Where is Anna?" he asked. "I mean, I can't make a reservation unless I know where we're going."

"Oh, Lord." Laurie sat down on the step and clutched her head. "Let me think. Her last letter was from Los Angeles. But the TV deal didn't work out, so she was going to spend a couple of weeks with those friends of hers at Palm Beach, unless her agent came through with something in New York. . . . This is ridiculous."

"She wrote me two weeks ago from Nice," Doug said.

"Nice! What the hell was she doing there?"

"She didn't say."

"Put the phone down," Laurie said irritably. "You look silly holding it like that."

"I'm going to try the New York apartment," Doug said. He began to dial.

"What for? If she's in the hospital—"

"I don't know where else to call," Doug snapped.

"Are you two quarreling?" Ida's gaunt frame appeared in the doorway. "What is it, Laura?"

"Oh, Aunt, I don't know how to tell you—"

Doug suddenly made a wide, sweeping gesture. His eyes opened wide.

"Hello?" he said. "Hello? Who is this? Anna?"

Laurie jumped to her feet.

"What? Who? Let me—"

Doug fended her off as she snatched at the phone.

"Yes, Anna, it's me. What's going on there? I hear voices yelling. . . . Oh." His voice dropped a full octave. "A what? You're having a party?"

Laurie staggered back to the stairs and sat down. Her aunt bent over her.

"What is going on, Laura? What is it you were going to tell me?"

"Forget it," Laurie mumbled. "I'll explain in a minute."

"Yes, I'm fine," Doug said. "I'm glad you're fine. No, I didn't call just to ask if you were . . . Yes, everybody here is fine too. Anna, for God's sake, will you shut up about everybody's health for a minute? We just got a phone call telling us you were in an accident. . . ."

He listened while the telephone gabbled and squeaked at him. His eyebrows rose.

"No, darling, I don't think the woman was referring to your cutting your finger on a piece of glass. Are you sure nothing happened tonight that might have led someone to . . . Oh, you've been home all afternoon. Yes, dear, I know what your cocktail parties are like. It must have been a wrong number.

Wait a minute. I think Laurie wants to talk to you. Yes, she's here too—and she is fine."

He handed the phone to Laurie. She was too bewildered to be very coherent; after a few comments she handed the phone back to Doug. There was certainly nothing wrong with Anna, except that she was in her normal state of cheerful inebriation. Not the result of alcohol; Anna didn't need booze to get drunk, she had been born in that condition.

Finally Doug hung up.

"Well," he said.

"Well," Laurie repeated.

"Anna didn't know you were here. I dropped her a note before I came, but apparently you—"

"No, I didn't." Laurie's head was aching. She rubbed her forehead. "That never occurred to me, Doug."

"It wouldn't." Doug's voice was hard, but Laurie knew his anger wasn't directed at her. "If someone dumps a shock like that on you, you don't stop to think."

"It couldn't have been a case of mistaken identity then." Laurie's wits began to function again. "Because if Anna didn't know I was here, her friends wouldn't know either."

Ida's eyes moved from one of them to the other.

"What happened?"

"Poor Aunt." Laurie giggled, a little wildly. "You keep asking that, and nobody answers you. Some woman just called me and told me Anna was mortally injured. She didn't give a name. If Anna had been a normal mother, with a fixed habitation, we might have gone rushing out into the night hoping to be with her at the end."

"But that is absolutely vile," Ida said indignantly. "Of all the cruel tricks—"

"I don't think it was a trick," Doug said slowly. "Or if it was, it was not motivated by idle malice. Laurie, I owe you an apology. Photos or no photos, I'm ready to believe in your theory."

Laurie leaned against the wall and enjoyed nostalgia. Six years . . . had it been that long? High schools had not changed. Except for a few minor differences in decor she might have been standing in the hall of Nathan Hale High, or Father Serra High, or . . . she had forgotten the names of the others. Thanks to Anna's peripatetic habits, Laurie had attended five different high schools, three of them in one year. It would have been easier for Anna to put her in a boarding school, but Anna had her fads; one of them was a baseless sentimentality about the good old democratic public high school, which had been good enough for her in her day.

The wall against which Laurie leaned was built of cinder blocks painted a pale nauseating green. Posters attempted to brighten this long stretch of mediocrity, whose original color was both faded and dirty. Apparently a school election was due. The posters blasted out directives to the reader: "A vote for Debbie is a vote for progress"; "Sam is the Man"; "Andy for Class President, he's Awww-right!"

The halls were deserted. From behind the closed classroom doors came the murmurs of muted voices. The school day was almost over.

Laurie yawned. The night watches were beginning to get to her. At least Doug was now on her side. The telephone call had convinced him that her far-out suspicions weren't so wild after all. There was a villain, and there was a plot. (Doug had used those very words, rolling them on his tongue with a certain relish.)

The only reasonable explanation for the phone call was that someone wanted them—both of them—to leave Idlewood. They had discussed it at length, trying to find other reasons. Admittedly, some people liked to play sick jokes, via the anonymity of a telephone. But the unknown woman had asked for

Laurie by name. None of Anna's friends or enemies—the two categories were by no means distinct—knew Laurie was at Idlewood. She had told no one in Chicago of her plans to come east, so that eliminated her friends and enemies, even if she could believe that any of them would stoop to such a thing.

Laurie's voice had faltered, momentarily, on that denial. Doug eyed her curiously, but she had not qualified it. Not even Bob would be that weird, she told herself. Besides, he didn't know where she was.

In these days of direct dialing there was no way of finding out whether the call had been local or long distance. Laurie had been too upset to notice anything distinctive about the woman's voice. Yet the fact that the call had been made was a clue in itself, and, as Doug pointed out, if someone wanted them to leave, then there was good reason for them to stay.

Laurie glanced at her watch. Only a few more minutes.

Another plus for an evening which had seemed to start so badly was that Jeff was now definitely involved. After accusing all and sundry of stealing her pictures, Lizzie had stormed out, so the others had been able to discuss the situation in peace. Uncle Ned refused to have anything to do with it. In his own way he was as obsessed as Lizzie.

Ida said little. Her grim silence bothered Laurie more than tears would have done. At one point she patted her aunt's bony hand and said,

"Cheer up, Aunt Ida. Don't you see, if someone is playing tricks it means that Aunt Lizzie isn't losing her mind—at least, no faster than she was already."

The feeble attempt at a joke produced no answering smile on her aunt's dour face.

"I cannot believe it," she muttered.

"It is hard to believe," Jeff agreed. He ran his fingers through his hair. The tangled black locks clung to his high forehead. There was genuine anger in his voice when he added, "How could anyone be that stupid!"

"What hangs me up is the question of motive," Doug said. "There is no sane reason why anyone would want to harm Aunt Lizzie; so we've got to face the fact that this creature may be moved by sheer malice and mischief. God knows it happens often enough these days. Are you sure, Aunt, that there's no local idiot who harbors a grudge, reasonless or not, against any of you? How about Mr. Wilson?"

"Jack Wilson?" Jeff let out a gasp of laughter. "A scheme like this would be totally beyond him, Doug. He has a mind like a crudely drawn child's map—flat and two-dimensional."

"He is an unattractive person," Ida said. "But he is sober and hardworking. He has always been an excellent tenant and we have had no quarrels with him. No, Douglas, there is no one."

That was all they could get out of her, although they continued to speculate fruitlessly for another hour. Yet when Ida excused herself and went up to bed, Laurie was left with the uneasy feeling that there was something she had not told them. Was it only her imagination, or had her aunt seemed to flinch every time the word "motive" was mentioned?

Now she dismissed such speculations with an angry shrug and glanced again at her watch. A bell shrieked. The children poured out of opening doorways like water under pressure bursting through a hole. They came in all sizes and colors and shapes: tall and short, black and white, male and female—but they shared a terrifying exuberance and a capacity to make incredible amounts of noise. Laurie's head echoed with the screams of dear friends greeting one another after an absence of two hours, with the sounds of locker doors banging and footsteps thudding in rapid retreat from the hated halls of academe.

As the stream rushed past her she wondered how she had ever expected to locate the Wilson girls in this chaos. Fortunately there was a bottleneck at the main door, where the children jostled and shoved to reach the long yellow buses drawn up outside. Rachel's height and her spectacular golden hair enabled Laurie to spot her. The girl would stand out in any crowd.

Rachel's clothing also differentiated her from her peers. Most of them, boys and girls alike, were wearing jeans or corduroy pants. Some of the girls flaunted the boots and calf-length skirts fashionable that year. Rachel's skirt was long, but it certainly wasn't stylish. The color, the cut, the fabric—everything about it was wrong. The skirt and the long-sleeved, high-necked blouse were designed to cover the girl as completely as possible. They did a good job of that, but it would have required a long black veil, like the ones worn by old-fashioned Moslem women, to render Rachel unnoticeable. Her exquisite face and silken flood of hair drew glances from the boys as she passed them, but none spoke or approached her.

Behind her, like a squat dark shadow, was Mary Ella, her arms piled with books. They were like the sisters in the old ballads, one fair and beautiful, the other dark and cruel. (And why, Laurie wondered, were the blondes always the good girls?) In the ballads the prince or the young squire usually fell in love with the yellow-haired, blue-eyed sister, and the brunette, driven by jealousy, shoved her sibling into the river or massacred her in some other fashion.

Laurie breasted the crowd with outthrust arms and shouted apologies. The kids made way for her good-naturedly when they happened to notice her, but she was almost trampled by an overgrown youth surrounded by an entourage of admirers—a star athlete, no doubt. Laurie followed the Wilson girls out the door and tapped Rachel on her shoulder.

The look of unguarded terror on the girl's face as she turned made Laurie forget the speech she had prepared.

"Hey, it's all right," she exclaimed. "I just wondered if you would like a ride home, Rachel. And you too, of course, Mary Ella."

Mary Ella said nothing. She looked like a little female gnome with her dark, lank hair covering her forehead clear down to her thick eyebrows.

"Oh, no," Rachel said. "We couldn't. If we don't get home on time—"

"But you will be. We can get you there before the bus could. Look, there's Doug with the car."

Rachel's blue eyes widened as she followed the direction of Laurie's pointing finger. Laurie smiled to herself. She had suspected Rachel wouldn't be able to resist that car. It had already drawn considerable attention from passing students, though Laurie fancied that some of the girls were not so much interested in the car as they were in its owner. Doug, leaning negligently against the front fender, appeared to be unaware of the admiring feminine eyes, but his pose was slightly self-conscious.

"Well," Rachel said hesitantly.

"Come on," Laurie said.

The two girls squeezed into the back seat. Laurie and Doug had agreed in advance on this arrangement, in case someone carried tales home to Mr. Wilson. Doug tried to be casual and avuncular, but he could hardly keep his eyes off Rachel. He sat staring into the rear-view mirror until Laurie kicked him, none too gently.

"Drive," she said. "The girls don't want to be late."

"Plenty of time," Doug said. "How about stopping for a Coke or an ice-cream cone or something?"

A look passed between the two girls. Rachel shook her head.

"Thank you, sir, but we better not. I have to get to my baby-sitting job, and there's chores to do first."

"Baby-sitting?" Laurie repeated. "But this is a school night."

"Oh, I do it every night," Rachel said. "It's Mrs. Wade's baby; she works the night shift at the plant. He's little, he sleeps a lot, so I can get my studying done there."

Doug was driving as slowly as he dared, but Laurie knew there was no time to waste, so she plunged into the heart of the matter.

"Girls, we didn't finish our talk yesterday. Now please believe you aren't going to get in trouble from this. I can see the subject irritates your father, so we won't come to the house again. We just wanted to find out how this business started."

"I told you yesterday," Rachel muttered.

"I'm still not clear about some of the details, Rachel. You met Miss Lizzie in the woods last summer?"

"Well, you see, we go out picking berries and things. . . . They don't mind; Mr. Ned said we could."

It took considerable prodding and reassurance before Rachel produced a coherent story. Boiled down, the narrative was simple enough. The girls did not have regular summer jobs because their father refused to let them work in evil places such as dime stores and restaurants. However, since the devil made work for idle hands, they were expected to keep busy. So, when they weren't helping with the farm they were out scouring the hillsides for unconsidered treasures. Berries in season, sour cherries from the trees of people who were too lazy to put up their own fruit, crab apples, persimmons—anything and everything that could be canned or made into jelly by the frugal Wilsons.

"You must get scratched pretty badly," Doug said. Laurie knew he was admiring Rachel's delicate skin, and resenting the thought of its being marred.

His warm, flexible voice reflected his feelings, and Rachel sensed them. Her responses to his occasional comments were much more relaxed than her replies to Laurie.

"Oh, I'm used to that," Rachel said, smiling. "But I sure do hate that poison ivy. I get it worse than Mary Ella. I just break out all over."

"Go on," Laurie said.

There was not much more to tell. Miss Lizzie liked to walk in the woods when the weather was nice.

Sometimes she would bring cookies and lemonade and other things to eat. Betsy was really too little to pick berries, so she got in the habit of sitting with Miss Lizzie while the others worked, and Miss Lizzie would tell her stories. Then Betsy started talking about actually seeing fairies. They laughed at her and scolded her, but she went right on doing it. Even after school began they continued to meet Miss Lizzie, and Miss Lizzie went on telling Betsy fairy tales, even when they asked her not to. She didn't understand that they were lies, and against the word of Jesus. At last the inevitable happened. "Poppa" overheard little Betsy babbling about the elves, and Poppa got very angry.

"Does he beat you often?" Doug asked abruptly.

Rachel bowed her head so that the shimmering veil of hair hid her face.

"Doug," Laurie said.

"Okay, I'm sorry. It's none of my business."

It wasn't their business. Rachel could not be considered a battered child, there wasn't a mark on any of the visible portions of her body—though admittedly very little was visible. All the same, Laurie knew what would happen if she and Doug went to the authorities with accusations of child abuse against Wilson. "Abuse? Ma'am, a man's got a right to spank his kids if they misbehave. Did you see any marks on the girl? Has she complained?"

Not that Laurie had any intention of taking such action. She hoped Doug would control his crusading instincts. Any attempt at interference would only make him look like a fool and would make matters worse for the girls. Doug's indignation, visible in his tight lips and rigid grip on the wheel, was all for Rachel. He hadn't expressed any concern for Mary Ella. But Mary Ella was eminently forgettable. Laurie realized, with something of a shock, that she had never heard the girl speak.

She turned, her arm over the back of the seat, and examined the younger child. She had to make a conscious effort to do so; Rachel dazzled like the sun, drawing all eyes, and Mary Ella hid behind her radiance. She was a pathetically unattractive child, with all the flaws to which adolescence is prone—bad skin, baby fat, protruding teeth. Her hair was stringy and lusterless, her eyes small and deep-set. Caught off guard by Laurie's sudden move, she met the latter's gaze for a moment, and then her pupils slid off to one side. They were her father's eyes—flat, muddy-brown, expressionless.

"Mary Ella," Laurie said, "do you own a camera?"

Mary Ella shook her head. Laurie became all the more determined to force her to speak.

"What were you doing while Miss Lizzie and Betsy were together?"

The girl's thick lips parted. As Laurie had suspected from the shape of her mouth, her teeth were in terrible shape—crooked, protruding. Naturally Wilson wouldn't favor orthodontic treatments. If God had wanted Mary Ella's teeth straight, he would have made them straight.

Mary Ella spoke. Her voice was surprisingly deep for a child of her age; and after a moment Laurie understood why she spoke so seldom.

"I was picking b-b-b-berries."

It took her forever to get the last word out. Laurie's hands clenched in sympathy. Good God, she thought; I wonder how the poor kid gets through a school day. Well, it's no wonder she stutters.

"I see," she said gently, when Mary Ella had finally expelled the word; then out of sheer decency she turned her attention back to Rachel.

"You say you didn't take any pictures, Rachel? Did you ever see any—photographs of the fairies, I mean?"

"No, ma'am."

"Did Betsy see them, or talk about them?"

"No, ma'am." This time the response was slightly less emphatic. Rachel raised melting blue eyes and added, "At least I don't think so. She's just a baby, ma'am. You can't trust what she says."

"That's true," Doug said.

Laurie knew that it was, but Doug's ready acquiescence irritated her. With wry amusement she realized that she and her brother were inadvertently following a well-known interrogation technique; he was the nice cop and she was the mean cop. Unfortunately he wasn't taking advantage of his role to ask meaningful questions. She tried a new tack.

"Did you ever meet anyone in the woods during that period?" she asked. "I don't mean neighbors, people hiking or picking berries—I mean some particular person whom you encountered often, who might have joined Miss Lizzie and Betsy while they talked."

"No, ma'am."

"Betsy never mentioned anyone like that?"

"No, ma'am."

Laurie could have shaken the girl, even though she knew it was partly her own fault that Rachel was not forthcoming with her. She had not really expected that this line of questioning would produce any useful information, but it was a possibility that had to be investigated.

Doug drew to a stop beside the Wilson's mailbox. Mary Ella was out of the car the moment the wheels stopped turning. She plodded off down the road without so much as a thank-you. Laurie watched the squat, shabby figure retreat, carrying with it an almost palpable dark cloud of despair. The child was supposed to be intelligent, but what kind of future did she have, barricaded from communication with a broader world by her emotional handicaps?

Rachel had gotten out on the driver's side. Laurie turned in time to receive the fringe radiation from the blinding smile the girl directed at Doug.

"Thank you, sir. We surely did enjoy the ride."

Then she was off, running to catch up with her sister.

Laurie jabbed her brother sharply in the ribs.

"Let's move on before Poppa comes along."

"What? Oh, sure."

Laurie sat back, folded her arms, and waited for her brother to get his wits back. They had gone some distance before he said, "I'd like to kill that cruddy Wilson."

"Then the family could go on welfare," Laurie said. "That would be a big help."

"It might be better than what that child endures now."

"Just like a man," Laurie said in disgust. "It's always the beautiful blondes that get the sympathy. Mary Ella's the one I feel sorry for. Rachel will escape eventually. She'll have Sir Galahads tripping over each other panting to rescue her. But Mary Ella—"

"Hey, cool it. I pity both the kids."

"How nice of you." Laurie was surprised at her own vehemence. "Oh, forget it. We can't do anything for either one of them. It wasn't a very productive interview, was it?"

"I wouldn't say that."

"Oh?" Laurie glanced out the window. "I see we're heading for good old Vi's, so I presume you are going to enlighten me."

"It's obvious, isn't it? Those kids haven't the sophistication to plan anything complicated. Somebody—some outsider—picked up a harmless little game and turned it into a plot."

"Who?"

"One name leaps to mind," Doug said.

"You mean Jeff, I suppose," Laurie said calmly. "Since I am not a complete fool, naturally I thought of him. He could have taken the snapshots—and he could have stolen them, he's in and out of the house all the time. But it can't be Jeff."

"Why not?"

"The caller was female," Laurie said.

"A confederate. Jeff's the kind of guy—"

"Who could talk a girl into doing anything he asked her to," Laurie agreed, so enthusiastically that Doug gave her a dirty look. "But why should he? He has no motive. He seems to like his job, and I'm sure he's fond of the old people."

"Like, schmike," Doug muttered. "So maybe he's a psycho. Gets his kicks out of tormenting old ladies."

"Nonsense. I just wish I could think of another suspect. No one seems to fit."

Doug was silent, and the quality of his silence made Laurie uneasy.

"Well?" she demanded.

Doug's shoulders lifted and subsided, so sharply that the car swerved. "We have to consider every possibility."

"What are you driving at? I can assure you I have an alibi. I can bring a dozen witnesses to prove I was—"

"Cut it out, will you? This is serious. I'm talking about Ned and Ida. Now wait," he said, as Laurie drew a sharp breath, preparatory to objecting, "think about it. They're getting old. Hell, they aren't getting there, they *are* old. One little screw in the brain gets loose and bingo, all the years of pent-up hostility start oozing out. You know how petty annoyances can grate until finally they pile up and become unendurable. I can see how Lizzie would be hard to live with. Ida has no patience with her fantasies, and Ned thinks she's ga-ga. Hell's bells, Laurie, I hate the idea as much as you do; but you must admit it's possible."

Laurie was conscious of a sick, sinking feeling at the pit of her stomach. She was remembering the expression on Ida's face the night before, when Lizzie had asked why anyone would want to hurt her.

Vi greeted them with the warmth reserved for old friends, and Sam, semirecumbent in his favorite booth, raised his head high enough to remark, "Thanks, don' mind iffah dew."

Vi lingered after she had served them, exchanging

heavy witticisms with Doug. Laurie suspected she had something on her mind and before long Vi, not the subtlest of women, came to the point.

"How are the folks?"

"Fine," Doug said.

"I heard Miss Lizzie was failing."

"Who told you that?" Doug demanded.

One of Vi's massive shrugs rippled down her body.

"I've known 'em for years," she said, with apparent irrelevance. "They're quality, the Mortons are. Shouldn't be alone out there, old as they are."

"They aren't alone," Laurie said.

"Oh, well. I mean family. What is it you do for a living, Doug?"

Irritation and amusement struggled in Doug's face as he assimilated this broad hint. Amusement won.

"I'm an architect," he said.

Vi's face fell. "Oh."

"Hard to make a living that way," Doug said, with a deep sigh.

"I guess. There's one in Frederick."

"One what?" Laurie asked, highly entertained by this exchange.

"Architect."

"How is he doing?"

"Starving," Vi said. She and Doug both sighed.

After Vi had gone, Laurie allowed herself to laugh.

"Vi doesn't have a good opinion of your profession. Why couldn't you have taken up something sensible, like carpentry or animal husbandry? What *is* animal husbandry, by the way?"

"I'll explain it to you when you're a little older. All the same," Doug said seriously, "I bet an architect could do all right here. The area is growing, and the old houses are being renovated. There's good money in restoration."

"You aren't thinking seriously of it, are you?"

"Not really. But it might not hurt to let the word get around that I was."

Laurie folded her arms on the table and gazed

thoughtfully at her brother. "You're taking this pretty seriously, aren't you? I'm not trying to beat a dead horse or anything, but not long ago you were ready to dismiss the whole thing as a wild-goose chase. What made you change your mind?"

"Your metaphors," Doug said, "are becoming zoological. Must be Uncle Ned's influence. What made me change my mind? The telephone call, of course. You'll forgive me for mentioning this—"

"Oh, don't spare my feelings."

"I never have, have I? Up to the time the unknown lady called to tell us of Anna's apocryphal accident, we had no concrete evidence whatever. You had seen the photos and the lights and heard the pretty music, but you were the only one who had. I had no reason to consider you a reliable witness. Then the photos conveniently disappeared. That made me wonder. But Lizzie could have hidden them, or you. . . . Well, I won't belabor that point. Then came the phone call. I have racked my brains, but I can only come up with one explanation that makes sense. That call was meant to get us away from here."

"It couldn't have kept us away long," Laurie said. "Sooner or later we'd have found out Anna was all right."

"That's what worries me. Sure, we'd have found out, and sooner rather than later. If Anna were a normal, sedentary-type mother, with a fixed address, we would have rushed off, found her healthy and blooming—and then what?"

"We would have realized the call was a hoax," Laurie said. "We'd have come back—"

"In a state of considerable agitation," Doug added. "The situation being what it is. But even if we took the next plane back here we would have been gone for twenty-four hours, give or take a few hours. A lot can happen in twenty-four hours."

His normally affable face was grim. Laurie stared at him.

"No," she said, denying, not the statement itself, but its implications. "No, Doug."

"I don't like it either."

"You're jumping to conclusions. Suppose this character is in a panic? If this thing started as a joke, it's gotten out of hand. Maybe he's scared. Maybe he's trying to—to cancel the joke."

"Maybe. But can we afford to take that chance?"

Laurie jumped to her feet. "Let's go home. Right now."

IV

They emerged from the artificial twilight of the tavern into the glow of a spectacular sunset. Long strips of slate-gray cloud crossed the western sky; as the sun dropped down behind them it rimmed their edges with molten bronze and cast a pale rosy wash over the landscape. More snow had come overnight, and it lay like strawberry frosting on the chocolate-brown furrows of the fields. From the crest of the ridge, mile on mile of rolling farmland spread out, enclosed by the dim purple-red curve of the far-off mountains. Houses and barns and silos, miniaturized by distance, looked like children's toys.

"Look," Laurie said, as Doug slowed for a turn, "that's one of my favorite views. The sweep of that one stretch of dark pines, up and over the hill, and one bright red barn, to the left of center—it's so perfectly designed it looks like a painting."

"Ugh," said her brother.

The sun hid behind the flanks of the hills and all light died. The fields were somber gray, the trees were black, the sky was the color of shadows. Laurie's spirits dropped again, after their momentary resurgence. Is there really someone out there in that pretty, peaceful countryside who wants to injure Aunt Lizzie? she wondered. And why do I find that idea so hard to believe when the sun is shining, and so horribly plausible after dark? I'm as bad as any savage, worshiping a primitive sun god. I'm afraid of the dark.

Doug was no help. Gloom and depression fairly radiated from him. He didn't speak the rest of the way home.

If Laurie had known what was awaiting her she would have been even more depressed. Having no premonitions, she did not sneak in the back, but walked boldly through the front door just in time to hear Lizzie announce in ringing tones, "Wait, I hear someone coming. I'll just see if it's Laura."

Laurie turned to flee, but she was too late. Lizzie peeped around the corner of the stair, saw her, and returned to the telephone. "Yes, it is Laura. You called at just the right moment. Now you wait, and I'll get her."

"Tell him I just dropped dead," Laurie said.

"Oh, darling, not so loud! He'll hear you."

Oh, well, Laurie thought, I may as well get it over with. I can't go on dashing out of the house every time the telephone rings. She took the phone from her aunt's hand. What an obscene shape it was, all black and curved and waiting. . . .

"Hello," she said.

The caller was, as she had suspected, Hermann.

Shortly thereafter she returned the telephone to its cradle and turned to her aunt, who was dusting a table in the hall and humming loudly to herself.

"Aunt Lizzie."

". . . tiptoe through the tulips. . . ." The humming formed words and then broke off. Lizzie turned an innocent gaze upon her niece.

"Oh, are you through talking, darling? I didn't hear a word you said, honestly."

"You did, too. I was caught off guard or I never would have . . . Aunt Lizzie, I can't stand that man. I don't want to have dinner with him."

"Then why did you tell him you would?" Lizzie inquired.

Laurie yearned to tell her why. Everybody was

conspiring against her, that was why. The implicit pressure and the explicit approval of the old ladies, and all those long years of trying to do what would please them ... Pleasing the aunts had become a habit as hard to break as alcoholism. She had been trapped by love.

"I don't know," she mumbled.

"You can wear my dress, the gold one," Lizzie said happily. "You look so pretty in it. Oh, darling, you'll have a nice time."

"I'll have a headache," Laurie said. "I'm getting one now."

CHAPTER
9

Laurie didn't have to feign a headache as an excuse to get home early. Her temples began to throb when Hermann started on his lobster, and by the time he had dissected that repulsive arthropod the headache was well developed. There was something horrible about the way Hermann ate lobster. Oh, he was neat—too neat—dabbing genteelly at his mouth after almost every bite. His plump pink fingers gripped the silverware with the precision of a surgeon, and the crunch, as he crushed the claw. . . . Every sliver was meticulously coated with butter and then inspected carefully before it was conveyed to Hermann's mouth, wherein it vanished with a slight snapping sound.

Laurie refused dessert. Hermann had cherry cheesecake.

Laurie refused a liqueur. Hermann ordered brandy, and added that it was really a man's drink, not suitable for ladies.

Laurie ordered brandy.

At least she didn't have to talk. Hermann did all the talking. He told her about his job and detailed the inefficiencies of the people who outranked him. He told her what was wrong with the President's anti-inflation policy and outlined the legislation that should have been passed. One day, he explained, he might consider running for office himself. It was high time the state had some good solid conservative representation.

Laurie had had a cocktail before dinner and several glasses of wine with dinner, though Hermann had drunk most of the bottle. She should not have ordered the brandy. She didn't even like brandy. It had an astonishing effect, however. After her first few sips she found herself staring at Hermann in mild astonishment. Why on earth had she worried about what she should say to this simpleminded egotist?

She put both elbows on the table and interrupted Hermann with a distinctly provocative statement about the ERA.

It took Hermann's slow wits some seconds to adjust to the change of subject. He gaped at her, and then chuckled.

"What a little tease you are. You aren't one of those feminists. You're too sweet and—er—feminine."

Often before, when she had been so challenged, Laurie had pulled in her horns. She didn't want to be identified with the extremist elements of the women's movement. As she had said, such advocates did the movement more harm than good by making it repellent, not only to men but to many women who might otherwise have supported its aims. But that wasn't the real reason why she had backed down. She had backed down because she didn't want to be considered unattractive and unfeminine—even by creeps like Hermann.

Now, without warning, a great gusty wave of reckless abandon swept over her.

"You're damned right I'm a feminist," she informed Hermann. Rising, she waved an imperious arm at the waiter. "More brandy here," she called.

The remainder of the evening was a triumph, if a shortlived one. Laurie would have been willing to sit on indefinitely, her elbows planted, debating women's rights. She found that by raising her voice slightly she could silence Hermann. He was afraid someone would overhear the vulgarities she was uttering. And of course her intelligence could run rings around his any day of the week, drunk or sober.

He got her out of the restaurant, finally, and dragged her to the door. Laurie knew she wasn't drunk. If she had been, the cold night air would have sobered her. Instead it inspired her to further enormities.

"Keep both your hands on the wheel," she said loudly, as Hermann, encouraged by the darkness and intimacy of the front seat, reached for her knee. "Men are such rotten drivers. Watch out for that patch of ice on the hill. Fifteen miles an hour is plenty fast enough. Look out, that's a dog. Oh; it isn't. Well, there might be a dog. The speed limit is thirty-five here; you're going forty."

Hermann made it fifty. He got her home in record time.

Laurie thanked him for a lovely evening and got nimbly out, while he was fumbling with his seat belt. Hermann was slow, but that final move drove the point home. He did not get out of the car. He departed, leaving Laurie standing on the steps.

Laurie giggled. She was in no mood to go in. The aunts would want to know why she was home so early and they would inquire minutely into the details of her date. Besides . . . She was *not* drunk. Not at all. It might be a good idea, however, to let the cold air steady her steps just a trifle before she confronted the aunts.

It was a beautiful night, cold and crystal clear. The stars blazed like scattered diamonds on black velvet. Her headache was gone. She felt wonderful. Even the high heels, which gave her such an admirable psychological advantage over Hermann, did not impede her walking.

Whistling between her teeth—and regretting she had not thought to display this vulgar accomplishment to Hermann—she strolled along the path that circled the house. She had no particular goal in mind, just a little walk in the lovely winter night. She would, of course, keep an eye out for elves. Laurie giggled. She seldom giggled, but tonight she felt like doing it.

At the entrance to the boxwood alley she hesitated, and a cold breath of sobriety dulled her euphoria. It was dark in there. Really, really dark. Maybe she had better go into the house.

No. Had she not announced, in ringing tones, that very evening, her devotion to the credo of the New Woman? I am strong—I am invincible! I can walk down icy graveled paths in tottery high heels anytime I feel like it.

She had not gone far before she began to regret her valor and suspect she was not as invincible as she had thought. The shoes were poorly adapted to walking on gravel. The thin heels caught and failed to find firm footing. The boxwood reached as high as her head. Not the faintest beam of light penetrated the interwoven branches. Laurie let out a gasp as the undergrowth ahead rustled. Light shaped itself into two small spots like staring eyes. She had to remind herself that the grounds were inhabited by small nocturnal animals—rabbits, possums, raccoons, rats. . . . Rats. She pursed her lips and produced a whistle. "I am strong, I am invincible. . . ."

The staring eyes vanished as she approached. Perhaps they had only been a trick of her imagination. Now she could see lighted windows ahead. My goodness, she told herself with false surprise, they must be Jeff's windows. Maybe I'll stop in for a cup of coffee. He said he wanted to talk about the Middle Ages.

Then something came out of the boxwood and ran straight at her.

It was, of course, one of the nocturnal animals she had postulated, a little more stupid or less wary than its kind; but Laurie's nerves failed to register this sensible theory until it was too late. The creature actually brushed against her leg. She let out a strangled whoop and began to run. After two steps she lost her balance and the run turned into a flapping, scrambling attempt to stay on her feet. She might have succeeded in that aim if an object had not loomed up in her path—a shape waist-high and squat, like a thick tree trunk, but shining faintly in the light from the window.

Unable to stop herself, Laurie plunged into it. It fell over backward with a metallic crash that echoed through the still night. Laurie followed it down onto the ground.

The echoes died. Laurie rolled over. Now that she was out of the dire shadow of the boxwood the light from Jeff's cottage enabled her to see more clearly, and her dark fancies vanished. She looked from the ruins of her nylons to the fallen object. What was a garbage can doing out in the middle of the path? Or could she possibly be *off* the path? She had lost one of her shoes. When she picked it up and shook out the gravel, the heel fell off.

Laurie's lower lip protruded. What kind of a place was this, where a person could practically break her neck and make enough noise to raise the dead, and nobody even came out to see whether everything was all right?

Jeff's door opened.

"Is somebody there?" he asked, without much interest.

"Me," said Laurie.

"Laurie? What the hell are you doing there? Are you hurt?"

He dragged her to her feet. Laurie tilted to one side and Jeff let out a wordless hiss of concern.

"It's my shoe," Laurie explained. She held it out to him. "The heel broke off."

Jeff peered at her suspiciously.

"Laurie, are you drunk?"

"I guess so," Laurie said placidly.

He scooped her up in his arms, bulky coat, broken shoe and all. He carried her into the house and put her in a chair. When he came back to her, after closing the door, she saw that his face was alight with laughter.

"I thought it was a coon or something," he explained. "Animals are always knocking over trash cans looking for food. Weren't you supposed to go out tonight?"

"I was out," Laurie said. "Boy, did I fix Hermann! I had a wonderful time. You know, Jeff, we missed the most obvious excuse of all the other day, when we were talking about how to get rid of Hermann. All I had to do was be myself."

"Your present self is all banged up," Jeff said, looking her over. "I'd better give you some emergency first aid. If you go in looking like that, you'll scare the old ladies into a heart attack. Uh—how about a cup of coffee or three?"

"I'm perfectly sober," Laurie said.

Jeff's eyes danced. "A few minutes ago you told me you were drunk."

"I just said that to be polite."

Jeff studied her, his hands on his hips, his lips twitching.

"Sit still," he said. "Don't move."

"I have no intention of going anywhere," Laurie assured him.

After two cups of coffee her mellow glow had subsided enough to make her conscious of the pain of scraped knees and bruised hands, but she still felt fine. One might be a feminist at heart, she told herself, but that didn't mean one could not enjoy someone's tending one's wounds. The only thing that annoyed her was that Jeff insisted that she remove her shredded pantyhose without assistance. Grumbling, she complied. Jeff's lean brown hands were gentle as he bathed the bloody scratches with warm water. When he had finished he sat back on his heels and contemplated his handiwork.

"So far, so good. But you can't walk, not in those shoes. How are you going to get back to the house?"

"Carry me."

"I guess I'll have to. Better put on a pair of my socks. It's cold out there."

Kneeling at her feet he slipped the socks on. Laurie wriggled her toes.

"Pretty," she said, admiring the bright argyle pattern of blue and crimson.

"Your aunt made them for me. Okay, let's go."

He picked her up. Laurie looped an arm around his neck.

"You're in an awful hurry to get rid of me," she said.

"Laurie—don't."

"Don't what?"

His lips were warm and hard and experienced. Laurie's head spun—but her eyes remained wide open. Bob had complained of this habit, probably, Laurie thought, because he liked his women to be swooning and semiconscious when he deigned to kiss them. Once she had asked him how he could tell her eyes were open if his were closed. He had not answered, and he had continued to be unreasonably annoyed even though she kept telling him she couldn't help it; it was an uncontrollable reflex, she didn't really *see* anything. . . .

On this occasion, however, she did see something, over Jeff's shoulder—a flash of movement and of color at the back window. Her muscles went rigid. Jeff let out a yelp of pain as her nails dug into his neck.

"Now what?" he demanded.

"Out there—" Laurie gestured. "Outside the window."

"What was it?"

"You won't believe me."

"Try me."

"It had golden hair," Laurie whispered. "And . . . and wings."

Jeff's grip relaxed. For a moment she thought he was going to drop her.

"I really saw it," she said. "Really."

"Okay." Jeff started toward the door.

Laurie knew she had affronted, not only his ego, but his intelligence. As soon as they were outside she stared wildly around, trying to catch another glimpse of the unbelievable thing she had seen.

"Stop wriggling," Jeff grumbled.

"I'm sorry. I really—"

"Okay, okay. I believe you."

He didn't, and she didn't blame him. It had moved so fast she had not gotten a good look, but she knew she had seen it; a flash of translucent, gauzy lavender, and a face distorted by staring eyes and a squared-off mouth into something not too unlike the faces in Lizzie's photographs.

As they approached the kitchen door it burst open and Laurie saw her brother. The very outlines of his body bristled with fury.

"What's going on?" he demanded.

"She fell," Jeff said briefly.

"Uh-huh." Doug grabbed at Laurie. Jeff resisted. For a moment she hung ludicrously between them, with Doug clutching her shoulders and Jeff retaining his grip on her knees.

"Hey," she said in feeble remonstrance.

Somehow—she was not quite sure how—Doug managed to get a firm hold on her. Jeff let go.

"I'll take care of her," Doug said.

"Thanks, Jeff," Laurie added.

"Any time." Jeff politely closed the door for them.

"He's mad," Laurie said. "You hurt his feelings."

"I'll hurt more than his feelings, if he . . ." Doug broke off. He peered more closely at her. "What's the matter?"

"I just saw a fairy, 'Tripping hither, tripping thither, nobody knows where or—'"

"Sshhh. Do you want to wake the whole house? Thank God the aunts are in bed."

"What time is it?"

"A little after eleven." Doug started up the stairs. "You've had quite an evening, haven't you?"

"I fixed old Herrrrrman," Laurie said with satisfaction. "Want me to tell you how?"

"I don't want you to tell me anything until you've slept it off."

"I'm not drunk."

"Oh, yeah? Not that I blame you."

"You're sweet," Laurie said. His grip was a little too hard for comfort, but at least it had some emotion behind it. Not like old wooden Jeff, she told herself, ignoring the fact that her own inappropriate comment had been responsible for Jeff's coolness. She nestled her head against Doug's shoulder. "You're a nice brother," she told him. "It's nice to have a brother. I never knew how nice it was to—"

"Oh, shut up." Doug dumped her on her bed.

"Help me off with my coat."

Doug did so. Then he stood stiffly with the coat over his arm like a well-trained butler.

"Now help me off with my dress."

"Drunks," said Doug viciously, "deserve to sleep in their clothes." He dragged the blankets over her and stalked out.

Laurie framed several witty, caustic retorts in her mind, but she fell asleep before she could say them.

I

She woke in the dead hours of the morning, every sense tingling.

With the unreasonable luck that often attends

drunks and children, she was wide awake and in full possession of her wits, without the slightest trace of the hangover she fully deserved. She knew what had awakened her, and as she sat rigid, her ears cocked, she heard it again: music. The same minor, haunting melody that had drifted out of the dark woods once before.

She shot out of bed as if propelled by a spring and reached for the light switch. The clock on the mantel said three thirty-five. The music went on, rising and falling in unending monotony. Its lack of resolution scratched at the nerves.

Laurie had no trouble remembering the events of the previous evening, a scant four and a half hours ago. The annihilation of Hermann, Jeff's kiss, the fairy at the window, Doug's anger . . .

She didn't blame him for refusing to help her undress. If Ida had walked in on them during that process, the poor old lady would have fainted dead away. Apparently, though, Doug had relented and returned after she fell asleep. The window had been opened a few inches. The icy breeze made her shiver, which was no wonder, because she was wearing only her bra and panties. Good old Doug . . .

The music rose to a pitch of plaintive appeal, and Laurie heard—or thought she heard—a rustle of sound from below, like bedclothes being thrown back. She snatched at the first garment that came to hand. It was the flowing, fur-trimmed golden robe Lizzie had tried to lend her for her date with Hermann. Laurie dropped it over her head and fumbled for her slippers. She would have preferred more practical attire, but apparently Doug had hung her dress up in the closet, for it was nowhere to be seen.

At least the robe wasn't too long. It hit her a good two inches above the ankles and did not impede her speed as she hurried down the stairs. Lizzie's door was closed. Laurie eased it open, and heard, with relief, the sound of slow, tranquil breathing. She must have imagined the sound of rustling bedclothes—or else Lizzie had stirred, rolled over, and gone back to sleep.

If the old lady had not wakened by now there was a good chance she might sleep on. Laurie had to hope for the best; there was no way of barricading the door. Dimly, through the closed window, she could still hear the plaintive music.

Holding tight to the rail, she ran down the stairs. Maybe if she hurried she could catch the musician and put an end to the whole business. Where the hell was Doug? There was a light in the kitchen, so she headed in that direction.

Head down on the table, his cheek resting on his arm, Doug slept the sleep of the just and weary. A gaudily jacketed paperback book lay beside his hand. Laurie considered trying to wake him and decided it would take time she could not spare. No wonder he was exhausted; she was supposed to share the night watches, and she had copped out on him. Snatching a coat from among the garments hanging in the entryway, she opened the door and went out.

The icy night air made her catch her breath. She fumbled in the pockets of the coat. No gloves, but there was a scarf, and she put it over her head, knotting the ends under her chin.

A pale, passionless moon slid through banks of gathering cloud and the shadows on the ground below shifted with it, shaping monstrous moving patterns on the snow. The bare black branches of the dormant roses stretched up like skeletal arms groping from a grave. Nothing moved except the shadows, but the music continued, so close now that it seemed impossible she could not see its source.

Laurie went forward. Instinct kept her in the shadow of the hedge—the old, primeval instinct that moves man to seek cover in the face of the inexplicable. She was fairly sure the musician was not hidden in the woods. They were too far away. He must be concealed in an outbuilding, or behind the boxwood. Laurie shivered. If something crouched in those shadows, piping music to the moon, it could continue its serenade undisturbed by her.

The windows of Jeff's cottage were dark. Naturally he was asleep at this hour. Any sane person would be. So what did that make her? Crazy. No question about it, she was out of her mind to prowl the night alone, while some maniac tootled on a flute. She should have awakened Doug.

Laurie came to a decision. She would go to Jeff's place. It was closer than the house. She need not traverse the boxwood alley, she could go around, past the garage and the toolshed.

Her slippers had rubber soles, good for walking on the slippery crust of snow, but not warm enough for a winter night. Her feet were already cold. She was grateful for the warmth of the long robe around her calves, expecially since the coat she had taken appeared to be one of Lizzie's. It barely reached her knees. She hugged it closer around her body and went on, trying to move quietly. She reached the toolshed and stopped to catch her breath. Her pulse was racing, though she had not walked fast. Then a nasty chill ran through her as she realized that the music was now very close.

It was not her imagination. The unseen musician must be within a few yards of her.

Her heart sank down into her slippered feet. Jeff's cottage was only a few yards away.

She didn't want Jeff to be guilty. But if he was the trickster, this was the time to catch him in the act. She didn't dare go back for Doug. The music had been playing for a long time, it might stop any second. Gritting her teeth, she tiptoed on.

She had almost reached the garage before she saw it. The empty square of darkness where the closed doors should have been would have warned her if she had not been so intent on her suspicions of Jeff.

She stopped to stare and to wonder, and as she did so the darkness took shape and rushed toward her.

Part of her mind shrieked in wordless archaic terror. Another part recognized the object for what it was, but the knowledge did nothing to relieve her fear. At the last possible moment she forced her paralyzed muscles to move; the fender of the car brushed her arm as she threw herself to one side.

For the second time that night she went sprawling on the gravel, and for the second time hard hands yanked her to her feet. Jeff's face was ghastly in the gray moonlight.

"Are you hurt? Did it hit you?"

"Just brushed me." Laurie was amazed at the calmness of her voice. "Hurry, Jeff. See who's driving."

She craned her neck to look past him as he continued to hold her. The car had rolled gently to a stop at the end of the curved drive, its bumper nudging the white-painted gate. The door on the near side—the driver's side—was closed. But Laurie thought she saw movement on the other side.

"Hurry," she said urgently. "Before he gets away."

Jeff stared wildly at her, his eyeballs gleaming. Then he ran.

Laurie sat down on the driveway. She felt quite composed, but she preferred to sit. The moon went in, behind a cloud. Her teeth began to chatter.

After an interval she heard a car door slam. Jeff came trotting back.

"Nobody," he said briefly.

Laurie squinted, trying to see his face. The moonlight flickered on and off like a faulty light bulb.

"Damn," she said. "He got away."

"Stand up, you'll catch cold." Jeff extended his hand. Laurie let him pull her to her feet. "Are you sure you're okay?"

"Just a few more inches of skin gone," Laurie said morosely. "Hey—what about footprints? If he sneaked out on the other side of the car, there should be t-t-t——"

"You're cold," Jeff said cleverly. "Get in the house."

"But the t-t-t-t—— The footprints!"

"I'll check as soon as you're inside." He looked at her inquiringly, and despite his obvious concern the corners of his mouth twitched with amusement. "T-t-t——?" he asked.

"Tracks!" Laurie got the word out.

He would have carried her, but she refused the offer. After all, a woman had to have some pride, and she had lost a good deal of dignity already. Her frustration about life in general focused on nearer objects; when they entered the kitchen and found Doug still placidly sleeping, she heaved him upright and shook him till his hair fell over his eyes.

Jeff watched for a while and then went out to look for footprints, remarking, "I hate sadism."

One of Doug's eyes opened. It glared wildly through his tangled hair like the eye of a cornered rat peering through dry grass.

A brief but animated dialogue ensued. Doug swept the hair from his brow with a gesture worthy of a Brontë hero.

"I can't believe it," he mumbled. "Never slept so hard . . . Wait a minute. Did you say you got hit by a car?"

"A near miss." Delayed reaction struck Laurie. She dropped into a chair, her legs extended, and contemplated the ruin of Aunt Lizzie's golden robe. Her bloody, dirty knees protruded through the rents in the skirt.

Doug stood up. He turned on the cold-water tap, stuck his head under it, and shook himself like a big dog.

"Speaking of dogs," he said, although Laurie had not done so, "where's that damned Duchess?"

"I don't know and I don't care. Don't you see, Doug—we're making progress. The musician was in the garage, that's why the music sounded so close. Little pixies can't drive cars. Somebody was behind that wheel, and it wasn't Jeff.".

"You're sure?"

"Yes, I'm sure. The car was still moving when he picked me up."

The door opened and Jeff came in. He met Laurie's questioning eyes and shook his head.

"Nothing."

"But how could anyone get out of that car without leaving footprints?" Laurie demanded.

Jeff answered slowly, "There isn't much snow by the gate, under those big cedars. What there is is crusted hard. Maybe someone could go on all fours, crawling.... But I'm not sure that's what happened, Laurie. It may be my fault. I might have forgotten to set the parking brake."

"And the car just happened to start rolling when Laurie was in front of it?" Doug demanded.

"There is a slight incline. Not much, but it might be enough to—"

"And the garage doors? Don't you usually close them?"

"Yes, of course. But ... damn it, I don't remember! I had intended to go out this evening. Miss Lizzie said she needed milk for breakfast and there's a store in Frederick that's open late. I got involved in my work and decided it could wait till morning. So—well, I might have left the doors open."

"I don't think the car could have moved unless the engine was running," Laurie reassured him. "I don't remember hearing it, but it idles very quietly, you know, and I was concentrating on the music. No, Jeff, I'm sure it wasn't your fault. It was a deliberate attempt to run me down."

A strangled, unpleasant gurgle drew her attention to Doug. He was staring at her, his eyes bulging, his forefinger rigid and quivering as he pointed. She would not have been surprised to hear him shout: *There's the culprit!*

"Look at her," he gasped. "Look at—"

"I know I look awful," Laurie said irritably. "Hadn't you noticed? I've wrecked Aunt Lizzie's dress and—"

"Lizzie's dress. Lizzie's coat. A scarf over your head, hiding your hair . . . Oh, boy. If that car was a murder weapon, it wasn't aimed at you, Laurie. The intended victim was Aunt Lizzie."

CHAPTER

10

In a jostling, jumbled rush they all headed for the stairs. Aunt Lizzie's placid breathing mocked their fears. She didn't wake even when Angel Baby raked Doug's ankles with teeth and claws, and he let out a muted scream.

Uncle Ned and Aunt Ida slept too. Duchess was in the library, under the table. She lifted one eyelid and thumped her tail agreeably at them before returning to her nap.

"It's like Sleeping Beauty," Laurie muttered. "Everybody in the whole damn place is unconscious. How did Duchess get in here?"

"She sneaks in when she gets a chance," Jeff answered. "Then she hides so Miss Ida won't throw her out. She must have fallen asleep and been shut in."

So that accounted for Duchess—though, Laurie thought, not entirely. Uncle Ned always put the dog out for a brief run before he went to bed and then left her to "guard" the house. Everyone seemed to have been unaccountably neglectful of their duties that night.

Doug insisted on inspecting the scene of the crime and was furious when Jeff said he had returned the car to the garage.

"I'm going to be in enough trouble when your uncle sees that dented fender," Jeff protested plaintively.

"What difference does it make?" Laurie demanded of her brother. "You think you're Sherlock Holmes? If our villian left a clue in the car it's still there, but I doubt he'd be dumb enough to forget his wallet or his glasses—"

"What makes you think he wears glasses?" Doug asked.

"I don't!"

"Well, if you don't think he wears glasses, why did you—"

"Forget it," Laurie said disgustedly.

Doug went out anyway. Laurie returned to her room and changed into a bathrobe. She came back to the kitchen to find Jeff making coffee. She got a pan of hot water and sat down to bathe her damaged legs.

"I'd offer to do that," Jeff said, "but I don't want Doug to come at me with a club."

"Curse Doug anyway," Laurie said. "I don't know what ails the man."

"Don't you?"

"He's crazy. Ow . . . that stings. We're all crazy," Laurie went on. "The whole family. I should have told Herrrrman that. It would have been the truth."

Doug returned in time to hear the last part of this speech. He nodded in sour agreement.

"There must be a strain of insanity somewhere in this family."

"Any luck?" Laurie asked.

"No wallet, no glasses, no nothing." Doug watched her for a moment. "You missed a section," he told her. "Want me to do that?"

"No."

"I'll get the iodine."

"I don't want iodine. It hurts."

Doug got the iodine. Ignoring Laurie's protests, he swabbed the scratches. Laurie held her robe modestly at knee level and let out yelping cries as Doug worked.

"A Spartan you are not," he remarked.

"I don't believe in—ow!—repressing my feelings."

"No, but seriously," Doug said, "aren't you beginning to wonder just a little bit about this family? Did you ever do any genealogical research?"

"Ow! Ouch!"

"Stop yelling, you coward. I'm not touching any of your scratches."

Laurie opened her eyes. Doug had painted faces on her knees—circles with dots for eyes and sweeping semicircles for smiling mouths.

"You're weird," she said.

"I think it's rather a neat effect." Doug replaced the stopper. "No, but seriously—"

"No, I never did any genealogical research. Why the hell should I?"

"We might find out that Great-great-grandfather Angus was a werewolf," Doug said.

"I'm going to bed," Jeff said.

"Not just yet." Still on his knees, Doug turned a critical eye toward the other man. "How come you were up and dressed when this happened?"

"I heard the music, of course," Jeff said. "Went out to have a look around."

"Find anything?"

Jeff shook his head. "It could have been a bird," he said stubbornly.

"A buzzard," Doug suggested. "It was driving the car."

"I'm going to bed," Jeff repeated. "Good night."

The painted faces on Laurie's knees grinned at her with imbecilic optimism.

"Why don't you get some sleep too?" she asked Doug. "I'll sit up for the rest of the night."

"There isn't much left of the night," Doug said. "Uncle Ned will be up in another hour."

"So sleep in."

"Maybe I will." Doug reached for his book. Laurie, who was closer, got there first.

The cover depicted a scantily clad female crouching at the feet of a man attired in tropical garb. Muscles bulged all over him in an unlikely fashion, and above his head he brandished a sword as tall as he was. His opponent had six arms. Two of them groped lasciviously at the prostrate girl, and the other four waved weapons at the hero with the sword.

"Adult bookstore?" Laurie raised an eyebrow. "The cover may be X-rated, but it looks like comic-book stuff to me."

"Science fiction," Doug said.

"Oh, yeah? There's nothing scientific about that woman's anatomy."

"All right, it's not science fiction, it's fantasy. A lot of intelligent people read this sort of thing. It's a sign of an active imagination and—"

Laurie opened the book.

" '. . . his mighty thews bulged as he raised the sword. Whop! A head flew in one direction, and a trunk in the other. A great fountain of blood spurted up. The girl shrieked as a slimy tentacle encircled her writhing, naked body. She—' "

"Give me that!"

"Wait a minute. This is getting good. He just cut off two more of the monster's arms and she—"

Doug snatched the book from Laurie.

"It's a fairy tale," she jeered. "A grown-up fairy tale, with monsters and brave heroes and endangered maidens. Really, Doug."

Doug retreated with great dignity, his nose in the air and his despised book under his arm.

Laurie toyed with the idea of resuming her interrupted slumber. Surely there would be no more danger that night; Uncle Ned would soon be up and about. But she knew she would not be able to sleep. They were making progress, toward a certainty of danger, but they seemed farther and farther away from a solution. Tomorrow they would simply have to interrogate the old people more closely. Reclusive and harmless as the Mortons seemed to be, they must have an unknown enemy. Uncle Ned's outspoken views and, upon occasion, corporal remonstration against poachers and hunters might have aroused ire. Ida's manner was not always friendly; if, for instance, she had caught a clerk trying to cheat her and had insisted that he be fired from his job . . . From such petty causes a sick mind could assume offense.

And what about the family history? Maybe great-great someone had cheated at cards, or seduced a neighbor's daughter, or embezzled the firm's money. Maybe Uncle Ned, in his youth . . .

Laurie grinned and shook her head. No, she couldn't picture that. Ned had always preferred animals to people.

Even as that fond, half-contemptuous appraisal passed through her mind, she revised it. She was making the same mistake young people often made about the elderly—not only that they were long past the stronger passions and emotions, but that they had never been subject to them. She ought to know better.

Fifty years ago. The nineteen twenties. Flappers, shingled hair, flattened breasts, and rouged knees. Try as she might, she could not picture Ida doing the Charleston in one of those skimpy, waistless dresses. It was easier to imagine Uncle Ned in plus fours and spats and a straw hat . . . or was that the wrong period? He was still a fine-looking man; in his long-gone youth he must have been quite a lady killer. As for Aunt Lizzie—strip off fifty or sixty pounds, turn her hair back to its original brown, remove lines and wrinkles—and *voilà!* She'd have made a wonderful flapper, Laurie thought, smiling affectionately.

Surely somewhere there was a family album. She would ask Ida if she might see it. The old lady would be pleased at her interest, and perhaps with the help of actual photographs she could envision not only how they had looked, but how they had felt about life and love and the opposite sex when they were young.

But before that she would have to explain to Aunt Lizzie how her precious robe had gotten ripped to shreds.

She was still sitting at the kitchen table wrapped in gloomy thought when Uncle Ned came downstairs. He looked surprised to see her, but only mildly so. Nothing ever surprised Uncle Ned very much.

" 'Morning," he said. "How about a walk?"

Laurie started to shake her head and then changed her mind.

"I'd like that. But none of your forty-mile hikes, Uncle Ned. I'm not as young as you are."

Her uncle acknowledged this witticism with a vague smile.

"Where's that fool dog?"

"She's in the library." Laurie started up. "I'll let her out on my way upstairs. I'd better put on some jeans."

She braced herself before she opened the library door. Duchess emerged in a brown whirlwind, tongue lolling, eyes gleaming, tail a furry blur. No prisoner, released after a lifetime in the Bastille, could have rejoiced more in his liberation. After sprinkling Laurie liberally with hair, Duchess bounded down the hall toward the kitchen. Laurie went to her room and changed. When she came back down, Ned was ready to go.

The sun was not yet above the horizon, but the eastern sky looked like one of Aunt Lizzie's fancier dresses, pale-azure gauze woven with gold and banded in turquoise and coral. The dog ran and rolled and then suddenly squatted, its brown eyes rapt in profound contemplation. This duty completed, it rushed at Ned for approval, danced heavily on Laurie's feet, and galloped off across the lawn.

The woods were magical in the early-morning light, with no suggestion of eeriness, only a beauty too perfect to be quite real. The shadows were exquisite shades of blue-gray and mauve. Ned didn't speak until they had reached his bird-feeding station. He filled the feeders with seed and distributed nuts and carrots. Then he sat down on the bench beside Laurie.

"Best place in the world," he said. "Can't imagine why anybody would want to leave here."

"It is beautiful. But didn't you ever want to travel, Uncle Ned?"

"Did. France. Not very pretty when I saw it."

"World War One? Weren't you awfully young?"

Puttees and flat tin hats, tight short jackets, trousers cut like riding breeches. She could see a younger Uncle Ned in that romantic costume. What she couldn't see was Ned carrying a gun.

"Lied about my age," Ned said briefly. "Damn fool," he added.

"Was that where you learned to . . . to . . ."

"Hate killing." Ned nodded. Laurie did not reply, but he sensed her sympathy; turning his head, he gave her a shy smile.

"Came back to an office job," he went on. "Didn't do too badly. Made a lot of money. Hated it. So . . . one day I quit. Never went back. Didn't have to work; why do something you hate?"

"You should sympathize with the kids today," Laurie said. "They don't believe in working at a job they hate either."

"Have to work unless you've got money," Ned said drily. "I was lucky. Well. I'm going on. You coming?"

"No, I'll sit awhile and go back to the house."

Ned tramped off, his stride long and free. The pom-pom on his red stocking cap bounced up and down.

Laurie made her way back to the house through

the newminted sunshine. As always she was aware of the beauty that surrounded her, but a new word and a new idea colored her vision that day. Money. All these acres so well tended, the old house meticulously maintained, the expensive car, Lizzie's splurges in the boutiques. . . . Where did the money come from? She had never thought of the Mortons as wealthy. They rented land to the Wilsons and perhaps to other families, but in these days of rising costs and higher taxes that income would not suffice. They surely weren't living on social security.

Money was a motive for crime. The root of all evil.

When she burst into the kitchen Aunt Ida was at the stove. She moved without her usual briskness, but when she saw Laurie she produced a bleak smile.

"I fear you must tolerate my poor cooking this morning. Lizzie is playing slugabed."

"You sit down. I'll cook." Laurie shed her coat, took her aunt by the shoulders, and propelled her toward a chair. The bones under her hands felt pathetically frail and brittle.

"I'm glad to have a chance to talk to you," she went on, prodding the sausages that were gently sizzling in the frying pan. "Does Aunt Lizzie have any money?"

She expected a dignified remonstrance at the vulgarity of the question. There was no answer at all. She turned to look with surprise at Ida.

"I feared you would ask that eventually," her aunt said with a sigh. "My dear Laura, Elizabeth has *all* the money."

"All?"

"Ned has his own income, of course. However, he contributes generously to the expenses of maintaining Idlewood, and he is ridiculously extravagant about his hobbies. Thousands each year to the various societies for the protection of animals, and—"

"You're rambling, Aunt Ida," Laurie interrupted. "That isn't like you. I'm surprised. I never

197

thought. . . . You know I'm not asking out of idle curiosity, don't you?"

"Yes, my dear. I know precisely why you are asking."

"Then tell me, please."

"You are aware, of course," her aunt began, "that there were four of us to begin with. Your Uncle Ned, Elizabeth, myself, and Mary, your grandmother. Poor Mary died young, God rest her—before our father passed on. You never knew your great-grandfather. You would not have understood him. He was an autocrat of the old school, with strong views about family and property. Yet in his way he was fair-minded; he made no distinction between his male and female offspring. We four were to share equally in his estate—which was, I might add, extensive. Then . . ." Her thin lips quivered. Laurie hated to see her so distressed, but she hardened her heart; this story might or might not be useful, she could not tell until she had heard it.

Ida regained control of herself and went on in a firm voice.

"As father grew older, he grew—as we all do! —more opinionated and more rigid. Your grandmother Mary's share of the property would ordinarily have passed to your mother, but Anna's way of living offended Father. When Anna divorced your father, Papa cut her out of the will."

"My father? Don't you mean Doug's father? Or did he allow her one mistake?"

Like another, more famous autocratic old lady, Aunt Ida was not amused.

"Certainly not. He was violently opposed to divorce. I meant her first husband, of course."

"So her share went back into the estate," Laurie prodded.

"That is correct. Ned lost his share when he retired from the office. Papa had no patience with a man who would not work."

"But how did Uncle Ned get the money to pay his share of the expenses here?"

"Ned did very well in business," her aunt explained. "I don't understand such matters myself." They are, her tone implied, too vulgar.

"So now we're down to you and Aunt Lizzie," Laurie mused. "Your father must have been a—"

"He had every right to do what he wished with his own," Ida said firmly. "He chose . . ." Her hesitation was only momentary. "He chose to leave everything to Lizzie."

"Why did he do that?"

"I have explained to you why he omitted Ned and Mary. His reasons for excluding me are irrelevant." She lifted a hand to silence Laurie as the latter started to object. "Believe me, Laura, they are."

"Couldn't you challenge the will?" Laurie asked indignantly.

"Certainly not!" Her aunt was equally indignant. "Father was in complete possession of his senses. The embarrassment and publicity of a lawsuit were out of the question." Her tone softened. "It has never made any difference, Laura. Your Aunt Elizabeth is very generous." She added, with no change of tone, "You are burning the sausages."

"Oh." Laurie flipped the sausages, with a reckless spatter of grease. She was now as reluctant as Ida to pursue the subject, but she forced herself to ask the question to which she already knew the answer. "Then who inherits when Aunt Lizzie dies?"

"I do, of course," Ida said. "And Ned. Elizabeth has always refused to make a will. Do you see now why I have been perturbed? If Elizabeth is losing her mind she will require skilled care; and an institution is out of the question, Laura, I could not bring myself to take her from her home. If there is a plot aimed at her sanity or her life . . ."

"Oh, my," Laurie said helplessly. "I see what you mean."

"A singularly useless comment," said a voice from

the door. Laurie turned. Hands in the pockets of his jeans, hair immaculate, Doug lounged against the doorframe.

"How long have you been there?" she asked.

"I heard most of it." Doug uncrossed his legs and went to Ida. Dropping to one knee, he put both arms around her stiff shoulders. "Get one thing straight," he told her. "I wouldn't believe you wanted to harm Aunt Lizzie if I caught you pointing a gun at her. I wouldn't believe it if Sherlock Holmes and Hercule Poirot and the combined police forces of greater New York, Baltimore, and Washington, D.C., told me so."

Even in that extremity Ida did not succumb to the weakness of tears or emotion. She only said, "Thank you, Douglas," but her expression as she looked at him made Laurie's throat tighten.

"Make that two of us," she said.

Doug squeezed his aunt's shoulders and rose to his feet. Laurie was feeling particularly fond of him at that moment; she noted with approval that he moved neatly, without Jeff's feline suppleness, but with a grace all his own. Yes, as brothers went, he was a good example.

"You are burning the sausages," he said.

"Oh, curse it."

"They're a lost cause, I'm afraid." Doug inspected the wrinkled, leathery dark-brown objects in the pan with a fastidiously lifted nose. "Get out of the way and let me cook. I can see I'll never get any breakfast if I depend on you emotional females. Where is everybody this morning?"

"We all slept late," Ida said.

Doug busied himself at the stove. Laurie got herself some coffee and refilled her aunt's cup. Having started a new batch of sausages and filled the toaster with bread, Doug said, "We had another bad night last night, Aunt Ida. Luckily Aunt Lizzie didn't hear it, but the fairy piper was at it again. Laurie sallied bravely forth to investigate and the musician tried to run her down with the Lincoln."

Ida's shocked exclamation was echoed from the hall. Lizzie stood there, her horrified face contrasting ludicrously with her frivolous lace-trimmed peasant blouse and ropes of bright beads.

"You are tact personified," Laurie told Doug. "It's all right, Aunts; I wasn't hurt, I just skinned my knees."

Deciding that Lizzie was the more perturbed of the two, she started toward her, bent on reassurance, but Lizzie waved her off and stumbled back. So might Macbeth have responded to the ghost of Banquo, his victim, and although Laurie knew her aunt's distress was genuine, she could not help noticing the streak of theatricalism that seemed to run in the family.

"Oh, dear," Lizzie gasped. "Oh, I never thought. . . . It isn't fun anymore. I can't let this . . . Wait here. Wait, I'll be right back."

She retreated at full speed, her dangling necklaces clashing.

The others exchanged glances.

"Oh, oh," Laurie said. "You don't suppose she planned it herself?"

"The thought did pass through my mind," Doug admitted. "But, damn it—excuse me, Aunt Ida—no, she couldn't have. Not alone."

Lizzie was back before they could pursue this theory in greater detail. Her beruffled bosom heaved agitatedly. She thrust an envelope at Doug.

"Here. Here, take them."

"You told us they were gone," Laurie exclaimed, as Doug removed a small sheaf of snapshots from the envelope. "Aunt Lizzie, you lied to us."

"Oh, my darling, how can you say such a thing! I would never tell you a falsehood. The photographs I had concealed in my secret place *were* taken. But . . ." She cocked her head and gave Laurie a sly glance. "You don't suppose I had only one set, do you? No, no, I had them copied. I pretended I had to go to the drugstore to buy aspirin. And, of course," she added virtuously, "I did purchase the aspirin, so that was not a lie."

"But, Aunt Lizzie—"

"Now don't scold me." The old lady's lip quivered. "It was just a game. Life gets so *boring* around here. But it can't go on, not if you are going to be hurt, Laura. Douglas must look at the photographs and tell us what to do."

"I wasn't hurt," Laurie assured her. "But I'm afraid your pretty robe is ruined, Aunt Lizzie. I'm sorry about that. I shouldn't have worn it, but I was in a hurry and I couldn't find my jeans, and . . . What are you looking at me that way for?"

"My robe?" Lizzie repeated. "The gold one?"

"I'm so sorry. And I'm afraid your coat is ripped, but that was just a seam, it can be—"

"My coat?"

"I'm really terribly sorry, Auntie."

Lizzie's worried look smoothed out into an expression of such profound stupidity that a casual observer would have supposed she had lost what remained of her senses. Laurie knew better. Lizzie was considering a new, startling idea, and planning what she should do about it. There was no use questioning her about it, she would be deaf and blind to external stimuli until she had worked out her plans.

Laurie turned to the photographs, which Doug had spread out on the kitchen table. They were the same ones she had seen before—or rather, if Lizzie was to be believed, copies of them. His elbows on the table, his chin propped on his hands, Doug studied the bizarre objects intently. Ida moved her chair so she could see them too. She could no longer afford to dismiss Lizzie's fancies with a sniff of contempt.

"They are most peculiar, are they not?" she murmured. "I have never seen such things."

"I have," Doug said.

"What?" Laurie exclaimed. "Where? How? Who?"

"They're very good," Doug said, with the judicious

202

air of a connoisseur. "Brilliant, in fact. Most fantastic art is out-and-out horror—buggy-eyed monsters or slimy what-nots from outer space. It takes genius to give a faint, shivery suggestion of something alien and malevolent in familiar form. Not many artists can produce work of this caliber. Doré, Beardsley, some of Ed Cartier's stuff. . . . Frazetta and the Hildebrand brothers are slick and commercial and popular, but I'm not overly impressed by them. They never gave me the shivers."

Except for the first name, Laurie had never heard of the people he mentioned. That was enough to give her a clue, however.

"These are not paintings," she protested.

"No, they're definitely three-dimensional. I don't recognize the medium. Some semitransparent plastic, I would guess."

Laurie dropped into the nearest chair.

"Sculptures—figurines? Is that what—"

"What else could they be, nitwit? I don't blame you for being impressed, though," Doug added generously. "You're not familiar with this field of art. It's become popular, with the general boom in science fiction and fantasy, *Star Wars* and Tolkien and their imitators. Most of the artwork *is* two-dimensional. Posters, calendars, book illustrations. There aren't many sculptors who specialize in horror and fantasy. And this guy is extraordinarily talented. Oh, yes, it's a guy, not a woman. I've seen his work somewhere. Wish I could remember his name."

"Where did you see it?"

"I forget. One of the sci-fi conventions, maybe. I've been to so many of 'em. He's not one of the well-known artists in the field. Probably an amateur who does this as a hobby and rarely exhibits."

Laurie was speechless. As she looked again, the true nature of the "fairies" seemed so obvious she could have blushed for her own gullibility. She was as bad as Lizzie; some subconscious part of her mind had wanted to believe in the wonders of the invisible world she had cherished as a child, when she had populated Idlewood's pastoral peace with fairy-tale characters. Yet the faked photos were cleverly done. The surrounding leaves and blades of grass had been arranged to suggest just-halted movement, so that the artificial intrusions blended with the natural background.

"Can we trace these things?" she demanded.

"Maybe. There are shops that specialize in fantasy. I don't know about Frederick; certainly D.C. and Baltimore might have such things. Getting the artist's name won't solve our problem, though. Presumably his work is for sale to anyone who walks in off the street."

"He can't have a large clientele," Laurie argued. "A dealer might remember who bought these, especially if they are one of a kind."

"Oh, I'll try," Doug assured her. "Don't expect quick results, though. I'm sure I saw these figures here in the East—I've never been to any of the Western or Midwest conventions—but that doesn't mean the artist is from this area. These little gems could have been bought in San Francisco or Nome, Alaska, for all we know. The fans keep in touch with one another, so I'm sure I can track the guy down eventually through local dealers. But it will take time."

Laurie made an exasperated noise. Doug grinned sympathetically.

"I know how you feel. I'm impatient too. So why don't we go to the source? Aunt Lizzie. Hey, Auntie, wake up and pay attention. The die is cast, the worms have turned. We want the truth now."

Lizzie started affectedly. Three pairs of hostile eyes focused on her. She began to retreat, step by step.

"Come on," Doug insisted. "You told us you got these from the Wilson girls. We know that isn't true—"

"Douglas, I do not tell lies! If you choose not to believe me, I won't talk to you anymore."

"Auntie, a child could not have taken these." Doug's tone became wheedling. "Come on, Auntie, be nice. You said you didn't want to see Laurie get hurt—"

"Laurie won't be hurt. That was ... It won't happen again. Dear me," Lizzie murmured, as if to herself, "I seem to have acted rather precipitately. It has always been my weakness." Her eyes shifted, with seeming casualness; when they came to rest on the snapshots Doug slapped his hand down on them. Lizzie sighed. "There is nothing to worry about," she assured them. "Nothing at all. Laura, darling, will you see to breakfast? I just don't seem to feel like cooking this morning. I think I will take a little nap."

"Stop her," Laurie exclaimed, starting up. It was too late. Lizzie had fluttered out, with the deceptive speed she could muster when she wanted to.

"What's the point?" Doug demanded. "I can hardly shake the truth out of her, can I? What made her change her mind?"

"She put two and two together, that's what," Laurie said. "Darn that woman! She's the smartest lunatic I ever saw. Don't you get it? When she thought I was in danger she was ready to tell us everything she knew. Then—dumb me!—I told her I was wearing her clothes and she realized she was the intended victim. She's enjoying this melodrama!"

"Or she knows who the villain is and thinks he wouldn't hurt her," Doug said.

"She could be wrong."

"She sure could. Damn ... Excuse me, Aunt. I just burned the second batch of sausages."

II

With Ida's help Laurie finally managed to get breakfast. Lizzie had barricaded herself in her room and refused to come out. When Doug knocked and demanded entry, a slim furry paw slid under the door and dug sharp claws into his ankle. He left, cursing cats, Lizzie, and old houses that didn't have properly fitted doors, and shut himself in with the telephone.

Ned came in and applied himself to his breakfast.

"Going into town," he announced. "Taking the car in. Fender's dented. Can't have it like that."

"Did Jeff tell you how it got dented?" Laurie asked.

"Must have forgotten to set the brake," Ned said calmly. "Even Atlas nods." He inspected Laurie. "You all right? You must be, you were walking okay this morning." He returned to his eggs.

Laurie looked at her uncle with exasperated affection. He was so disinterested in the ordinary cares of life that he seemed inhuman at times. At least after their talk that morning she had a clue as to why he was that way. Plunged into the insanity of war, some men became hardened to slaughter and cruelty. Ned had become oversensitized to pain and protected himself by trying not to care too much.

Doug joined them.

"Guess what?" he demanded, grinning.

"Don't tell me you found the artist!" Laurie registered appropriate surprise, pleasure and admiration.

"I got his name. Frank Fulkes. Sound familiar?"

"Never heard of him."

"I doubt that he's our villian." Doug perched on the edge of the table and began nibbling absent-mindedly on the last sausage. "He lives in upstate New York. Hasn't produced anything for several years. But the second place I called—the Cimmerian Bookshop, in Baltimore—used to handle his work. If I take in the snapshots they may remember who bought those pieces."

Neither of them expected Ned to demonstrate any curiosity about this speech; nor did he.

"Going to town," he told Doug. "Have to take the car in. Big dent in the fender."

"You're not driving, are you?" Doug asked apprehensively.

"No. Jeff. I have to go along, make sure they do the job right."

Doug looked inquiringly at Laurie. His uncle's Olympian calm seemed to bewilder him.

"Jeff forgot to set the parking brake," she said.

"Anybody can make a mistake," Ned remarked. "Offered to pay for it. Can't allow that, of course. I'm going now."

He left. Duchess, abandoned, let out a sharp, indignant bark. She was soothed by the remains of the sausage, proffered by Doug, and settled down at his feet.

"You going to Baltimore?" Laurie asked.

"Uh-huh."

"Want me to come along?"

"You'd better stay here and keep an eye on Lizzie. God knows what she'll do next."

"That was odd, wasn't it? That she's the family heiress. I never would have suspected it. I wonder how much money is involved."

"Almost any amount of money can constitute a motive for someone," Doug answered. "But do you believe that's the reason for all this?"

"I don't see how it could be. The only one who profits is Aunt Ida, and nobody in his right mind would suspect her. She must know that. Why do you suppose she's so upset?"

"She isn't worried about being suspected. She's worried about the next heirs."

"The next . . . Oh! You don't mean—"

"I do mean. Us, my darling sister," Doug said. "You and me."

Left to herself, Laurie attacked the dishes, in an effort to get her mind off that last revelation. She and Doug probably were the Mortons' heirs. Well, she thought, that eliminates the profit motive. Neither of us would . . . Anyway, it wasn't possible that . . .

She paused in the act of scouring a particularly loathsome frying pan—the one in which the sausages had burned—and stared blindly out the window, her brow furrowed. Much as she hated to admit the idea, it was possible. What did she know about Doug, after all? He was practically a stranger. A glib, charming stranger, to whom she had become rather attached—but that didn't mean he was incapable of skulduggery. All he would need was a confederate, on the spot, to supply him with information and manipulate a few props. He had, by his own admission, friends in town. Suppose one of them had told him, jokingly, about Lizzie and Baby Betsy and their games? Doug's interest in fantasy suggested an inventive, far-out imagination. He of all people might see the possibilities in that innocent game. Obviously he had access to the type of artwork that had been used to fake the photographs, and the fact that he had admitted as much, with seeming candor, was no proof of innocence. He had not made the admission until after Lizzie had produced the snapshots, and he must have known that sooner or later Laurie would figure out that the elves were sculptured shapes. She was an idiot not to have realized that earlier; but without the photographs it would have been very difficult for her to trace the artist, unfamiliar as she was with the field of fantasy.

And now Doug had the photos and was on his way to some apocryphal bookstore. . . . No; the bookstore was probably real. He would run no risk in tracing the local buyers of Frank Fulkes' work if he had himself acquired the pieces elsewhere.

Horrified at the direction her thoughts were taking, Laurie tried to stop herself, but her mind continued remorselessly piling up evidence. Doug was broke, failing at his profession. He had expensive tastes. He was certainly attractive to women, capable of persuading a naive local girl into waving colored lights around the woods, making a telephone call. He could even have driven the car the night before. She had walked for several minutes before going to the garage—plenty of time for Doug to nip out and get behind the wheel. And he could have been back in the kitchen before she and Jeff got there. If Doug had been the driver it would explain one point that had worried her—how had the unknown gained possession of the car keys? She was convinced that the engine had been running. The car was heavy, it would take more than a push to get it moving.

With genuine dismay she contemplated the picture she had constructed. It fit together with the neatness of a jigsaw puzzle—motive, means, opportunity. The only missing piece was the identity of the poor fool who was Doug's assistant; but that was a minor point. The girl might be innocent of everything except gullibility.

Still, there was no proof. Laurie was enough of a historian to know that several different, equally convincing theories can be built from the same scraps of evidence. Anyway, why should it horrify her so? A lot of people had relatives who were in jail—or who ought to be in jail.

A muted whine from the dog made her start. Duchess was dreaming of bones or beefsteak or something equally delectable; her jaws had relaxed into a broad grin. So much, Laurie thought, for the theory that dreams might be messages from another world, premonitions of blessings and disasters yet to come. Did the spirits of departed ancestors come to dogs, warning them to steer clear of traps and highways? Duchess looked like a canine caricature of a medium Laurie had once visited; the woman had twitched and moved in the same way.

The house was so quiet. For the first time in her life Laurie did not feel at ease within its walls. Perhaps it knew she was harboring vile suspicions about the young heir.

She snatched up a coat and went outside. No comfort there either; even the sun had gone back on her. Heavy clouds barricaded the sky. Laurie put her hands in her pockets. Why couldn't she ever find a pair of gloves? She walked along the path. Insensibly her steps turned toward Jeff's cottage. Should she confide her suspicions to him? It would be the basest of betrayals, pure treason against the family name; but if Doug really was the miscreant responsible for the attacks on Lizzie, he had to be stopped.

Avoiding the boxwood alley she circled the tool-shed and paused for a long suspicious look at the garage before proceeding. The doors were closed. She had forgotten; the car was at the body shop, and so was Jeff.

A flicker of movement where there should be none made her draw back in the shelter of the shed wall. No, her eyes had not deceived her; the curtain moved again, as someone had lifted a corner in order to peer out. Someone was in Jeff's cottage.

Doug was on his way to Baltimore, Uncle Ned had gone to Frederick with Jeff. . . . Her mind ran down the list of possible allies before facing the unpleasant conclusion that she would have to deal with this herself. By the time she returned to the house, called the police, and waited for them to arrive, the intruder would probably be gone.

At least she could provide herself with a weapon. She eased open the door of the toolshed and surveyed its contents. Quite an arsenal—shovels, axes, picks, rakes. Dismissing the sharper, more lethal instruments, she selected an ax handle which had lost its head and was, presumably, awaiting repair. It was light enough to be easily wielded and heavy enough to stun an adversary without seriously maiming him.

Her heart pounding, she scuttled across the open space between the shed and the cottage and stood on tiptoe to peer in the window. But the curtains were drawn; she could see nothing. As she stood debating her next move, the doorknob started to turn. Laurie flattened herself against the stone wall, her club ready.

The door opened about four inches. A head appeared. Laurie bit back an exclamation. The face was monstrous—solid, dead black, with white banding the staring eyes and the circle of the mouth. A ski mask made quite an effective disguise.

The burglar would have seen her if he had bothered to look in her direction, but apparently he was not anticipating an ambush. He stepped briskly out and turned to close the door. Laurie brought her club down.

At the last possible minute she realized that there was something hauntingly familiar about the pattern of the plaid shirt and the posture of the long legs. She let out a cry of surprise, and tried, not altogether successfully, to alter the direction of her swing. The intruder whirled and threw up his arm. The club hit it with a resounding thwack. The burglar staggered and sat down.

"Damn it," Laurie exclaimed. "I thought you'd gone to Baltimore."

Doug pulled off the ski cap. His hair stood on end and his eyes bulged with fury.

"I told you to stay in the house! My God, I think my arm is broken."

"Let me see." Laurie squatted. Doug shook his head violently and tried to retreat without standing up.

"Oh, don't be silly. I didn't know it was you." She pushed his sleeve back, took his elbow in one hand and his wrist in the other and tried to bend the part in between. Doug objected loudly.

"It's not broken," Laurie said. "Why the hell didn't you tell me what you were going to do? And what were you doing?"

Doug did not answer the first question. "Searching the place, of course," he snarled.

"Why the ski mask?" Laurie answered her own question.

"You couldn't resist the fun of disguising yourself and playing master spy. I don't suppose you found anything, did you?"

211

"No."

"He's too smart to leave evidence lying around," Laurie said contemptuously. "You mustn't judge others by yourself, dear brother. Why don't you get up?"

"I'm thinking of fainting," Doug said.

"You aren't hurt." She looked at him more closely. He *was* a little pale. "Are you?"

"I think it's a greenstick fracture. But never mind." Doug got to his feet. "Get back in the house, will you?"

"Where are you going?"

"Where I said I was going. Baltimore. See you later."

He lifted the garage door, ostentatiously favoring his right arm, and vanished inside. The car started with an ill-tempered roar, as if echoing its owner's sentiments, and departed with gravel spurting out in all directions.

Laurie waited until Doug was out of sight before she tried the door of the cottage. It was unlocked. Fine burglar he is, she thought; he didn't even have to pick the lock. The fact that Jeff didn't bother to lock his door argued that his conscience was clear— or that he had been careful to dispose of any incriminating clues. All the same, Laurie decided she might as well have a look.

Since she didn't know what to look for, she found nothing of interest. Jeff was fanatically neat; his shoes were lined up in a straight row, his clothing arranged in symmetrical piles. He even squeezed his toothpaste from the bottom of the tube and rolled it up as he used it.

Laurie sauntered toward the typewriter. She had always been curious about Jeff's novel. Here was her chance. After all, she told herself, she had to find out whether he was really a writer. Maybe the pages were blank. Maybe he was typing out *Gone With the Wind,* to give an illusion of industry.

The page she picked up was numbered 375. It was

a rough draft, crisscrossed with X's and blurred by typos. The heroine was named Lady Isabeau. She had the face of an angel from heaven and the heart of a devil from hell. At least that was what Raimond thought of her. Raimond's identity was not clear, but his intentions were. His jerkin open to the waist, displaying his broad hairy chest, he stood over her, his hands on his lean hips, as she cowered against the wall of the castle keep. Her hands fluttered, vainly trying to cover her bare . . .

"Hmm," Laurie said. She turned to the next page.

Some time later she reached the end of the completed part of the manuscript. Jeff had run out of steam on page 396, and Lady Isabeau was still vainly trying to cover herself with her clouds of silken blond hair, Raimond having removed the alternatives piece by piece. He had also mentioned a few incidents in the lady's career which justified his appraisal of her character, and Laurie couldn't conjure up much sympathy for her, despite the fate that lay in store for her—probably on about page 415, at the rate Jeff was going.

Laurie was tempted to go back to the beginning, but her conscience was bothering her; it was a dirty trick reading someone's manuscript without permission. He might have a best seller on his hands at that. His style wasn't particularly polished, but the readers of this brand of fiction did not demand polish.

Having restored the papers to their original condition, she left the cottage. Maybe she ought to drop Jeff a gentle hint about keeping his door locked, if she could do so without giving herself away. The aunts would swoon if they ever got a look at a page of that manuscript.

Or would they? She was falling into the same old error of thinking of them as petrified people, without emotions or human instincts. She had promised herself she would avoid that kind of youthful ignorance. Perhaps this would be a good time to ask Ida if she might look at the family album. There was nothing more she could do at the moment, except watch over Lizzie and hope Doug would find a clue in Baltimore. Assuming, of course, that Doug wasn't the guilty party himself.

She found the aunts in the parlor, busy with their fancywork. Ida's pink knitting was a good ten inches long, but her needles did not click with their usual brisk rhythm. Lizzie was also heavy-eyed and lethargic. Laurie admired her needlepoint, a complex, if saccharine, depiction of furry kittens. Lizzie looked at her suspiciously.

"Thank you, darling, it is kind of you to say so, but if you are hoping, by means of flattery, to make me forget the trick you played on me this morning—"

"What trick? Oh—you mean persuading you to show Doug the pictures? I didn't plan that, Auntie. You misunderstood."

"Never mind," Lizzie said, more graciously. "We'll just forget the whole thing, darling."

"I wish we could, Aunt Lizzie. I still think—"

Lizzie raised her hand. "Now not another word. I don't intend to refer to the subject ever again."

Laurie recognized the technique. It was the same one Lizzie always employed when one of her enthusiasms had run its course. Like a repentant drunk the morning after, she wiped out all memory of her excesses and refused to refer to them. The system had always worked before, but this time, Laurie feared, Lizzie had started something she could no longer control.

"Auntie," she began.

"Sit down, my dear, you look tired," Lizzie said. "You may stroke Angle Baby if you like."

Laurie sat, but declined the offer of Angel Baby. The cat was looking particularly seductive and that, Laurie knew, was often the prelude to a vicious attack. Ida's old Siamese was curled up on the couch. Laurie patted her, thinking as she did so that it was too bad human beings didn't age as gracefully.

Sabrina's blue eyes had lost their sapphire brilliance and there were white hairs around her muzzle, but she had held up a lot better than her mistress, though her age in cat years was almost as great. She opened one eye when Laurie stroked her, gave a brief, rusty purr, and went back to sleep.

Ida was delighted to produce the photo albums—not one, but several of them.

"I am glad you are taking an interest in the family history," she said. "As the last of the Mortons—"

"Doug wouldn't like to hear you say that." Laurie smiled.

Ida blinked. "The last of the Morton women, I meant to say. Men do not care for such things, more's the pity."

Laurie remembered having seen the albums before, but that had been years ago, when she was small enough to find the old-fashioned costumes hilariously funny and the youthful versions of her aunts and uncle quite unbelievable. Now she studied the faded photos with sympathetic interest, although there were many faces she did not know. Ida insisted on naming each of these and giving a brief biography, so the viewing went slowly. Lizzie didn't even pretend to be interested. She went to get lunch, and Ida proceeded methodically through album after album.

Ida's father had obviously been an enthusiastic amateur photographer. There were dozens of shots of the aunts and Uncle Ned as babies and children. Propped against pillows, swathed in yards of lace-trimmed muslin, they stared at the camera with round, unsmiling eyes. The family resemblance was clear even at that tender age. All the fat, lace-enveloped babies might have been the same, though even then Lizzie was decidedly plumper.

The babies grew into children, holding dolls or rolling hoops. The girls were all pretty, though Lizzie was the beauty of the family. Mary, Laurie's grandmother, had a sweet, gentle face. Her wedding picture was charming, despite the short white dress and kid slippers; her eyes shone with happiness, and her tall young groom reminded Laurie of Anna, especially around the eyes.

But the real surprise was Uncle Ned. Having outgrown the chubby cheeks and gap-toothed smile of childhood, he became a strikingly handsome boy. The Morton heritage was pure Scot, virtually undiluted by other nationalities; yet Ned's high cheekbones, finely cut lips, and thin nose suggested a Latin strain—a grandee of old Granada turned buccaneer, ravaging the coasts of Britain and the female inhabitants thereof.

"He's gorgeous," Laurie exclaimed.

"We have always been considered a handsome family," Ida said. "The Morton features are quite distinctive."

Lizzie called them to lunch then, and afterwards the aunts went to take their naps. Laurie returned to the parlor. She felt restless and ill at ease. The weather might be partially responsible for her mood; the skies were somber, suggesting snow.

The albums were still lying on the table. She opened one at random. There was nothing for her here, just sad reminders that youth must fade and beauty wither.

Laurie stared with melancholy fascination at a snapshot of Uncle Ned. He held what was obviously a brand-new bicycle; his wide smile radiated the pride of ownership. He must have been about sixteen when the picture was taken, Laurie thought.

As she continued to look at the picture she became conscious of a strange sensation at the pit of her stomach. Uncle Ned's face. Particularly his smile. . . . What was it about his smile?

The answer struck her with an almost audible click, as if she had been probing clumsily at a lock with a hairpin and had finally struck the crucial spot. No—no, she thought, it can't be! But supposing it were. . . . Her mind raced wildly, picking up the pieces—the same bits of evidence she had considered earlier that day. But this time they clicked neatly into place, with no empty spaces to distort a damning picture of guilt.

The album slid unregarded to the floor as Laurie got to her feet. Moving like a robot, her dazed mind still molding her fantastic theory into shape, she went to get her coat. Duchess, dozing under the kitchen table, leaped up and began bounding up and down. Coats meant that people were going out, and sometimes they took her along.

Hastily Laurie scribbled a note and left it on the kitchen table, weighted down with a salt shaker. She considered the hopeful dog for a moment and then shook her head. There was no danger in the errand she planned now, no need for a guard dog, even if Duchess had qualified for that title. And there were practical difficulties as well.

"I'm sorry," she told Duchess. "I'd take you if I were driving, but I guess I'll have to walk. You'd run off and get lost."

With both cars out she had no alternative but to walk. She was in no mood to wait. Not only was she curious to discover whether her theory was really correct, but she was concerned about Lizzie. The amiable, dotty old lady seemed to feel that she had the situation well in hand, but her niece feared that this time Lizzie had raised demons that would not be easy to exorcise. If this new idea was right she might be able to nip the plot in the bud that very afternoon, before Lizzie got into more trouble.

But as she closed the door on Duchess's long, reproachful face, a thought occurred to her. It was worth looking, at any rate.

She was in luck. The big garage held another car, a rusty, aged Ford. She had thought Jeff might have some means of transportation; he wouldn't use the Lincoln for personal errands, and there were no buses in this rural area.

She found an extra set of keys, carefully labeled, in one of his dresser drawers. Laurie thanked heaven for his neatness. Now if the car would start . . .

It was worn on the outside but, like all Jeff's possessions, it did the job it was supposed to do. The engine started right away. Laurie drove out.

The snow had not yet begun to fall, but if she was any judge of weather it would before long. The clouds were the color of dark slate. In the sullen, threatening light the Wilson house looked like something out of a horror film, a dismal bastion of smug complacency and prejudice. Even if it's true, Laurie thought, I can't entirely blame her. She must feel like a trapped animal. Anything—anything!—to get away. They're all egotists at that age, the don't feel for other people—especially old people.

Wilson's truck was not there. With bad weather approaching, he would surely work until the last possible moment. His presence would not have deterred Laurie, however. He was a fat, stupid bully, and in her present mood she had no doubt of her ability to stand up to him.

She had brooded over the photo albums longer than she had realized. The girls were already home from school. When Mrs. Wilson opened the back door, Laurie saw Betsy at the table, smearing jam messily on a piece of bread. Mary Ella sat next to her.

Laurie pushed past Mrs. Wilson with scant ceremony.

"Where is Rachel?" she asked.

"Why, at her baby-sitting," Mrs. Wilson answered. "Miz Wade wanted to do some shopping before work, so she picked Rachel up at school. What's the girl done now?"

She wiped floury hands on her apron. Pinkly clean and scrubbed, they were big hands with thick fingers like uncooked sausages. Laurie pictured them clamped on Rachel's shoulders, shaking her till her slender neck arched in pain, and the image was so distasteful that she came to an abrupt decision. Perhaps she could handle this without involving Rachel after all.

"Why should you suppose Rachel has done anything?" she asked coolly. "Actually, it was Mary Ella I wanted to talk to, about—about some work she might do for me. Can we go to your room, Mary Ella?"

Mrs. Wilson looked as if she wanted to object; and indeed, Laurie's manner was less than courteous. But Laurie had counted, correctly, on the woman's desire to keep on good terms with the Morton family. She gave her daughter a grudging nod, and Mary Ella rose obediently and led the way to the back stairs.

Narrow and dark, they rose at a steep angle and opened onto the second-floor hall. Laurie looked around, trying to get the plan of the house clear in her mind. It was not complex: two bedrooms on each side of the hall, with a small bathroom at the front. The parents would have one of the front rooms, Laurie supposed. Baby Betsy, the pet, probably had a room of her own, but the Wilsons surely wouldn't waste space on the other girls. The fourth bedroom would be the "spare room." Her hunch was confirmed when Mary Ella, still mute, opened a nearby door, displaying a bleak, cheerless room with small windows. The walls were painted a dark, drab olive. A braided rug, in shades of blue and white, was the only attractive object, and Laurie knew it was a sign of economy, not aesthetic appreciation. The blue came from Mr. Wilsons' faded overalls, the white from his undershirts. The Wilsons wasted nothing. The fact that the result was pretty was purely accidental.

There were no curtains at the windows, only cheap paper shades. The spreads on the narrow beds were a bleached white cotton. The straight chair in front of the desk had obviously been designed to give the sitter a backache. A row of books stood on the top of the desk. They were all textbooks, except for a copy of the Bible. The single nonutilitarian object in the entire room was a sort of sampler on the wall, worked in violent red and somber black yarn. "The wages of sin are death," it assured the reader.

Laurie stood in the doorway looking around.

"If I had to live here, I'd cut my throat," she said.

The comment jarred Mary Ella out of her stolidity. She gave Laurie a startled glance.

Laurie closed the door. "Sit down, Mary Ella. Sit on the bed. I'll take the chair—for my sins."

Mary Ella obeyed, though not without a fearful glance at the door. Sitting on the bed was probably a sin. *Sitting* was probably a sin, in that house.

On the way upstairs Laurie had planned what she would say to Mary Ella in order to persuade the girl to tell her the truth. The sight of that horrid, sterile room affected her so strongly that she threw her speech out the window and said impulsively,

"I'd like to help you get away. Nobody should live like this. And it's worse for you. You're a reader, aren't you? You know there are other worlds out there."

Mary Ella's eyes remained fixed on her clasped hands, which rested genteelly on her lap.

"You borrowed books from Aunt Lizzie," Laurie went on. "You couldn't bring them home. Your father doesn't approve of reading for pleasure. But you could read there, in the woods, last summer. Rachel covered up for you; she picked nuts and berries enough for two. Mary Ella, what did you do in return—for Rachel?"

Mary Ella didn't stir. A squat, unresponsive lump, she continued to sit with folded hands and downcast eyes. Perhaps it was the very hopelessness of her pose that moved Laurie. It made her all the more determined to reach Mary Ella. Both girls were physically imprisoned, but this girl's mind and imagination had been walled in too. And that was the worst kind of tyranny, worse than stone walls and iron bars.

Laurie leaned forward and took the girl's limp hands in hers. "I will help you, Mary Ella. I can do it. Your parents won't dare interfere; they won't risk losing their lease. Nor, if I know them, will they turn down a chance to make money. I'll tell them I want to hire you to help with the housework. You can come every afternoon, and read. There's a good library at Idlewood. And when you're ready for college I'll lend you the money—coach you—help you get aid or a scholarship, whatever it takes."

It was like watching a statue come to life. The blaze of dawning hope in the girl's eyes almost made Laurie regret her reckless promise. Who do you think you are? she asked herself. God? Pygmalion?

"What do I have to d-d-d——" Mary Ella began.

"You don't have to do anything. I'll help you in any case. I promise. But Rachel is in bad trouble, Mary Ella. I want to help her too. So far nothing serious has happened, but if this goes on, someone is going to get hurt. You covered for her, didn't you? She could get out at night—down those back stairs—but she couldn't do it without your knowledge. Don't you see, he's using her, making her do wrong things.

She's still a minor; no one will hold her responsible. But he must be stopped."

"He's going to m-m-m-marry her."

"Maybe that's what he told her. But even if he would—even if he *could*, she's underage—would you really want her to marry a man like that? A man who would seduce a young girl and try to injure a harmless old lady who has always been good to him?"

As she spoke she realized that the ideas she was presenting were not new to Mary Ella. The girl was not stupid; in fact, she was probably a lot smarter than her older sister. But Rachel would have resisted the voice of reason and caution, and Mary Ella would have no choice but to support her. The alternative would have been for Mary Ella to betray Rachel to their parents.

"B-b-but what can I do?"

"Nothing. You've confirmed what I suspected. That was all I wanted you to do." Laurie stood up. "Maybe I can keep you girls out of this. I'll try. If there is trouble, you come to me, understand? Straight to me. Now tell me how to get to Mrs. Wade's house."

Mary Ella gave her directions. Emotion seethed in her pitifully homely face now and Laurie sensed, with some dismay, that part of the emotion was admiration for her. She felt like the unfortunate Chinese gentleman who, having saved a drowning man from the river, had found himself stuck with the rescuee for the rest of his life. She meant to keep the promises she had made, but how she was going to do it she did not know; like Scarlett O'Hara, she decided to think about that tomorrow. She started toward the door. Mary Ella tried to speak.

"B-b-b-be c-c-c——"

"Careful? I will, don't worry. I won't say anything to your mother."

"N-n-no! I m-m-mean. . . . I want to t-t-t——"

Laurie patted her on the shoulder.

"I'm in a terrible hurry, honey. I want to get this settled. We'll talk later, okay?"

When she reached the kitchen Mrs. Wilson was cutting out biscuits with the stolid efficiency of a machine. Laurie gave her a bright smile.

"Mary Ella says it's fine with her," she announced. "I'll come back and talk to you and your husband about it another time—tomorrow, maybe. I want to get home before it starts to snow."

Fine sleety flakes stung her face as she ran across the yard toward the car, but she scarcely noticed the threatening weather. It would have taken more than a little snow to stop her now. The chance of talking to Rachel privately was too good to miss. The situation was bad—in fact, it was a horrible mess—and a lot of people were going to be hurt before it was over. Yet Laurie's dominant feeling was one of relief. It could have been so much worse.

She had no trouble finding the Wade house. It was one of a group of cheap modern homes in one of the small subdivisions that had sprouted like mushrooms among the fields. She rang the bell. Through the flimsy walls she heard voices, male and female, raised in heated argument, and felt a stab of alarm until she realized it was the television set. So poor Rachel gorged herself on soap operas whenever she got the chance. Such shocking frivolities were undoubtedly forbidden at home. Laurie wondered how Mr. Wilson had been persuaded to expose Rachel to a household whose standards were so relaxed.

She was about to ring again when the door opened a crack. A wide blue eye appeared in the opening.

"I can't let anybody in," Rachel said.

"That's a very sensible rule, but it doesn't apply to me. No one could possibly object to your letting me in."

"I promised Miz Wade I wouldn't."

The door started to close. The opening was too narrow to admit Laurie's foot, and she assumed the door was on the chain. She spoke quickly.

"Rachel, I know all about it. Didn't you realize you were committing a crime?"

Rachel was no longer visible—even her eye had disappeared—but Laurie heard her quick intake of breath. For a moment nothing happened. Then the chain rattled and the door opened wide.

"I don't know what you mean," Rachel said.

For an instant even Laurie half believed her. The upturned, flower-fair face, the shining azure eyes, the cloudy aureole of hair . . . It's a good thing I'm not a man, Laurie thought cynically.

"Oh, yes, you know," she said firmly. "Let me in. We can't talk here." The girl continued to bar the door, and Laurie went on, "I don't blame you, Rachel. You're young, and he can be very persuasive. Maybe we can figure out some way of putting a stop to this without going to the police."

Alarm flared in the girl's face at the mention of the word. She stepped back. Laurie followed her into the house and closed the door.

She was in a tiny foyer with doors on two sides. Silently Rachel led the way into the room at the right—a living room, with an imitation fireplace on one wall. The cheaply built house, surely only a few years old, was already showing signs of wear, and if Rachel's duties included housecleaning she had not yet begun the day's chores. The wall-to-wall carpeting, an impractical cream color, was sadly spotted and stained. The furniture needed dusting. The floor was littered with toys and the coffee table was covered with magazines, most of them devoted to the intricacies of daytime TV. The house smelled faintly of spoiled food and of another odor Laurie could not immediately identify. Clearly, Mrs. Wade was what Aunt Ida would have called a slattern. But she was a cheerful slattern; for all its disorder the house had a warm, comfortable atmosphere quite unlike the cold neatness of the Wilson home.

"Where is the baby?" Laurie asked. She had to raise her voice to be heard over the TV drama.

"Asleep."

"He must be a darned good sleeper. Turn that off, Rachel, will you please?"

Rachel complied. When she turned to face Laurie she was more composed than the latter had expected, although her pretty mouth was not as pretty as usual.

"Did you mean that, about the police?"

"Now, Rachel, you can't be that naive," Laurie said, in mingled pity and exasperation. "I don't suppose he told you what he intended to do—"

"It was a joke!" Rachel wrung her slim hands. "I guess it wasn't a very nice joke, but—"

"It wasn't a joke. He wants the money."

"Only what's coming to him."

"So you do know that much."

Rachel's eyes fell. Her long, thick lashes were tremulous against her cheek.

She'll be all right, Laurie thought. There isn't a policeman or a judge in the state who'd believe anything evil about her. I don't believe it myself. But was I ever as stupidly trusting as she is? Oh, Lord, I suppose I was.

"I'll be honest with you, Rachel," she said. "I haven't decided what to do yet. I just figured this out a little while ago, and I'm still dazed. I would rather not go to the police. I never thought I entertained any of those corny old ideas about the family honor and the family name, but I guess I do. It will be a horrible shock to the aunts, to learn that one of their own flesh and blood . . . He hasn't done anything so far that would demand a criminal charge—except for trying to run over me, and he'd probably claim he only meant to frighten me."

She was talking to herself rather than to Rachel, trying to clarify her confused thoughts. Rachel watched her from under her lashes, her hands tightly clasped.

"The important thing," Laurie continued, "is to make sure he's stopped—that he can't ever profit from this situation. I can arrange that. . . . Or can I? I'll have to tell Aunt Lizzie the whole story. Damn, this is more complicated than I thought."

"I'll help you," Rachel said suddenly.

"What?" Laurie had almost forgotten the girl as she wrestled with her dilemma. "How can you help?"

"If I do, you'll have to promise not to tell Poppa," Rachel said.

"I don't want to tell him, but I don't know—"

"Please!" Rachel lifted her clasped hands as if in prayer. Her wide cornflower-blue eyes entreated. "I've got something you can use to keep him from hurting Miss Lizzie. It's a—a plan, like, that he wrote out, in his own handwriting. So if anything did happen to Miss Lizzie, they could prove he did it and then he wouldn't get the money. Once he knows you have the paper . . ."

"Hmmm." Laurie eyed the girl thoughtfully. "You aren't as naive as I thought. You're right, a person cannot profit from a crime. You really have such a thing—practically a signed confession?"

"Yes." Rachel nodded vigorously. "He wrote it down so I wouldn't forget what to do. Come with me and we'll get it right now."

"Where is it?"

A delicate rose-pink blush stained the girl's cheeks.

"In a place we had. A place where we used to meet and . . . I'll show you. It's not far."

"But—" Laurie caught the girl's arm as she started toward the door. "Rachel, we can't just walk out. What about the baby?"

"I'll run next door and ask Miz Filcher to come over for a few minutes. We can be back in half an hour, honest. And then," Rachel said, "you'll have the proof. He won't be able to hurt anybody."

She ran out.

Laurie tried to collect her wits. Obviously Rachel feared one thing above all else—that her parents would learn about her pathetic love affair. "A place where we used to meet, and . . ." No need for the girl to finish that sentence. Laurie didn't blame Rachel for being frightened, or for betraying her lover with such unattractive promptness. In Rachel's eyes, and in that of her parents, attempted murder was far less reprehensible than fornication. That's what Wilson would call it, along with a number of other forthright biblical nouns. Laurie shivered as she pictured Wilson's rage. He'd beat the girl half to death. No, she did not blame Rachel.

The girl was back almost at once, flushed and panting.

"Hurry," she begged, tugging at Laurie. "She's coming over as soon as she finishes peeling the potatoes. Let's go, right now."

"Are you sure—"

"She said she'd come. Please hurry. Please!"

They stepped out of the door into a cloud of white. The snow was coming fast and there was already a slick coating on the driveway. The bad weather gave an additional reason for haste.

"How far is it?" Laurie asked, as they got into the car.

"Only a few miles down the road. Turn right when I tell you."

The turn was into a woodland track, rutted and slippery. Laurie fought the wheel as the car skidded. When they had gone a short distance, Rachel directed her to turn off the track and stop in a small clearing. The girl jumped out.

"This way," she said. "It's not far."

Laurie got out of the car, feeling stiff and slow and elderly by comparison to Rachel's quicksilver movements. She was beginning to have doubts about getting out of the glade; the car had settled into its resting place with a cowlike stolidity and a squelch of mud. She comforted herself with the knowledge that she couldn't be too far from home. If worse came to worst, they could walk and someone could drive Rachel back to the Wades.

The snow clung to her eyelashes and blurred her

vision. Rachel was so far ahead that she was barely visible; the curtain of white flakes gave her slim figure an eerie look of semitransparency, and her cloud of pale-gold hair was the only bright spot in the gathering gloom.

There was a path of sorts. Tall pines leaned in overhead and cut off some of the snow, but there was enough of it on the ground to make walking treacherous. Laurie was about to shout at the agile little figure ahead and announce her intention of giving up for that day when Rachel stopped. Her face was pink with cold and her eyes danced. Of course, Laurie thought; she's relieved to have this almost over. She knew she was doing wrong. She just didn't know how to get herself out of it.

"We'd better come another time," Laurie said. "I don't think—"

"But we're there," Rachel said.

Laurie had been so intent on keeping her footing that she had given scant attention to her surroundings. Now she saw that the path had gradually descended until high banks closed in on either side. This must be an old streambed. The banks were rocky in some places and in others were thickly covered with tough wild vines, seemingly impenetrable, even in winter. Twists of honeysuckle, tough as wire, writhed over the corpses of the fallen trees they had strangled. The stark black-and-white landscape, the lowering gray sky suggested the setting for one of the more morbid Grimm fairy tales.

Rachel reached out a mittened hand. Laurie blinked. For a moment, to eyes blurred by moisture, it had seemed like magic. A black hole had appeared amid the tangled honeysuckle.

"A cave," she exclaimed.

"It's really big inside," Rachel said. "Come on. I'll show you."

Before Laurie could protest Rachel had dropped to her hands and knees and crawled into the hole. Her voice echoed hollowly: "Come oooooon. . . ."

229

Laurie had no intention of following.

"Get your paper and come back," she yelled. "We haven't got time to fool around. Hurry, before—"

She never finished the sentence. It was interrupted by a muffled crash and a shriek.

Sometime later, when she had been called upon to defend her decision, Laurie insisted that she had had no choice but to enter the cave. If Rachel had been injured, she might require immediate attention. At the time she didn't think so clearly. In fact, she didn't think at all; she simply responded to the wordless demand of that cry of pain.

After the first few feet the surface under her hands was rock, not dirt, and even in the darkness she sensed that the tunnel had opened up into wider spaces. She called the girl's name, and winced back as a thousand mocking echoes answered. Surely Rachel couldn't have gone much farther. . . .

The sudden flare of light was as startling as a blow. Laurie's eyes closed involuntarily. She did not see the rock fall, but she felt it, in a sharp burst of pain on the back of her head, before the blackness of unconsciousness engulfed her.

CHAPTER

12

"Stupid," Laurie told herself. "Dumb. Idiot. Fool."

She was calling herself names, but she wasn't doing it aloud because her mouth was filled with nasty wet cloth. Her wrists were tied behind her, and her feet were also bound. She was so cold her teeth would have chattered if they had had room to do so. Someone had removed most of her clothes. The chill, harsh stone of the cave floor scraped her bare back as she wriggled, trying to free herself. It wasn't as cold inside as it had been out in the open air, but it was cold enough.

The bonds that held her were not rope or wire; they felt like soft cloth, but they did what they were designed to do, and the fact that they were fairly comfortable, even when she strained against them, was not reassuring. Quite the reverse. They confirmed a theory she had formulated as soon as she woke up to find herself half naked and half frozen. Once the freezing process was complete the bonds would be removed, leaving no telltale marks, and she would be dumped somewhere in the woods—fully clothed, of course—a victim of exposure and her own folly.

How had he known they were coming to the cave? Rachel might have telephoned him when she ran next door to ask the neighbor to watch the baby, but Laurie didn't think the girl had had time for that.

At that point in her reflections she remembered the note she had left on the kitchen table. "Stupid" was too feeble a word. Not only had she mentioned that she was going to the Wilsons, but she had added: "I think I've got it!" She couldn't wait to rub it in. . . . Why hadn't she had the elementary common sense to realize that a note could be read by someone other than the person it was addressed to?

Because she was stupid. Because she had never really believed he meant to harm any of them, even Aunt Lizzie. There were other ways of getting what he wanted—safer ways that did not necessitate murder. Theoretically anyone was capable of killing, given the proper provocation—in self-defense, or to protect a loved one. But to kill for money—surely that presupposed a degree of emotional sickness that should have been visible to a smart observer—such as herself. He didn't seem like that kind of person.

The only sound she could produce was a groan, so she groaned, and the mocking darkness moaned back at her in a hundred voices. To think that she had called Rachel naive!

Her last, faint hope of survival was based on that very naiveté of Rachel's. She couldn't believe that Rachel had deliberately led her into the clutches of a killer. Nor was it likely that he would hurt Rachel. He must believe the girl to be thoroughly under his spell, and he wouldn't want to risk too many "accidents." There was a chance that he had simply sent Rachel back to her baby-sitting, trusting that a combination of fear and love would keep the girl quiet. But she might not keep quiet. She had been visibly shaken by Laurie's mention of the police. If the note was found . . . if they went to the Wilsons and then to Mrs. Wade's, following her trail . . . if they could force Rachel to talk. . . .

If she didn't freeze to death first, and if *he* didn't come back to finish the job he had begun. . . . Too many ifs for comfort.

Lizzie had been right all along. There were inhuman things in the dark woods—the misshapen, malevolent goblins of greed and madness. Too bad Lizzie had not responded to temptation like her namesake in the poem. "No, their offers should not charm us; Their evil gifts would harm us." The moral was clear: people who messed around with the fairies got in trouble. Trouble was definitely what she was in, thanks to Lizzie's meddling. Laura and Lizzie, two little girls victimized by goblins. "Fruits like honey to the throat, But poison in the blood. . . ." Odd, how readily the words came back to her after all those years.

A sound penetrated her fading consciousness, and she came back to her senses with a start of terror. Her thoughts had been wandering as her body sank into the deadly, ultimate sleep of cold. There was no point in conjuring up imaginary nightmares, the real situation was nightmarish enough; and no point in waiting supinely for death. Maybe she could find a jagged rock or a piece of glass and cut through her bonds. Heroines in thrillers managed to do things like that.

Before she could put this brilliant scheme into execution the sound came again, and this time she was alert enough to understand what it meant. She forgot she had decided to be a heroine and tried to shrink into the smallest possible space.

In that instant, as the unseen person inched closer, her mind played one of the tricks minds play under stress. She remembered the odorous, messy Wade house where Rachel had been baby-sitting, and she identified the vagrant smell that had been part of the general aroma of sloppy housekeeping.

Until that moment she had believed she had fitted all the pieces of the puzzle into their proper places. This revelation revealed new gaps whose existence she had not suspected and supplied the missing pieces. She would have screamed then, if she had been able to do so.

Her sense of hearing, magnified by the absence of sight, told her that the person was now in the cave, so close she could hear his heavy breathing. When the flashlight flared she closed her eyes; but in the dazzle she had caught a glimpse of a face—the face she had once feared, and now hoped to see. Was it too late? Had the girl come with him?

"Oh, my God, I was afraid. . . . Laurie, darling. . . ." Jeff's voice, harsh with fear, Jeff's hands, pulling the cloth from her mouth.

He gathered her up into his arms, holding her so tightly she couldn't breathe or talk. The warmth of his body against her chilled flesh felt heavenly, but Laurie fought to free her face from the muffling folds of his wool jacket. Why didn't the idiot untie her?

"Don't," she croaked. "Don't do that—"

"It's all right," Jeff muttered. "You're all right now. I'll get you out of here, love. Thank God I was in time."

Laurie considered trying to bite him, but abandoned the idea. His jacket was too thick. She had enough fragments of cloth clogging her tongue as it was. "Untie me," she mumbled. "Quick, quick."

"Right." He lowered her gently to the floor and began working on the knots that bound her wrists. Laurie held herself still with an effort. She wanted to squirm and yell. Her mouth felt as dry as flannel. A thread was caught between two teeth, and the minor irritation almost drove her frantic.

The flashlight, resting on the ground, gave her her first sight of the cave. The rough, uneven walls arched up into darkness. From her prostrate position Laurie could see very little, but what she saw brought a wry smile to her lips. A small Coleman stove, kitchen utensils, and canned goods stored in a wooden crate; a heap of gaudy pillows, a box fitted up as a dressing table, with mirror and piles of cosmetics. It was a child's playhouse, furnished with pilfered or scavenged scraps—a place for make-believe, for pretending, for the fairy-tale fantasies of an immature mind playing at romance.

She was unable to enjoy the sad, sardonic humor of the setting because of the fear that made her numbed nerves tingle. The flashlight beam failed to illumine the mouth of the cave and Jeff's agitated panting drowned out lesser sounds, but she could have sworn someone was coming. The sense of an ·inimical, imminent presence was overwhelming.

"Hurry," she gasped.

As she spoke her hands fell free and Jeff shifted position to work on the cloth that fastened her ankles. "Hurry," she said again. "We've got to get out of here before—"

"Sweetheart, don't worry," Jeff said. "I'm here. I'll take care of you. I love you—"

"Oh, shut up," Laurie exclaimed. "Shut up, Jeff."

It was too late. Her instincts had not been wrong. Someone was coming. . . . No. Someone was already there, and had heard. In the dim, remote boundary of the light she saw a face and knew it—the same face she had seen outside Jeff's window in the dark of midnight.

No wonder she hadn't recognized it. Jealous rage distorted the features and gave the skin a livid flush. It scarcely resembled a human face, much less that of a lovely young girl. But I should have identified the hair, Laurie thought. What was she wearing that night, to give the impression of gauzy lavender wings? Some exotic negligee ordered for her by an infatuated lover? Or a costume, for the further be-guilement of poor Aunt Lizzie?

The scream she tried to utter stuck in her throat, but her convulsive movement made Jeff look up. He tried to turn. His position was too awkward and

Rachel was too quick. The blade of the knife burned in the light before it was buried in his upflung arm. The two bodies went down together, in a tangled, writhing mass.

Laurie scratched frantically at the knots holding her feet immobile, but her hands were so numb with cold they refused to obey her will. One of the most horrifying aspects of the struggle was its silence. Jeff's injury and Rachel's insane fury made them equals in strength, so that they lay almost motionless and neither had spoken or cried out. Then Jeff's voice rose in a hoarse, urgent shout. "Run! Quick, before she—"

The speech ended in a grunt and a horrible soggy thud as his head hit the floor.

Kneeling over him, her tumbled hair masking her face, Rachel remained unmoving for a few moments. Then she flung her head back. Her hair lifted like a pale, soaring flame before it settled around her shoulders. Its silky fairness framed a face as coldly beautiful as that of Andersen's Ice Queen. Very slowly, still on her knees, she turned until she was facing Laurie.

Laurie had not prayed aloud since childhood. All she could remember at this moment was "Now I lay me down to sleep," and that didn't seem particularly appropriate. At least she hoped it would not prove to be appropriate. But she felt like praying. She had never seen anything, on or off the screen, that frightened her as much as Rachel's face.

She continued to pick at the knots but she knew she wasn't making any progress. Jeff lay still, his eyes closed, a trickle of dark blood puddling out from his arm. Laurie swallowed, cleared her throat, and screamed.

She did it to relieve her feelings, not because she expected a response. When a voice answered, she almost toppled over in sheer surprise.

"Laurie! Laurie, where are you?"

"Here! Hurry! Help!"

Rachel, caught in the hypnotic web of her deadly intent, appeared not to have heard the exchange, but when a heavy body forced itself into the cave she was jarred out of her reverie. She got to her feet in one smooth movement. She held the knife in her right hand, and even in her absorption in her own prospects of survival Laurie was sickened at the sight of the dark, wet blade.

"He-e-elp!" she shrieked.

"I hear you, I hear you," her rescuer said irritably. "Stop yelling. The echoes in this place are fierce." He rose cautiously to his feet.

"Hi there, Rachel," he said pleasantly. "Give Uncle Doug the knife, okay?"

Rachel backed away. Her foot struck the pathetic makeshift toilet table. The mirror crashed to the floor.

"Now see what you've done," Doug said. "Seven years' bad luck. Give me the nasty knife before you hurt yourself."

He put out his hand. Rachel slashed at it. The movement was almost careless—the petulant slap of an angry child, rejecting authority—but a dark line sprang up across Doug's palm and blood began to drip from his fingers. He didn't look at it, or lower his hand.

"Now, now, mustn't do that." Out of the corner of his mouth he added, in a lower voice, "Am-scray, sis. What are you hanging around here for?"

"I can't walk!"

"Hop, then. Or crawl or wriggle or squirm. Just move. Don't worry about your clothes, Uncle Ned's waiting. Good thing it's him and not Ida. Wouldn't she be shocked. . . ." In the same quiet voice he went on, "Okay, Rachel, time to go. Want to ride in my nice pretty car? Maybe you'd like to drive. You're a good little driver, aren't you?"

He had been slowly inching forward, so imperceptibly that Laurie had not noticed until she realized he stood between her and the girl. No dream lover of her wildest fantasies had ever looked as good to her as Doug did then, his hair wet with melting snow, his tall body tense despite its appearance of relaxed confidence. She knew she was safe now. The way to the exit was open. She started moving toward it, but she didn't crawl into the tunnel until she had seen Rachel drop the knife and collapse, sobbing, into Doug's waiting arms.

II

"It does seem unfair," Doug remarked, "that you haven't even caught a cold."

"Cold! I feel as if I'd died and gone to. . . ." Laurie caught the eye of her eldest aunt and omitted the last word.

She was swathed in blankets clear up to the chin. They weighed her weary body down so she couldn't even wriggle. She was in her own white bed and the lights shone serenely on the familiar furniture—the ruffled shades, the Beatrix Potter prints, the rows of brightly bound fairy tales in the bookcases.

Uncle Ned had forgotten to take off his red knit cap. The pom-pom nodded absurdly as he leaned over to pat the place where Laurie's hand might have rested if she could have gotten it out from under the blankets.

"Everyting's all right now," he said. "You're fine."

"I'm fine," Laurie agreed.

"Good. I'm going to feed Duchess." He stood up. "Get some sleep," he said. "Dear."

He was almost out of the room before Laurie realized what he had said.

"Uncle Ned . . . give Duchess a big fat bone for me, will you?"

"Well, she deserves it," her uncle said calmly. "Might not have found that hole in time without her."

The door closed quietly behind him.

"You know," Doug said, "he is the most uncanny character in this whole scenario. Out of this world."

"Shut up," Laurie said. Uncle Ned had called her "dear." In any other man, the emotion that had produced that word would have expressed itself in extravagant endearments and embraces.

"Ned suffered in the war," Ida said. "He has never been the same since."

"I like him the way he is," Laurie said. She added, "I like all of you the way you are."

They sat alongside the bed, all in a row, like spectators at a play. Ida had selected a straight chair. She sat bolt upright, her hands folded. Her face was a mask of wrinkles and her eyes were sunken, but they had a peaceful look Laurie had not seen for some time.

Aunt Lizzie was still wearing the peasant blouse and embroidered skirt. Fake jewels festooned her ample bosom. Her hair was agitated and her eyes avoided Laurie's.

"Oh," she murmured, "don't you think we might have a little snack? The stress of the day . . . And dinner will be late, I have not had the opportunity to—"

"Not now, Aunt Lizzie," Doug said. "We have a few things to discuss first."

He sat on a footstool, his long legs bent, his knees absurdly elevated. Laurie smiled at him. "My heroic rescuer," she said.

Doug grinned. "Don't bother soothing my male ego. You can brag all you like, you're entitled. This is the last scene and you get to play the detective. Tell us, O great sleuth, how you figured it out—and almost got yourself killed."

"Just good old feminine intuition," Laurie said. "I couldn't have proved anything. Luckily Rachel didn't know that. What did you find out from the bookstore in Baltimore?"

"I found out that Jefferson Banes had bought

those figurines. The proprietor didn't know his name but she remembered *him* very well."

"That was careless of him," Laurie exclaimed. "He should have known we might trace them to him."

"Sure he knew. Why do you suppose he was so anxious to get rid of the snapshots? But I doubt that he had any scheme in mind when he bought the figures, or even when he took the pictures. It did begin as a joke, just as the kids said."

"Not the kids, just Rachel," Laurie said. "With some help from Baby Betsy, who is going to turn out to be a real menace someday. Why is it we can't think of a golden-haired infant as a monster? And I'll never believe Rachel meant it as a joke."

"You're rambling," Doug said. "Start from the beginning."

"At the beginning I suspected you," Laurie said, and had the mean satisfaction of seeing Doug's jaw drop and his eyes widen. "You'd be suprised what a solid case I built up. I even wondered if you were really who you said you were. I hadn't seen you for a long time, and I didn't recognize you at the airport, and—"

"How absurd," Ida said crisply. "Did you suppose we would not know our own nephew?"

"I realized that, eventually," Laurie said. "But—"

"Don't go on," Doug groaned. "I don't want to hear any more about that part of your brilliant deductions."

Laurie decided she had better not go on. To justify her suspicions by explaining that she had never felt for Doug as a sister ought to feel would sound . . . It might be misunderstood.

"Didn't you suspect me?" she asked.

"Not for an instant."

"I think that's an insult."

"Forget it," Doug said. "When did you realize that my pure nature and innocent face made your foul suspicions impossible?"

"Not until I was looking at the photo album and

realized that Jeff looked astonishingly like Uncle Ned. The same high cheekbones and long nose, the same smile. I'd have seen it much sooner, only . . ."

"Age changes people," Ida said drily. "You were not to blame for failing to see the resemblance, Laura. You did not know us when we were young. Your mother resembles her father, not the Mortons. But that I should not have seen it . . . Perhaps I did. That dreadful subconscious mind you young people are always talking about—I liked him without knowing why. Without wanting to know why."

"He was very likable," Laurie said gently. "I'm sure he was telling the truth when he said it wasn't his idea to hurt Aunt Lizzie. It was Rachel's. She was responsible for all of it—the music, the lights in the woods, even the car, that night it almost hit me. She was driving it. She had stolen the keys from Jeff."

"Why did he come here, then?" Ida demanded. "Why should he seek us out unless—"

"He wanted money," Laurie said. "He admitted that. And it wasn't hard for him to find out who he really was. Modern psychologists feel that adopted children have the right to learn about their natural parents. I guess it's a good idea, generally. Not many cases turn out like this one.

"In the beginning Jeff was motivated by normal, understandable curiosity: Who was my natural mother? Why did she give me up? But that last question can lead to considerable resentment—even to hate. Jeff's adoptive parents died years ago, leaving him almost nothing. When he traced you and learned that there was a lot of money in the family . . . Well, he decided you owed him."

"We did," Ida said.

"Maybe so, I can't argue that. But the method he chose. . . . He meant, I think—though he never would have admitted it—to indulge in a little blackmail. You'd have paid it, wouldn't you?"

"I don't like that word," Lizzie complained, wrinkling her brows. "Naturally we would have given the dear boy—that is to say, he was a dear boy, if it had not been for this unfortunate—"

"I understand," Laurie said. "But I'm afraid he didn't. He didn't realize that you would have acknowledged him joyfully and shared ungrudgingly, especially after he had earned your affection and trust. It's such a tragedy, when you think how it could have been—comfort and security and love for all of you. All lost, because of his weakness."

"That's water over the dam now," Doug said. "Go on."

"I know. I just can't help regretting. . . . Well, anyway, after I spotted the resemblance I realized that Jeff might be—er—related to the family. And if he was, then he had a motive. I had always known he had the means and the opportunity to play the tricks on Aunt Lizzie, but I had never considered him a serious suspect because I couldn't figure out why he would do such things. The only thing he couldn't have done was make that telephone call, and I had already realized that the villian, whoever he was, must have enlisted some girl to do that for him—"

"He!" Doug exclaimed, in pretended outrage. "So naturally you thought of me—the notorious Don Juan, the Casanova of the architectural profession."

"Rachel thought you were pretty cute," Laurie snapped. "I saw the way she looked at you. And how about Sherri? Not to mention Vi, and heaven knows how many other—"

"Vi is my real dream girl," Doug said. "I'm planning to let her support me with the profits from her disreputable trade while I pretend to set up an office."

Laurie didn't have the heart to continue the badinage. She had been skirting around the core of the solution, knowing how it was going to hurt; but sooner or later the words would have to be said. The aunts knew what was coming. Both sat staring down at their tightly clasped hands. For once in their lives they shared a common emotion.

Laurie took a deep breath and plunged in.

"Jeff could have proved the—er—relationship," she said. "I'm not sure how . . . Don't they take fingerprints, or footprints, or both, at hospitals?"

Ida cleared her throat. She did not look at her sister, who was pleating the fabric of her skirt with shaking fingers.

"Papers were signed," she said steadily. "The proof did exist, yes."

"Then Jeff had a legal claim, assuming there was no will that specifically cut him out. I haven't checked with a lawyer, but I suspect Jeff would be considered the nearest heir, superseding Doug and me. Illegitimacy is no bar to inheritance these days."

Lizzie was crimson from throat to forehead. The evil word had been uttered. Relieved that it was over, Laurie hurried on.

"It was at this point that I went completely astray. I assumed Jeff had seduced poor innocent Rachel and forced her to help him. Actually it was the other way around.

"I don't know how you explain a person like Rachel. Psychiatry will point triumphantly to her dreadful, sterile home life, the suppression of all her natural instincts. When she saw a way out she grabbed at it. I can't blame her for that. Jeff did promise to marry her. He would have promised anything, given her anything." Laurie turned a critical eye on her brother, who was looking very pensive. "You can understand that, can't you?" she demanded.

"Oh, yes," Doug murmured. "Well—almost anything. The girl has a certain natural . . ." He glanced at his aunts, and refrained from finishing the sentence.

"Hmph," Laurie said. "Jeff certainly felt it; but he had nothing to offer her. He had no source of income, no job except this one, and they couldn't have stayed here. Her father would have raised Cain, taken her back, by force or by law. In order to be together they would have had to run away to another state, and live in poverty. Rachel might have been willing to do that to escape her parents; but then Jeff told her the truth about himself, and she saw a way to gain a fortune. It must have been a dazzling temptation—herself the mistress of Idlewood, with a handsome, indulgent husband, pretty clothes, jewels, all the things a young girl dreams of. And the cost was so small—the life of one old lady who was bound to die soon anyway.

"When Aunt Lizzie met the girls in the woods last fall, Rachel and Jeff were already involved. It was Mary Ella's turn to pick millions of berries, so that the lovers could meet in their cozy cave. That was when Rachel got her brilliant inspiration—and I have to admit it was clever. She didn't want to attack Aunt Lizzie directly. She knew that if there was the slightest hint of foul play Jeff couldn't claim his rights to the estate without becoming a suspect. Nor could she arrange a convincing accident at that time of year. The weather was mild; hikers, nature lovers, hunters were roaming the woods. But if she could set up a situation whereby Aunt Lizzie could be lured out of the house during the winter months. . . .

"Betsy's chatter about fairies may have suggested the idea, but I suspect it was that book of Conan Doyle's that allowed Rachel to develop her scheme fully. Mary Ella was borrowing books from Lizzie, remember? If she mentioned the story to Rachel—the parallels are really too close to be coincidental. The girls in *The Coming of the Fairies* played their tricks for the fun of it, but Rachel saw how the same idea could be used to trap Aunt Lizzie. She persuaded Jeff to take those photographs. According to him, she told him she wanted them for her little sister. Maybe he believed her; people can be pretty dumb when they're in love. When he realized what she was doing he tried to stop her. There is some evidence to substantiate that claim; he did try to keep an eye on Aunt Lizzie after it dawned on him she could come to harm chasing fairies. But he couldn't bring himself to betray Rachel, not to the police, nor to her parents."

"I don't know that I can blame him for that," Doug said thoughtfully.

"Oh, nobody can blame anybody for anything these days," Laurie said rudely. "I'm tired of finding excuses for crooks and criminals. Rachel is deformed. I know she had a wretched life, but so do lots of other people who don't see the murder of a harmless old woman as the key to the prison door."

"I never thought she would do those things," Lizzie murmured.

"Who would? We're all suckers for a pretty face. Even after she knocked me on the head and left me in the cave to die of exposure I didn't suspect her. When I heard Jeff in the tunnel I was sure he had come to finish me off. Then all of a sudden I remembered something—a particular smell I had noticed in that house where Rachel was baby-sitting."

"I am surprised you could isolate a single odor," said Ida, her long nose lifted fastidiously. "I am told that Mrs. Wade is a very poor housekeeper."

"Even a poor housekeeper wouldn't leave her stove turned on without making sure it was lit. That was what I smelled—gas. There were stories in the newspapers a few years ago about a baby-sitter who used to hold the child over the gas jet for a few minutes, just long enough to stupefy it so it wouldn't bother her while she was watching TV."

"Good Lord!" Doug's face hardened. Laurie was pleased to observe that this revelation had removed some of the glamour that still clung to his opinion of Rachel. "You mean she—"

"I wondered," Laurie said, "why the baby was so quiet. Rachel not only had all night for her activities, she had all afternoon and evening too. If the baby had started yelling while she was out, the neighbors might have heard it and come to investigate. Those houses are built of cardboard. Rachel did a lot of stupid things and took a lot of chances; she's too young to be a very well organized criminal. But that was one risk she didn't take. She gassed the baby."

"Good Lord," Doug repeated. "What's going to happen to that girl?"

The two old ladies exchanged glances. Then Ida said, "She will receive the best possible care, Douglas. I assure you of that. I have already spoken with Mr. and Mrs. Wilson. They were only too happy to have us take responsibility."

"I'll bet," Doug said. "Wilson is probably obliterating Rachel's name from the family Bible right now."

" 'If thy right hand offend thee, cut it off,' " Laurie agreed. "In a way this might be the best thing for Rachel. I'm not enthusiastic about psychiatric hospitals, but it's the girl's only chance. A couple of years from now she'll be eighteen, old enough to be on her own. She may be one of those people who resorts to crime only when they can't get what they want any other way. With a face and figure like hers, Rachel shouldn't have any problems. No. She's getting off easy. It's Jeff I feel sorry for."

"Oh, do you?" Doug gave her a hostile stare.

"Well, he's less culpable than Rachel. I'm sure he did try to stop her. Remember that night when you were all so strangely sleepy? Jeff drugged the after-dinner coffee. He was getting desperate; he couldn't watch Aunt Lizzie all the time, and that way he made sure she would sleep through the night and not go wandering in the woods. I was out with Hermann, so I didn't get any of the coffee."

"I wondered about that," Doug admitted. "And of

course Jeff was the only one who could have doctored the coffee. In fact, he was my prime suspect all along. I'm still not convinced he isn't passing the buck to Rachel."

"You're prejudiced," Laurie said indignantly.

Doug's brown eyes met hers, and she was surprised to feel herself blushing. At least it felt like a blush, though she was so warm she couldn't be sure.

"Jeff saved my life," she went on. "He led you to me—"

"Well, I persuaded him a little," Doug murmured.

"It was most exciting," Lizzie said brightly. "Just like those criminal dramas on television. Douglas took poor Jefferson by his collar and literally lifted him off the floor. However, Douglas, I must say that your language was not quite the thing. Mr. Kojak *never* used words like those, even when he was interrogating a psychopathic mass murderer."

"Auntie, I was upset," Doug said apologetically. "When I found out Jeff had bought those figurines I came tearing back here. The roads were getting slippery, so I couldn't make good time; but it gave me a chance to think, and I realized that Rachel must be involved. Auntie had insisted all along that she got the photos from the Wilson girls. That meant Rachel. Jeff wouldn't have used Betsy; a child that age couldn't be trusted to keep her mouth shut. And Mary Ella wasn't his type. So when I read that stupid, boastful note of yours, Laurie, I started to get a little worried. You had left it on the table, where anybody could have read it, and if Jeff thought you were closing in on him. . . . But I didn't get really scared till I had gone to the Wilsons and talked to Mary Ella. What did you do to that kid, hypnotize her? She spilled the whole story to me, right in front of her parents, she was so worried about you."

"I told her I'd help her get away," Laurie said. "I meant it, too."

"You should. You owe her. I told Wilson I'd beat
247

the daylights out of him if he laid a hand on her, but there are other methods of torture, and after he has recovered from his initial rage against Rachel he won't spare Mary Ella. She's known for some time that Rachel wasn't quite right. She said she tried to warn you."

"So that's what she was trying to say," Laurie exclaimed. "I was in a hurry, and that awful stutter—"

"We'll take care of her," Doug promised. "Anyhow, I went tearing over to the Wades', looking for you. Kicked the door in—"

"Doug, you didn't!"

"Wasn't hard. Cheap lock. All I found was one groggy baby badly in need changing. I did not oblige, I'm sorry to say, but I got one of the neighbors to come over. Told her it was an emergency. It was."

"Rachel told me she had asked the woman next door to come in," Laurie said. "I should have known she was a liar."

"It's just as well for that smelly infant that we removed his sitter," Doug said. "She wasn't exactly improving his chances of living to a ripe old age. Anyhow, by that time I was frantic. Nobody knew where you were; your trail ended at the Wades'. So I came back here. I will say," Doug admitted grudgingly, "that when I explained the situation, Jeff didn't hesitate. He thought Rachel might have taken you to the cave. It was the only place where she could be sure of privacy. He led us there—Uncle Ned and me—but he was in such a hurry we lost him in the snow and dark and we couldn't find the cave entrance until you screamed and good old Duchess went burrowing into the bank."

"It was too close for comfort," Laurie said, with a reminiscent shiver. "Where was Rachel all this time?"

"She'd been a busy little bee. First she got the car keys from your pocket and drove the car deeper into the woods. He had taught her to drive—among other things—last fall. Then she went looking for him. Do

248

you realize how close all these places are to Idlewood, especially if you know the shortcuts through the woods? Rachel knew them well. She was not very coherent about the next part, but I gather she was outside while Jeff and I were having our little discussion about your possible whereabouts. She went tearing back through the woods and got there about the same time he did. I don't know what she had in mind. I doubt that she knew herself. But when she caught you and Jeff making out—"

"Douglas," Ida exclaimed. "Please don't be vulgar."

"I tried to shut him up," Laurie said. "I was afraid she might overhear. She was crazy with jealousy. That's why she tried to run me down the other night. She knew it was me, all right. The funny thing is, I don't think Jeff was in love with me, not really."

"You aren't that closely related," Doug said coldly. "Anyway, what difference does a spot of incest make?"

"Don't be vulgar," Laurie said, anticipating Ida's comment. "I admit I found him very attractive. Any woman would. But I didn't fall for him. I'm sorry for him, though. What's going to happen to him now?"

"You could wait for him while he's in stir," Doug suggested.

"Now, Douglas," Ida said. "There is no question of prison, thank goodness. The police had to be brought in, of course, but they know only that that unfortunate girl had become infatuated with Jefferson, and had quarreled with him. Thanks to Ned's promptness in removing Laurie from the scene, the rest of the story need never come out. Rachel is incoherent and Jefferson has every reason to remain silent. He will not be charged. He will leave this part of the country and never return." Her lips twisted, as if in a brief spasm of pain, but she went on in a steady voice. "Tomorrow, Elizabeth will see our lawyer and make the will she ought to have made years ago."

"I don't want to make a will," Lizzie said rebelliously. "Douglas and Laura will have the money eventually, so what difference—"

"You will do as you're told," Doug said. "And I'll be on hand to make sure you behave yourself from now on. I'm opening an office in Frederick."

"How nice," Lizzie said, beaming.

"A wise decision," Ida remarked.

"Are you crazy?" Laurie demanded.

"Not yet," Doug said. "But in a few years, if Aunt Lizzie keeps on the way she's been going. . . ."

Lizzie hoisted herself out of her chair. Her lower lip tried to express hurt indignation, but she was so pleased she couldn't help smiling.

"Douglas, you are such a tease. I must see about dinner now, or we'll never eat tonight. In the meantime, what about a little nibble of something, and a hot cup of tea for our sick girlie?"

She trotted out, still talking to herself.

Laurie looked at her brother, who was studying his bandaged hand with unnecessary concentration. She knew why he had made his decision. With Jeff gone, the old people would be alone. Someone had to be there. She realized, with considerable astonishment, that the idea was not without its attractions. Mary Ella needed and deserved attention; it would be exciting to help that thwarted character and mind develop. No reason why she couldn't write her thesis here, as Aunt Ida had suggested. With Herrrrrman under control and Doug livening the place up. . . .

Doug cleared his throat.

"Now that Lizzie's gone we can finish this," he said. "I can't talk to her without screaming; her habit of wriggling out from under questions drives me up the wall. How much of this do you suppose she had figured out?"

"You can't describe Aunt Lizzie's thought processes," Laurie said. "They're too weird. She's like a medieval theologian; she can believe two contradictory things at the same time. And she's so darned innocent she'd never believe anyone meant to harm her. Especially her own son—"

"Her son?" Ida turned to stare at her. "My dear Laura—Douglas—have you been under the impression that Jefferson is Elizabeth's son?"

"Yes," Laurie said in surprise. "Certainly I did. That was the whole point of the plot—that Jeff would have inherited instead of us because we're only Aunt Lizzie's great-niece and -nephew, while Jeff—"

"No, no." Ida shook her head. "I cannot allow you to remain under that misapprehension. It would be unjust. Jefferson is not Elizabeth's son. He is her nephew."

Both auditors were struck dumb. Laurie knew, from Doug's bemused expression, that he was thinking the same thing she was. Uncle Ned?

Her aunt's face gave her the clue. Ida's cheeks might be a little redder than usual, but there was no contrition, no shame in her face. She sat very straight, her hands in her lap, and met Laurie's astonished gaze without avoidance.

Thirty years ago, Laurie thought. Thirty years, more or less—she had never known Jeff's precise age. . . . Ida would have been in her mid-forties. A susceptible age, she had heard. And that would explain why stern old Great-grandfather Morton had cut his erring daughter out of his will.

"It was just after the war," Ida said. "He was an officer, stationed nearby. He was married, with a family. I knew that from the start."

Her lips closed. So far as she was concerned, that was the whole story. There would be no explanations and no excuses, no regret, no expression of suffering or loss. That was not the Morton style. Nor was it necessary for her to go into such details. Laurie could imagine what it must have been like for her. A sudden overmastering passion, at an age when she had probably thought herself safe from such weakness—and the unexpected, catastrophic result. She would not have told her lover, not Ida. But she had to confide in her family because she had no means of her own. There was no alternative in those days but to bear the child; and no alternative, for a Morton, but to give it up for adoption. What else could she have done, even if she had wanted to defy the traditions that had molded her—penniless, middle-aged, unemployable?

Laurie struggled furiously and managed to get one hand out from under the blankets. She laid it on her aunt's folded hands and squeezed hard.

"Oh, my dear," she said.

"You need not feel sorry for me," Ida said. "There were compensations. . . . The basic point of your argument is not altered by this, you understand. If Elizabeth had predeceased me, the estate would have been divided between your Uncle Ned and myself, since Elizabeth has always refused to make a will. My portion, and probably Ned's as well, would have passed to Jefferson in due time. Or," she added, "before my due time, if that perverse young woman had decided not to wait."

"You're a wonder, Aunt Ida," Doug said. "Have I mentioned lately that I love you passionately?" He leaned over to give her a resounding kiss on the cheek. "Now I'm going down to help Aunt Lizzie. Laurie, could I talk you into a little—er—sherry?"

"I'd love it," Laurie said.

"How tactful he is," Ida said, after Doug had gone. "He wishes to spare me embarrassment."

"You're not embarrassed, though, are you?"

"No," Ida said. "It was all so long ago. And frankly, now that it is out in the open, I am actually relieved. You understand, I would not care to have the entire neighborhood know; but I could endure even that with equanimity so long as you and Douglas do not think less of me."

"You know how we feel."

"Yes. And I thank you. I ought to have trusted you both, but in all sincerity, Laura, it never for a

252

moment occurred to me that there could be the remotest connection between my youthful folly and the present situation."

"No reason why it should have occurred to you," Laurie assured her. "It is a wild, far-out plot, Aunt. I'm only sorry he turned out not to be . . ."

"A dutiful son?" Her aunt's lips curved in an ironic smile. "My dear girl, let's not pretend to be sentimental. I'm really too old to become a mother. And— you must know this—you and Douglas are very dear to me. No other relationship could alter that."

"Doug is nice, isn't he? You know, Aunt Ida, when I realized that Jeff was the guilty party, I was actually relieved. I had been so afraid it might be Doug. I didn't realize how fond I was of him until I suspected him. I've been thinking—maybe I'll do my dissertation here. Doug and I could get an apartment in Frederick, and—"

"An apartment!" If she had suggested entering a bordello her aunt's horror could hardly have been greater. "Out of the question, Laura. You can stay at Idlewood, with us."

"Auntie, I love you all, but I'm not sure I can live with you. I'd get fat on Aunt Lizzie's cooking and you'd worry if I stayed up late studying and Uncle Ned would roust me out at dawn to go bird-watching, and—"

"And I would interfere with your social life." Her aunt smiled ruefully. "I understand, Laura. I have not completely forgotten what it is like to be young. Very well. I can see why you might prefer to be independent, but for you and Douglas to live together would be . . . You cannot do it!"

"I don't see why not. It's silly for us to have two places, when we could share expenses."

"Oh, dear." Ida sighed. "I suppose I must tell you. Anna should have done so years ago, but she was always lax about her duty, and I never felt I had the right to interfere. However, I have no choice now.

My dear Laura, you cannot live with Douglas because it would be improper. He is not your brother."

"What?" Of all the shocks she had had that day, this hit Laurie the hardest. She fought free of the covers and sat upright. "What did you say?"

"He was adopted," Ida explained. "Your mother is not a maternal woman, but she was slow to realize that. Her desire for a baby was similar to the yearning of a little girl for a doll. When she believed herself incapable of producing offspring in the conventional manner, she rushed out, in her impetuous way, and procured an infant as one might purchase a toy. I can't even be sure that she and her current husband went through the proper channels and formally adopted the lad, though they always regarded him as their own. He is the son of a theatrical friend of Anna's, who perished miserably of an excess of alcohol and other indulgences. Shortly after she obtained the baby she became enceinte. I am told that often happens. So you see, Laura, you and Douglas are not related to one another at all. So far as we are concerned it makes no difference. He is our dear nephew and always will be. But you can hardly. . . . I am so sorry to be the one to tell you this. I fear it comes as a shock."

Laurie collapsed against the pillows. She wondered if Doug knew the truth. Somehow she rather thought he did. Even at the airport in Baltimore— that greeting had been a little warmer than brotherly affection would explain. As she thought back over the past days, casual, seemingly insignificant looks and comments came back to her with a new meaning.

Yes, Doug knew, and she could hardly blame him for not telling her. "Speaking of elves in the woods, you and I are not brother and sister." Not an easy topic to introduce, no—especially if it had become complicated by other, unexpected emotional developments. . . .

She smiled. Her aunt, watching her anxiously, gave a little sigh of relief.

"I am so glad you are not too distressed. Yet I am afraid you must be disappointed."

"Well, I wouldn't exactly sat *that*," Laurie murmured. "No, I can't honestly say that I'm disappointed. I don't have too many old-fashioned prejudices, but I do draw the line at incest."

"Laura," her aunt said, "please don't be vulgar."

THRILLS * CHILLS * MYSTERY
from FAWCETT BOOKS

☐ THE WALKER IN SHADOWS by Barbara Michaels	24450	$2.50
☐ THE PELICAN'S CLOCK by Robert Middlemiss	14426	$2.50
☐ DEATH IN THE AIR by Agatha Christie	04041	$2.50
☐ CASEBOOK OF THE BLACK WIDOWERS by Isaac Asimov	24384	$2.25
☐ THE BLOOD BOND by Emma Cave	24402	$2.50
☐ THAT MAN GULL by Anthony Stuart	04637	$1.95
☐ THE GREEN RIPPER by John D. MacDonald	14345	$2.50
☐ MURDER IN THREE ACTS by Agatha Christie	03188	$1.75
☐ NINE O'CLOCK TIDE by Mignon G. Eberhart	04527	$1.95
☐ DEATH OF AN EXPERT WITNESS by P. D. James	04301	$2.75
☐ PRELUDE TO TERROR by Helen MacInnes	24034	$2.50
☐ INNOCENT BLOOD by P. D. James	04630	$3.50

Buy them at your local bookstore or use this handy coupon for ordering.

COLUMBIA BOOK SERVICE, CBS Publications
32275 Mally Road, P.O. Box FB, Madison Heights, MI 48071

Please send me the books I have checked above. Orders for less than 5 books
must include 75¢ for the first book and 25¢ for each additional book to cover
postage and handling. Orders for 5 books or more postage is FREE. Send check
or money order only. Allow 3–4 weeks for delivery.

Cost $_____   Name _____

Sales tax*_____   Address _____

Postage_____   City _____

Total $_____   State _____ Zip _____

*The government requires us to collect sales tax in all states except AK, DE,
MT, NH and OR.

Prices and availability subject to change without notice.   8208